HEDGEWITCH

SKYE MCKENNA

Illustrated by Tomislav Tomic

WELBECK
FLAME

Also available in the Hedgewitch series:

Hedgewitch

Woodwitch

Seawitch (from 2024)

This paperback edition was first published in 2023 by Welbeck Flame
An imprint of Welbeck Children's Limited,
Part of the Welbeck Publishing Group
Offices in: London – 20 Mortimer Street, London W1T 3JW &
Sydney – 205 Commonwealth Street, Surry Hills 2010

www.welbeckpublishing.com

Design and layout © Welbeck Children's Limited
Text © 2022 Skye McKenna
Cover illustrations © 2022 Saara Katariina Söderlund
Interior illustrations © 2022 Tomislav Tomic

Skye McKenna has asserted her moral right to be identified as the Author of
this Work in accordance with the Copyright Designs and Patents Act 1988.

A CIP catalogue record for this book is available from the British Library.

ISBN 978 1 80130 068 1

Text designed by Perfect Bound Ltd

Printed and bound by CPI Group (UK)

10 9 8 7 6 5 4 3 2 1

For my mother,

who taught me that

whatever we imagine,

we can make real.

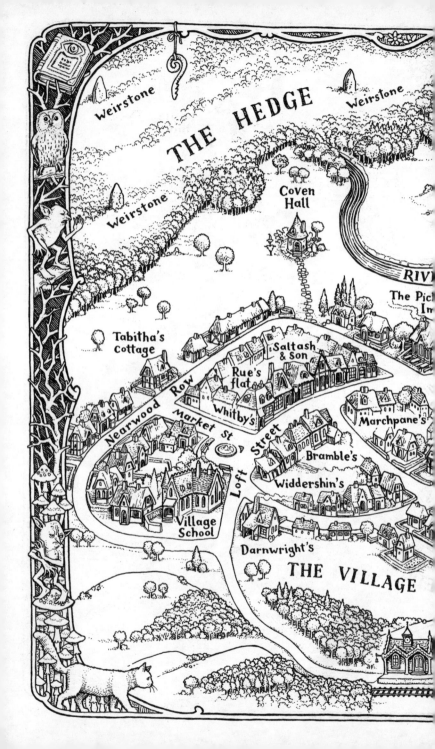

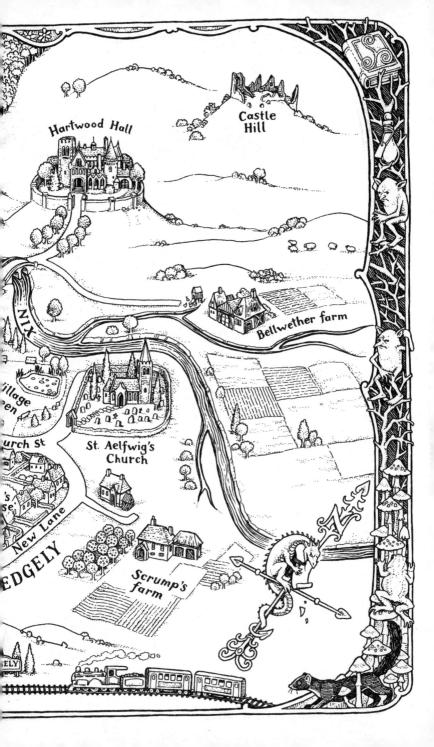

Hartwood Hall

Castle Hill

NIX

Bellwether farm

Village Green

Church St

St. Aelfwig's Church

New Lane

EDGELY

Scrump's farm

ELY

Chapter One

The Invisible Girl

Cassandra Morgan was hiding in the broom cupboard. It wasn't a bad place to hide, all things considered; a narrow window provided light to read by and an upturned bucket served well enough as a seat. If she ignored the smell of mildew and the odd inquisitive mouse, it was almost cosy.

Cassie knew all the best hiding places in the school: the dormitory roof, the hedges behind the gym, the unused classroom in the east wing. The broom cupboard had been nearest just then, when she'd heard the sound she dreaded most in the world: the horsey laughter of the hockey team, coming back from practice. She had slipped into the cupboard just in time, the clatter of sticks and squelch of wet gym shoes passing by.

Her heartbeat returning to its regular speed, Cassie settled into a corner and pulled a book from her satchel. The dust jacket read *Intermediate Algebra*, but under the false cover the book was bound in purple cloth, with the title *Tales of Faerie* embossed in silver. The book had cost her a chocolate bar and half a bag of mint humbugs, sweets being the unofficial currency of Fowell House. Cassie had worked hard for her confectionery, doing other girls' prep for months, yet she would happily have given a hundred chocolate bars for this book. It was not at all like the other 'faery books' she'd read, full of dainty creatures prancing about on lily pads. The stories it contained were wild and strange; youths whisked away by faery queens and maidens who danced all night in toadstool circles; fiddlers who wandered into green hills where they played music for a night, only to return and find a hundred years had passed; and children who stumbled upon secret doors that led to cities of starlight.

Cassie didn't believe in faeries, not exactly, she was much too old for that. But she did wonder where the stories had come from. She had looked under **398.4 Paranatural and legendary phenomena** in the school library and found only a single book on the shelf: *Faerie and Other Fallacies*, by A. B. Iffy. According to the author, sightings of faeries could be explained away by unusual weather phenomena or eating cheese before bed.

But it didn't really matter if the stories were true or not: for a few stolen moments each day, between classes or buried under the covers at night with a torch, Cassie could escape the hockey team, maths and tapioca pudding to walk in woodland glades beneath the moonlight.

The story she was reading just now was about a woodcutter who'd been given three wishes by a faery. Of course, he'd wished for useless things like fame and riches and to marry a princess.

If Cassie were offered three wishes, she knew exactly what she would ask for. First, she'd wish for more books. Fowell House had a library but it was full of dull textbooks and the girls weren't allowed any reading material that wasn't strictly educational. Their teachers argued that students had plenty of prep to keep them busy and ought to be improving their minds with practical, useful knowledge – not make-believe.

In spite of this, Cassie had managed to build her own secret library. There was a loose panel in the floorboards beneath her bed and under it was just enough space to hide a few books. The only problem was that she'd read them so many times she knew the words by heart.

Cassie's second wish would be to go on an adventure, like the girls and boys in her stories. Nothing interesting ever seemed to happen at Fowell House and she was not allowed to go beyond school bounds. In class she often daydreamed about flying through the window, out over the high iron fence. Once free, she would travel the world, encountering friends and foes and saving the innocent from the wicked.

Cassie's third wish was something she rarely allowed herself to think about. It was her dearest longing, but over the years she had found it harder and harder to believe it would ever come true. The certainty she'd once felt had dwindled to a small trickle of hope. Cassie wished, more than anything, to see her mother again.

The school bell clanged. Cassie closed her book and gathered her things.

Fowell House was made up of two separate buildings: the lower school, where Cassie had lived until she turned eleven, and the upper school, where she went now. The upper school was built of red brick and had four wings extending from the main hall, like a great red beast with legs sticking out on either side. All the windows had bars on them and rumour had it that Fowell House had once been a prison, which Cassie found all too easy to believe.

The dining hall was in the centre of the school, the belly of the great beast. Cassie made it just in time to join the queue for dinner. They were served the same thing they had every Monday: mutton stew; a grey mass of watery gravy with some lumpy bits in it, which might be meat if you were lucky. For vegetables they had potatoes, mashed without any butter so they had the consistency of wet sand, and cold peas. It was an unappetising prospect, but as Cassie had traded the last of her chocolate for the book, there was no question of skipping dinner.

She looked for a seat. The hockey team had the best spot, beside the only radiator in the hall. The other girls sat in groups or pairs, chatting about their day or playing with their food. Cassie found a seat as far from the hockey team and, unfortunately, the heating, as she could get. The two girls next to her shuffled away but Cassie was used to this and paid no notice. She loaded her fork with a lump of potato and steeled herself for the first mouthful.

As a junior, Cassie had made a few friends. They had all started together and been homesick for parents and familiar things. Yet every summer and Christmas the other girls went home to their families, leaving Cassie behind. She couldn't invite them to stay with her during holidays and wasn't allowed to leave the school and go out to tea with them when their mothers came to visit. Thus, Cassie had never been popular and, as the years passed, she spent more and more time alone. She had managed this well enough, kept company by her books and daydreams, until she'd entered the upper school the previous year. It was then she'd made her fatal mistake – Cassie had angered the Bleacher.

Lizzie Bleacher was the most popular girl at Fowell House. She wasn't pretty, or clever, or even particularly good at Games, despite being captain of the hockey team. No, a solid girl, with arms like bolsters and a black belt in judo, Lizzie ruled the upper school with sheer terror. It was wise to stay on the Bleacher's good side if you liked the current shape of your nose.

Having your bloomers tied to the flagpole or your head flushed in the loo by Lizzie and her chums was just part of initiation into the upper school. You were supposed to put on a brave face and cry later into your pillow. You were *not* supposed to talk back and you certainly were not meant to correct the Bleacher on her use of the word 'dilemma'.

This act had cost Cassie the last poor remains of her happiness at Fowell House. Before, she'd been simply unpopular, now she was untouchable. To be seen with Cassie was to be added to the Bleacher's blacklist and she couldn't blame anyone for wanting to avoid that. The other girls would not make eye contact with her in the halls. If she asked them to pass the salt at dinner, they pretended not to hear. No one would share a book with her in class or pair up with her in Games.

If she was going to be invisible, Cassie decided, she'd make the transformation complete, so she kept her head down in the classroom, sat on her own during meals and spent most of her free time in hiding. After a while, even the teachers stopped noticing her. Sometimes she wondered what would happen if she disappeared. How long would it take before the school realised? Would they even notice?

'Girls, your attention please!' called a squeaky voice from behind her.

Every head turned towards the doorway. The woman standing there had grey hair in a poodle cut and was dressed head to toe in beige. It was Miss Pike, Cassie's least favourite teacher, although at Fowell House that was a tough competition.

It was unusual to see a teacher in the dining hall. They had their own common room upstairs where, rumour had it, they ate sausages and bacon for breakfast and sometimes had lemon drizzle cake for tea. Miss Pike stood in the doorway, looking down her long nose at them.

'I have come to inform you of that which you will no doubt hear about from your fellow students soon enough. We wish to prevent exaggerated rumours and unnecessary panic.' Miss Pike cleared her throat. 'The situation is under control and there is no cause for alarm or hysteria. All of your parents shall receive a letter from the headmistress explaining the circumstances and making it clear that the school is in no way responsible for what has happened. The police will visit us briefly tomorrow and you are not to bother them. If they speak to you, you shall give them your full cooperation. In the meantime, no student will be permitted to leave the grounds under any circumstance. Are there any questions?'

The girls exchanged wide-eyed glances. Cassie was just as curious as the others but unwilling to draw attention to herself by asking. Finally, one of the sixth-formers put up her hand.

'Please, miss, what has happened?'

'Did I not already tell you? A girl has gone missing.'

Chapter Two

There's No Such Thing as Faeries

The missing girl was a first-former named Jane Wren. Jane wasn't in Cassie's dormitory, but Cassie knew her from geography, where she sat in the front row. Jane had been out shopping and was left alone in the park, eating liquorice, while her mother went into a dressmaker's. When she returned, Jane had vanished.

Cassie heard all the details soon enough. *Everyone* was talking about Jane. They whispered in the halls between classes, compared rumours while brushing their teeth and were still talking about it after lights out, so that

Matron had to come in three times to tell them to hush.

Everyone wanted to know what had happened to Jane. Had she simply run away? This was Cassie's first thought, given that she considered it herself at least three times a week, but, by all accounts, Jane had been happy at school. She had friends and was good at lessons and Games. She'd done nothing to attract the attention of the hockey team and had a loving family who came to visit her every second Sunday and took her out for shopping and tea in town. No, it seemed that wherever Jane had gone, it was against her will.

The school buzzed like a beehive with rumour and speculation, for Jane was not the first child to go missing that year. Children had been disappearing all over London. Only a week before, two little boys had vanished from a theatre while their father went to buy tickets. In March, a brother and sister had disappeared from Charing Cross station and, just before Christmas, a girl had gone missing in Kensington Gardens. Her parents took out advertisements, but she was never found. It was in all the papers and word had spread even to the inmates of Fowell House.

For months now, the students had been talking about the missing children, inventing outrageous stories to explain their disappearance. Theories ranged from mad scientists needing subjects for their experiments to a pack of hungry hyenas escaped from London Zoo. But now the missing children were no longer a story in the newspaper, or a game the lower-school girls played at break. The threat was real and far too close for comfort. Whatever had happened to Jane Wren could have happened to any one of them.

By far the most exciting outcome of Jane's disappearance was the investigation. The following day, the police turned up at Fowell House. There were two constables, a detective in a grey suit and a warden. The warden wore a long black cloak, studded with badges, and carried a sword. Her arrival caused a flurry of excitement and fresh speculation. Girls stuck their heads out of windows to get a glimpse of her, they followed her down hallways and crowded outside the door of the classroom she was using, their ears pressed to the wood. The younger girls were terrified of her; Jane's friends came out of their questioning looking pale and uncertain.

Wardens were a rare sight in London, a secretive and ancient branch of the police – or the military, no one was really sure. They never appeared in newspapers or on the wireless, but there was always a warden present when the king made a public appearance and their distinctive uniform commanded a certain amount of respect. Although the students of Fowell House had no idea what the mysterious wardens actually *did*, they treated the presence of one in the school with equal parts fear and fascination.

Cassie did her best to stay out of the way. She was as curious as any of the girls, but far too comfortable in her invisibility to risk being questioned by the police. That afternoon, she was hiding in a tree behind the north wing. It was a plane tree, one of the few on the school grounds big enough to climb and one of Cassie's favourite places to sit and read. She felt safe there; in summer its leaves sheltered her from view and even in winter she found passers-by were unlikely to look up and see her.

Cassie had her new book and a peppermint to suck on and was generally feeling quite content until she heard voices below.

'I still say it's an ordinary case of kidnappin'. Posh girl goes missin', ransom note'll turn up in a few days, mark my words,' said a male voice.

'All this iron, it's as if the school was built to keep them out. Of course, they took her from the park, off school grounds. Have your men searched the area she was last seen?' asked another, this one female.

"Course! Several times over. Not a hair left behind. No footprints neither, of the girl or whoever took her. Bit odd that, I'll admit, but then maybe they were careful, kept to the gravel like.'

They were talking about Jane Wren. Cassie found that by twisting slightly, she could see them through the overlapping branches. There was the detective, he'd taken his hat off and was running a hand through his sparse hair. Across from him was a tall woman in a black cloak. The warden. She stood with her back to the tree and Cassie could not see her face, only a cloud of golden hair.

'I've spoken to the girl's teachers and friends, they know nothing. I can only assume she was taken by chance, as the others have been. The poor girl was simply in the wrong place at the wrong time.'

'You don't think it's related, surely?' asked the detective, raising his bushy eyebrows.

'Most certainly,' said the warden. 'That is, after all, why I am here. Now, I had better speak with the headmistress,

she must take extra precautions for the safety of her girls.'

Cassie wished the woman would turn round. This might be her only chance to get a glimpse of the warden without being seen herself. She leaned out further and her movement disturbed the branch she was sitting on. A single dead leaf, left over from autumn, floated softly to the ground and landed at the woman's feet. Cassie held her breath.

'She'll be wantin' to keep her name out of the papers, I expect; they'll be all over this once they realise your lot are involved. S'prised the place isn't crawlin' with reporters already. Well, I'd better round up the boys then. We'll take one more look about the place and then head off, I should think.'

Cassie watched the detective replace his hat, nod to the warden and stride away. The woman in black did not move.

'You can come down now,' she said.

Cassie froze.

'I promise I won't bite.'

She was caught. Whatever the warden intended to do to her, she might as well get it over with. Tucking her book into her satchel, Cassie swallowed the last of the peppermint and scrambled down.

The warden stood waiting. Her uniform cut an imposing silhouette. At her waist hung a slender sword with a basket hilt. She was younger than Cassie had expected and she was smiling. A robin had perched on the branch above her, its head cocked to one side. There was a glint of gold in its beady eye and something about its gaze that expressed more than the usual boldness of robins. When the warden spoke, it did not fly away.

'What were you doing up that tree? Nothing suspicious, I trust.'

'No, ma'am. I was just...' Cassie tried to think of a convincing excuse and failed. 'I was hiding.'

The woman's eyes crinkled at the corners. 'Not from me, I hope?'

'No, ma'am.'

'Oh, please don't call me that, it makes me feel a hundred years old. My name is Renata Rawlins. What is yours?'

'It's Cassie, Cassandra, I mean.'

'Now, you won't go telling the other girls what you heard, will you?'

Cassie shook her head. It wasn't as if she had any friends to tell.

'Good, I trust you to keep your word.' Renata winked at her. 'I don't suppose you can tell me anything about the disappearance of your schoolmate?'

'I didn't know her, I'm sorry.' Cassie summoned up her courage to ask a question, 'Miss Rawlins, you said we were all in danger. What did you mean by that?'

'Do you know what wardens do, Cassie?'

Cassie shook her head.

'Well,' said Renata. 'We have a duty to investigate peculiar happenings. We're here to help people, to protect them.'

'Like the police?'

'Yes, although the police only protect you from other humans. We come in when something... stranger is involved.'

Cassie liked the idea that the warden was there to protect them, but she still couldn't understand what they needed protecting from.

'I suppose there is something strange about all those children going missing,' said Cassie, hoping this would encourage the warden to divulge more. 'Do you think you'll be able to find Jane?'

'I hope so, but it may already be too late. There are some places even we wardens cannot go—' Renata stopped and frowned. 'That's an interesting necklace you have there.'

Cassie realised her key had slipped out from beneath her jersey as she climbed down the tree, flashing gold in the sun. She tucked it away quickly. 'It was my mother's,' Cassie explained. 'She gave it to me, before she left.'

The bell rang. It was the signal for afternoon classes and Cassie had maths on the other side of the school. She was going to be late.

'I'm so sorry, I have to go!' Cassie began to run in the direction of the west wing. Feeling rude, she turned and waved. 'Nice to meet you!'

Renata waved back and Cassie noticed that the robin had flown down to perch on her shoulder.

Despite the excitement shared by the student body in the wake of these events, life quickly returned to normal at Fowell House. There was still prep to finish, hockey matches to win and classes to stay awake through. The teachers were even more irritable than usual and quick to punish any student who interrupted class to ask about Jane Wren.

Friday afternoons were particularly dull for Cassie,

who had double history with Mr Hastings. Cassie thought she might like history, if she had a chance: there were kings and queens, knights and battles, shipwrecks and gunpowder plots. The sorts of things that filled her favourite books, only these stories were true.

Unfortunately, Mr Hastings was not interested in storytelling. What he taught was dates. They had to memorise the dates of battles, births, coronations, executions, treaties and royal weddings – endless lists of numbers; it was almost as bad as maths.

'Right,' said Mr Hastings, entering the room as the last of the girls rushed to their seats. 'New topic today, chaps, books open at page 624! Having covered the Glovemakers' Rebellion of 1853 and the coronation of Queen Cordelia the following year, we will review the significant events of the reign of another great English queen, Elizabeth the Glorious: born 1533, died 1603.'

Mr Hastings was dressed, as always, in khakis and knee-high socks and carried a cane tucked under his arm. He never hit anyone with it, but he liked to crack it on the desk if anyone nodded off during class.

'What's that, Johnson? No, you may not be excused, should have used the latrine before class. You'll just have to hold it in!'

Mr Hastings had taught at a boys school before coming to Fowell House. If a few more of his students had braids and hair ribbons now, that made very little difference to him. He strode to the front of the room and squinted at them as though he were assessing the ranks of his own personal army. Probably, Cassie thought, he was trying to remember their names.

'Willis, is it? You with the spots. The list of key dates, beginning with the War of the Two Queens. Nice loud voice!'

April Wilson began to read slowly and painfully from the textbook. As usual, Cassie found herself skipping ahead.

1565: **The Battle of Rushwick.** The people of the sunless lands, led by the Shadow Queen, invade England through the Great Western Wood and lay waste to Worcester.

1566: **The Siege of London.** Surrounded by invading forces, Queen Elizabeth and the Black Knight take sanctuary in the White Tower.

Cassie propped her chin on her hands. This was beginning to get interesting.

1572: **The Battle of Morden.** Led by the first warden,
Jane Godfrey, the English army successfully defend
London and drive back the invaders. The Black Knight
is fatally wounded.

The Treaty of Rosehill, signed by both queens,
bringing an end to the war. The treaty grants peace
on the condition that neither party should attempt to
cross the border or claim the other's realm.

Who was this Shadow Queen? And where were the 'sunless lands'? Cassie shook her head, there was something else bothering her, the names sounded familiar, as if she'd read them somewhere else recently.

April Wilson droned on. The rest of the class were scratching at their desks or staring out the window at the uninspiring weather. Mr Hastings had his feet up on the table and was watching a spider crawl slowly across the ceiling.

Carefully, Cassie extracted the storybook from her satchel. Looking up every few seconds to make sure she was not observed, she turned the pages. There it was! The story about the queen, who'd taken a knight with her into Faerie. There was a picture of them riding through a dark forest, the knight asleep in his beetle-black armour, which looked rather uncomfortable, and the queen, radiant and terrible, holding a long white wand. The caption confirmed Cassie's suspicions: 'The Black Knight is taken to the Sunless Lands'.

Cassie could not say what came over her in that moment. Certainly, she forgot who and where she was, consumed with the need to know if the story could really be true. She raised her hand.

Mr Hastings didn't notice at first but, as April Wilson finally finished with a sigh of relief and sank back into her chair, he saw the small pink palm waving like a flag at the back of the class.

'Morton, what is it?' he asked, squinting in Cassie's direction.

She stood up. Chairs scraped as every girl in the room turned to look at her. Cassie could have escaped, even then. She could have asked to go to the lavatory, or the sanatorium or to get a drink of water. Her heart was beating hard, she swallowed.

'Please, sir, the invading army, the Shadow Queen, were they...' she began. 'Does this mean that faeries are real?'

For a long minute the room was silent. April Wilson's

mouth gaped like a fish. All of the girls stared at Cassie.

'They... I—' stuttered Mr Hastings.

The students began to giggle.

'That's not the word we use! You are here to learn facts, not faery tales— I mean, children's stories.'

A trickle of laughter passed through the seated class. Mr Hastings turned a violent shade of beetroot.

'There's no such thing as faeries!' he bellowed.

But the class was enjoying the scene, laughing and whispering to each other, turning to stare at Cassie.

She sat down, flushed and kicking herself under the desk. What had she been thinking?

'Quiet! That's enough!' called Mr Hastings, trying to restore order to the class. 'What you need to remember for the exam are the facts. When was the Treaty of Rosehill signed, anyone?'

'1572,' said Mabel Burren, with a smirk in Cassie's direction.

'Very good, Brown!' said Mr Hastings. 'You can read the next page for us.'

Cassie hunkered down over her book. What had possessed her? She'd undone all her hard work, months of trying to be invisible.

When the bell finally rang, Mr Hastings called out,

'Morton, stay behind, please.'

This garnered more smirks and whispers from the other girls as they filed past her. Cassie packed her books into her satchel and dragged herself to the front of the class. Mr Hastings scribbled Cassie's name and Monday's date on a slip of pink paper and handed it to her.

'Detention?' asked Cassie. 'What for?'

'For disrupting the class,' said Mr Hastings. 'I will not have my subject taken lightly. No more nonsense about imaginary beings, do you hear me?'

Cassie frowned. It wasn't fair that she was being punished for asking a question, however silly it might have been.

'Yes sir.' She sighed. After all, detention was now the least of her problems.

Chapter Three

The Awful Anniversary

The story of Cassie's humiliation passed through the school faster than head lice. Cassie had, for one day at least, replaced Jane Wren as the most talked-about girl in school. All her efforts to become invisible were in vain. She felt as though someone had pulled off her armour, leaving her exposed and vulnerable once more.

The hockey team were thrilled with this new opportunity to taunt Cassie.

'Seen any pixies lately Morgan?' they sneered as she passed them in the corridor.

They crept up behind her at meals to whisper, 'Hey Morgan, I think there's a unicorn under my bed. Want to check?'

When she tried to escape, Lizzie Bleacher shouted after her, 'Where are you going Morgan? The elves are that way!'

Word had obviously spread amongst the teachers too and they seemed to be keeping an especially close eye on Cassie, which made her nervous about her clandestine reading.

At night, Cassie had confused and troubling dreams about black knights chasing her with hockey sticks and Mr Hastings dressed as the faery queen, wielding his cane in place of a wand.

On Monday morning Cassie woke with a sick feeling in her stomach. That was the usual effect of Fowell House dinners, but today felt different. She lay in bed staring at the grey ceiling and the weak wash of light that crept in through the dormitory window, striped by the iron bars.

The five other girls she shared the room with were still asleep. Beatrice Hartree was snoring. It was not Beatrice who had woken Cassie, however, it was the strange and sudden sensation that something was wrong. Cassie felt as though she'd gone to take a step, from sleep to waking, and found the step missing, throwing her into the day with a sickening lurch. Of course, Cassie had detention that evening, but there was something else. She lay there and waited for her memory to stir. There were no exams yet, term had only just started. She had no overdue prep and Games Day wasn't until June. Cassie sat up and peered at the wall calendar which showed a drooping daffodil. It was April 30th, the anniversary of her arrival at Fowell House.

Cassie fell back against the mattress, which squeaked in surprise. She didn't care if she woke anyone. Today was the worst day of the whole year. Worse than her birthday, which no one remembered, or Christmas, when she sat alone in the dining hall picking at dry turkey while everyone else went home to family and presents and pudding.

Today marked seven years since she'd come to live at Fowell House and seven years since she'd last seen her mother.

Cassie tugged at the cord around her neck and fished out her key. The chain had broken years ago and string was more inconspicuous anyway. Jewellery was another item on the long list of things forbidden at Fowell House so, although she wore the key always, she never let anyone see it. It was no longer than her index finger and green-gold in colour. The bow was shaped like the spiral of a fern frond, unfurling into a straight stem with little leaflets forming the bit at the end.

Cassie had many theories about what the key might open: a treasure chest, a secret vault, the door to the home she and her mother would someday return to. Yet it was also a promise and a reminder of the commitment she herself had made. Her mother had given her the key on the day she left, begging Cassie to wait patiently for her, and Cassie had promised she would. At the time, she could never have imagined just how long that would be. Whenever she held the key, she drew on the small well of hope deep inside her heart, but when she reached for it now, she found the well was nearly empty. Another year had passed and she found it harder and harder to believe her mother was ever coming back.

Cassie moved through the day in a daze. She walked mechanically down the halls, ignoring the taunts of the hockey team. In class she sat and gazed out the window, watching three jackdaws fight over a biscuit. She spent her free hour curled up behind the gym, plucking at dead grass and staring at the school gates. She didn't even feel like reading, in fact, she was trying very hard not to feel anything at all, to squash down the creeping sense of despair and just get through the day.

Cassie would have preferred to have skipped dinner and gone to bed early that night. The sooner the day was over, the better. However, she had detention to get through first. She considered pretending to be ill, but even if she could convince Matron they'd just give her something worse the next day. Perhaps washing pots or pulling weeds or whatever they had in store for her would distract her from her own thoughts.

Cassie made her way to the entrance hall, where a queue of half a dozen girls were already waiting outside Miss Pike's office. When Cassie's turn came, she handed over her pink slip and was given a bucket of soapy water and a toothbrush.

'North-wing lavatory, cleaning duty,' said Miss Pike, with a sneer. 'Make sure you get in between the grout.'

The lavatory was empty when Cassie arrived. No one used the north wing if they could help it, because the only toilet that flushed did so with a strangled cry like a drowning sheep.

She set down the bucket of soapy water, which sloshed on to the dirty green tiles. There was nothing else for it but to get to work. The sooner she finished, the sooner she could crawl into bed where sleep would erase the last of that awful day.

Scrubbing floors is not, generally speaking, a pleasant task. You have to do it on your hands and knees and the water quickly turns brown and mucky. Scrubbing toilets is worse. Cassie had been at it for an hour or so and had made a fairly good start on the job when the door creaked open.

She looked up from the tiles to see three pairs of boots walking towards her. The boots were attached to the legs of three members of the hockey team. One of them was Lizzie Bleacher.

'Hullo, what have we here?' said Lizzie. 'Something nasty crawled out of the toilet?'

The other girls sniggered.

Lizzie strode across the floor as if she owned the place.

'Oh, you missed a spot,' she said and kicked the bucket of dirty water, spilling its contents across the tiles and soaking Cassie's skirt. All three girls laughed as Cassie got to her feet and tried to wring out the water.

Lizzie sneered at her. 'Didn't anyone tell you this was my territory?'

'I'm doing detention for Mr Hastings.'

A fresh smile spread over Lizzie's broad face as she remembered the cause of Cassie's punishment.

'That's right, you're the faery girl. Found any loo faeries down here, then?'

The others laughed while Lizzie, evidently pleased with her own wit, went on.

'Better hold her tight, she might grow wings and fly away.'

The two girls dragged Cassie to her feet again, gripping one arm each and pinning them behind her. Cassie bit her lip, she would not give them the satisfaction of hearing her cry out, even as her arms were nearly wrenched from their sockets.

Lizzie stepped in close, her face hovering above Cassie's own. She had an unpleasant view up the older girl's nostrils and tried to look away, but Lizzie's huge hand reached out and grabbed her by the neck.

'You thought I'd forgotten you?' she growled. 'Sneaking around and hiding in holes like a scared little rabbit.'

31

Cassie, who *had* hoped that might be the case, tried to shake her head but Lizzie's fingers were cutting into her windpipe and it was all she could do to draw rasping breaths.

'Well, maybe I've just been waiting for a good opportunity, an opportunity just like this,' she smiled. 'Nice and quiet, down here. No one to bother us. No one to hear you squeal.'

Cassie knew that Lizzie was just trying to scare her; the problem was, it was working. Like a dog, Lizzie could smell the fear of her prey. She let go of Cassie's throat and stood back with a satisfied smirk.

'Don't suppose anyone would care much if *another* girl went missing.' Lizzie tried to look thoughtful – an expression to which her face was unaccustomed. 'They'd just say it was kidnappers, or whoever it was that took poor little Jane.'

Cassie was quite sure that Lizzie had nothing to do with the disappearance of Jane Wren, whatever she might like to insinuate. However, she did not like the direction this conversation was taking.

'It's not like anyone would miss you, eh, Morgan? Not got any friends, have you. No one to blub when you don't show up for breakfast tomorrow morning.'

Cassie gritted her teeth. It was mostly Lizzie's fault she didn't have any friends and Lizzie knew it.

'You haven't got a mummy or daddy either, have you? Poor little orphan.'

'I'm not an orphan,' Cassie hissed under her breath. 'I have a mother.'

'What was that? I didn't hear you.'

One of the girls gave Cassie a shove from behind, sending her stumbling forward.

All the feelings Cassie had been pushing down that day, all the hurt, anger and frustration, were welling up inside her, a furious tide, ready to overflow.

'I said, I have a mother!'

Lizzie leaned in so close that Cassie could smell her breath. 'Where is she then, off with the faeries?'

The two girls who were holding Cassie roared with laughter. She seized the moment to break free of their grasp. Diving past Lizzie, she made for the door. Cassie was small and nimble and she might have outrun the bigger, slower hockey players if she'd not had eyes full of tears, vision too blurry to see the pool of dirty water.

She hit the tiles hard, sliding across the soapy floor until she slammed, headfirst, into a cubicle door. She lay there, curled up on the floor, smarting from bruised elbows and knees, her head ringing.

'You're not going anywhere, not until I'm finished with you.' Lizzie crouched down in front of her. 'You're done for, Morgan.' She raised a fist. 'And there's no faery godmother coming to save you.'

The lavatory door creaked open again. All four girls turned to see the pale beige shape of Miss Pike standing in the doorway.

The teacher examined the scene before her, taking in the three older girls looming over the small, crumpled form of Cassandra Morgan.

'Miss Bleacher, girls, the dinner bell rang five minutes ago. I suggest you make your way to the dining hall if you wish to eat tonight.'

'Yes, Miss Pike,' they chorused and headed for the door, Lizzie glaring at Cassie over her shoulder.

Once the older girls had left, Miss Pike entered the room, her heels clicking on the tiles as she navigated her way around the puddle.

'Miss Morgan, when I sent you to clean the lavatory, this is not what I had in mind.'

Cassie pulled herself up from the floor, her head aching.

'And what have you done to your uniform? You look as though you've been dragged through half the gutters of London. Still, you haven't got time to change. We can't keep her waiting. Up you get, follow me.'

They were halfway down the hall before Cassie had a chance to ask where they were going.

'Did I not already tell you? The headmistress wants to see you.'

Chapter Four

The Garm

The headmistress of Fowell House had an office on the third floor. From there, like a spider poised in the heart of her web, she oversaw the running of the entire school. Very few students had ever glimpsed the headmistress. The stories that were told about her did little to cheer those called to her office. Some said she locked students in cages suspended from the ceiling and left them there to starve. Others said she kept a pack of big black dogs which she let out at night, to roam the halls looking for errant students. One particularly gruesome rumour claimed that she ate the hearts of girls who failed their exams for breakfast – although no one believed that except the juniors.

Her name was Miss Griselda Garman but the students all called her the Garm.

Cassie followed Miss Pike down long corridors and up three flights of stairs. She was thinking furiously about what she might have done. She'd only broken four school rules that week and, as far as she knew, no one had seen her. Even if word of her foolish question in history made it to the headmistress's ear, surely she wouldn't send for Cassie on that alone? If Cassie only knew *why* she had been summoned she could prepare some excuse, some alibi to cover herself.

'Wait there until you're called for,' said Miss Pike, indicating a wooden bench against the wall. Cassie sat and watched the teacher disappear back down the stairwell, almost wishing she would stay. Miss Pike was hardly a comforting presence but anything would be better than going into that office alone.

The bench faced a wooden door. It was a very ordinary door. Cassie didn't know what she had expected – something like the entrance to a dungeon, with heavy bolts and metal teeth? She didn't like to look at the door all the same, so she got up to examine her surroundings. There were six framed photographs on the wall, a picture of the king, and a series of frowning women in austere dresses, presumably past headmistresses. There was no portrait of the Garm, but an empty hook and a lighter rectangle on the wall revealed that a picture had been removed recently.

The door opened and a girl emerged. She was a junior, maybe eight or nine years old. The girl had wide brown eyes behind round glasses and a nose buried in her handkerchief. She was trembling all over.

'Are you all right?' Cassie asked. The girl drew back, took one terrified glance at the door and ran for the stairs. Cassie could hear the skitter of her shoes going down.

The door stood half open. Cassie loitered in the hall, unsure what to do.

'Come in,' called a woman's voice. It was a demand, not an invitation.

Cassie took a deep breath, held up her chin and stepped into the Garm's office.

The room was dimly lit by the red glow of a desk lamp and a few burning embers in the fireplace grate. The walls were papered with a pattern of red poppies and hung with long framed mirrors. These reflected the view from the window, which looked out over the playing field. Cassie realised that from her window, the Garm could observe all the outdoor activities of her students. How many times had Cassie crossed the grounds below without knowing she was being watched?

Cassie approached the desk, her gym shoes squeaking on the polished boards.

The headmistress was bent over some paperwork, her pen scratching away while Cassie waited. A shadow shifted in the corner of her vision. It was a big black dog, lying in front of the fireplace, its two front paws crossed. The dog lifted its head to look at her. It had the profile of an Egyptian statue, with sharply erect ears and slanted golden eyes. Cassie edged away from it.

The headmistress put down her pen and folded her hands on the desk. She was younger than Cassie had imagined, surely younger than most of the teachers at Fowell House. Her short black hair framed a sharp face. It was a beautiful face, but not a pleasant one. Everything about it was too thin; you could see blue veins beneath her pale skin.

'Miss Morgan, is it?' she asked, looking Cassie over. Cassie could see her own crumpled, dirty reflection in one of the mirrors. She nodded.

'Your mother is dead.'

She said it just like that. No condolences, no suggestion

that Cassie ought to sit down and prepare herself. A simple statement, as if she had announced they were out of milk.

'No, she isn't,' said Cassie in a small but calm voice.

'She isn't what? Complete sentences, if you will.'

'Dead. My mother isn't dead,' Cassie repeated, louder this time.

The headmistress drew her mouth into an even thinner line.

'You may choose to disbelieve me, but the facts are these: no one has seen or heard from Rose Morgan for seven years.'

Cassie was well aware of that, she'd been trying steadfastly not to think about it all day.

'According to the law, a person who has been missing for seven years is declared dead. I have a letter stating so.' The Garm held it up.

'That's ridiculous!' said Cassie, her fists clenched tight.

'And what would a twelve-year-old girl know about these matters?'

Cassie frowned. 'I know a piece of paper can't kill my mother. I know you can't say someone's dead when you don't know for sure and I know she isn't!'

'How do you know?' asked the Garm. 'Do you know

where she is? Have you seen her even once since she left you here?'

'No.'

'She hasn't communicated with you in any way? Letters, phone calls?'

Cassie felt it was rather unfair to insist that her mother was dead one minute and then expect Cassie to explain her whereabouts the next.

'I don't know where she is, but that doesn't mean she's dead.'

'You know very little, that much is clear. As of today, you are an orphan. The question remains as to what we are to do with you.'

Surely, if it was true, Cassie would know, she'd feel different. She tried to believe the worst – just for a moment – but something inside her refused to allow it. There was no way she could accept that her mother was dead.

'Are you listening, Miss Morgan? I asked if you have any other relatives.'

Cassie shook her head. 'No, there's no one.'

Cassie had never known her father. Whenever she'd asked about him, her mother had always said he was a good man, but speaking of him made her so sad that

41

Cassie had stopped asking. She thought that he'd either died or gone away, somewhere they could not reach him. It didn't bother her though, not having a father, because she'd never known what it was like to have one. Her mother was different, she could remember her mother all too well.

'We cannot keep you here on charity, you realise. Your mother's accounts have been cut off. There's no money to pay for your schooling. You have nothing.' The Garm leaned forward, her eyes searching Cassie's face. 'She didn't leave you anything, did she? Anything... valuable?'

Cassie's hand nearly flew to her chest where the key lay hidden beneath her uniform but she stopped herself in time. If she showed the key to the Garm, she'd be admitting to breaking school rules and might have it confiscated. She shook her head, her hands falling empty at her sides.

'Arrangements will have to be made. I've been speaking to a Mr Burnhope, of Burnhope's Home for Children. They have been good enough to offer you a place there.'

An orphanage, they were going to send her to an orphanage. Cassie had read enough books to know the fate that awaited her was even worse than Fowell House.

The headmistress went on to explain the paperwork and formalities, but Cassie wasn't really listening. She was lost in a fog of disbelief and struggling to find some scrap of hope to cling to.

'Mr Burnhope will send someone to collect you in the morning. You needn't attend classes. You will pack your things and wait in your dormitory until called for.'

Cassie felt like two separate people. The Cassandra on the outside was calm; she nodded in reply to the headmistress's words. The other Cassie, trapped inside, wanted to throw a first-rate tantrum, to shout at the woman sitting so placidly at her desk, to rage and cry and scream at the world for the unfairness of what was happening, but she knew it wouldn't make an ounce of difference.

'That is all, you are dismissed,' said the headmistress.

The dog lifted its snout from the ground to watch her go.

Like a ghost, Cassie passed through the halls and down the stairs. Nothing she touched felt real. The Bleacher, classes, tests, everything that had been troubling her now seemed as insubstantial as smoke. Somehow, she found her way back to the dormitory. Laying on her bed, hands folded on her stomach, she looked up through the small window at the heavy clouds.

In her hand she clutched the key and thought about promises; the promise her mother had made, that she would come back for her, Cassie's own promise that she would wait. That vow was the only reason she'd stayed at Fowell House, yet when she'd made it, she could not have known just how long she would have to wait. Year after year, she'd clung to that promise.

But now she couldn't wait any longer.

Cassie rose from her bed and went to the window. The sun was setting behind the clouds, turning the sky mustard-grey. She wrapped her fingers around the cold bars.

Then it struck her – she was free. It wasn't the iron bars or the teachers or the school rules that had kept her here all these years, it was her promise. Now she could no longer keep that promise because she was being forced to leave. If she had to go, why not on her own terms? How many nights had she spent lying on that bed, planning her escape from Fowell House, only to wake up the next morning and go about her day as always? Well, this time she would follow through with her plan. She would run away.

It didn't take Cassie long to pack; she had very little to call her own. Her coat, her grey school hat to cover her tell-tale red hair, her toothbrush and some clean handkerchiefs. She managed to cram all of this into her school satchel. Cassie considered making a sack of her pillowcase but quickly discarded this idea. If she were caught, it would be impossible to pretend she was only out for a stroll. Finally, she prised up the loose floorboard beneath her bed. She could not bring all her books with her – there wasn't room and the weight would slow her down. She ran her fingers across their spines, it hurt to think of leaving them behind. They'd been her only company at Fowell House, her true teachers and companions. Finally, she chose the newest in her collection, *Tales of Faerie* – she hadn't finished reading it yet. Cassie crammed the book into her satchel and stowed it beneath the bed.

When the other girls returned to the dorm they found her apparently asleep, the covers pulled up high over her face. They chatted and laughed, fought over whose turn it was to use the bath first and generally made a racket until Matron came in to turn out the lights. Throughout all of this, Cassie did not stir. She waited, listening as the breathing in the darkened room grew slower and Beatrice Hartree began to snore. When she was quite sure they were all asleep, Cassie threw back the covers, still fully dressed. Grabbing the satchel and her coat, she slid through the door, shutting it silently behind her.

In her daydreams, Cassie had been able to skip over some of the more bothersome elements of her escape. By nine o'clock at night, all the doors were locked, the teachers having retreated upstairs to their parlour. The entrance hall was a lost cause; the great doors were barred and bolted. Cassie would need to find another way out. A window might work, if she could find one that had been left unlocked. She tried the first few classrooms she encountered, but all the windows were barred. Downstairs she fared no better. Then she remembered the broom cupboard

Cassie crept through the silent hallways, keeping to the walls. The only light came through the moonlit windows, turning everything black and grey, but Cassie could have found her way around the school blindfolded. Crossing the west wing corridor she heard footsteps and was forced to duck into an empty classroom, waiting for them to pass. It seemed not all the teachers had gone upstairs yet.

Once, she thought she heard the click-clack of claws on floorboards and the heavy panting of the headmistress's dog. She held her breath for a whole minute until the hall was silent again.

At last she reached the cupboard; it was pitch black inside. Cassie heard something scuttle away as she opened the door but she had no time for squeamishness. Switching on the light, she dragged the bucket that had served as her seat over to the window. It was unlocked. Struggling to pull herself through the narrow frame, she ripped her stocking on the catch. It was only a short leap down to the ground outside.

The night air was cool and heavy with moisture, the grass damp where she landed. Cassie found herself behind the north wing. She could see the school gates in the distance, but there was just one problem – she had to cross the playing field to get there. Cassie now knew that the Garm could see the field from the window of her office.

Crossing the path to the gym, she used the building's shadow for cover. There were still lights on in the teachers' common room. Above that was the headmistress's office. She wasn't sure, but she thought she could make out a faint red glow from within.

Cassie thought back to her recent visit. The Garm's desk had been facing away from the window, so if she was sitting at it she would not be able to see the field below. If, on the other hand, she chose this moment to get up and look down, Cassie would be spotted immediately, a dark shadow on the empty moonlit field.

From the other side of the gym she heard a snuffling sound, then the scratch of claws on pavement. There was no other way out, she'd have to chance it. Pulling on her hat to hide her hair and face, she broke cover and ran.

Cassie made it halfway across the field before she heard the howl. The sound gave her goosebumps. She turned to see a dark shape coming after her in great leaping bounds, all black legs and a flash of white teeth.

Cassie ran, pushing forward with all she had. The dog growled, waking some deep instinctual fear that urged her on. She forgot about stealth and silence, her breath rasped in her throat. Her only thought was to reach the school gates. Cassie leapt over a small hedge, her hat flying off, and fell on to the drive. She picked herself up, her shoes crunching on loose gravel. She could hear the dog panting behind her, it was catching up, and a new, unwelcome thought had occurred to her. The gates were just ahead, but they would be locked.

Cassie turned to face her pursuer. The dog's hackles were raised, its head lowered. The animal's eyes were fixed upon her and its teeth were bared in a snarl. It growled at her, a low sound like approaching thunder, but held its ground. Cassie gasped for breath, backed up against the gates. She watched the dog, waiting for it to strike, but it did not approach.

Cassie examined the gates, keeping one eye on the dog. She had to find a way under or over or through. The gates were of wrought iron, with spikes on top. She could climb, perhaps, but she'd lose some skin in the process and a fall would end in a broken leg or worse. Squeezing underneath would be impossible; the bars scraped the gravel with sharp points.

The gates were sealed with a huge, heavy padlock. Cassie reached for it and the dog began barking wildly. Glancing towards the school, she saw more lights coming on.

As her hand closed around the lock she felt a strange sensation, a spreading warmth that started just over her heart, as if she'd taken a sip of hot cocoa on a cold night.

The sensation passed and the lock, unbelievably, swung open in her hand. Cassie stared at it for a second, but she didn't have time to wonder at her luck. The dog was barking furiously. She pushed the gate open; it was heavy and the hinges squealed, but she got it wide enough to squeeze through. She dragged it closed behind her with a clang. The dog pranced and snarled in a frenzy, but did not come any closer. Cassie snapped the padlock shut again. With one last glance at the dark shadow of the school, she ran down the hill, the dog's howling cry fading behind her.

Chapter Five

Flight

T he suburb of Trite looked just like any other on the outskirts of London. The winding streets were lined with rows of neat little red brick houses, each with a neat little garden bounded by a neat little fence. Some were lit from inside, their inhabitants shadowy figures moving behind drawn curtains. Cassie wondered what it would be like to live in one of those houses. To come home from school each day and have your mother and father waiting for you. To sleep in your own bedroom, surrounded by toys. It seemed as strange and unreal as anything in her storybooks.

The streets were quiet, the few people she passed frowned and turned to watch her go. A girl in school uniform wandering around after dark was suspect. She needed to find somewhere to hide until the morning.

If Cassie had been allowed to go out to tea or the pictures, like other girls in her school, she might have known her way around. As it was, she found the winding streets confusing, the names on the signs unfamiliar and the dark corners and back alleys frightening.

Finally, she stumbled upon a park. It wasn't much of a park, just a square of new-mown grass bordered by neat rows of primulas. In the middle of the park was a gazebo – a small round building, decorated like a birthday cake, with steps leading up to it. She saw with relief that it was completely deserted.

Cassie sat on one of the benches inside, feeling safer with a roof above her head.

She was tired but elated. She'd escaped Fowell House, outrun the Garm's dog and somehow broken through the school gates – she was free!

Cassie pulled her coat about her. She made a makeshift bed on the bench, using her satchel as a pillow. As she lay there, the excitement of her flight began to wear off and worrying thoughts crept in. The dog must have woken half the school with its barking. Even if the teachers didn't realise she was missing until morning, they would start searching as soon as the sun rose. They might even call the police. She had to get out of Trite, she had to get far away where no one from the school could ever find her.

When Cassie had planned her escape, she'd only thought as far as the school gates. Now, alone in the dark night, the world seemed far bigger and more threatening than it had from the dormitory window. She had no money, no clothes beside her uniform and only a half-empty tin of peppermints to eat. She couldn't ask anyone for help in case they handed her back to the school. The only plan she had was to look for her mother. Unfortunately, Cassie had no idea where to begin. Lying there in the darkness, exhaustion finally overcame her and she drifted off to sleep.

Cassie woke with a start. It was still dark and she had no idea how long she'd slept. A deep silence had fallen over the streets and her clothes and hair were soaked with dew. She looked out over the shadowy park. Not a single leaf stirred and yet she knew that someone was out there. Her skin tingled.

Whoever it was, they were hiding, waiting, watching. Cassie could feel her heart thumping. She was wide awake now and fighting to stay calm and clear headed. She didn't fancy leaving the shelter of the gazebo and walking out into the night, but she doubted she could go back to sleep with that creepy-crawly feeling of being watched.

Cassie gathered up her things slowly, as if nothing were amiss. She set off at a casual stroll, aiming for the streetlights and the apparent safety of the red brick houses. She did not look back.

She must not run, she told herself, but as she reached the pavement she heard soft footsteps behind her. She picked up her pace, the footsteps quickened. Cassie wished that a car would drive past or that someone might come out of one of the houses – perhaps that would drive the footsteps away, but it was too early in the morning, the road was silent and the windows dark. She reached the end of the street and stopped. The patter of feet came to a halt behind her. Cassie took a deep breath and turned round.

Emerging from the shadows into the artificial light were half a dozen men. They were no taller than Cassie's shoulder but they carried knives and nets. The men watched her with round yellow eyes that reflected the light of the street lamp, like a fox's. One of them grinned, revealing pointed brown teeth.

For the second time that night, Cassie found herself running for her life. If Mrs Harrow, the games-mistress, could only see her now she might even have put Cassie on the hockey team. But terror is a powerful motivator: from behind her came a wicked, inhuman laughter that echoed off the buildings.

Cassie turned left, then right, hoping to lose them in the bends and turns of Trite's back streets, but they kept up. There was a whirring sound and something scraped across the pavement at her feet.

'Ya missed, Kripper!' called one of the men.

'She's a slippery little thing, in't she?' said another.

'I likes it when they run! Makes it more fun.'

'How's about you stop your yappin' and catch her?'

Cassie couldn't keep it up for much longer, her legs ached and a stitch was developing in her side, but she pushed herself on. She followed the street lamps down Trite's high street. On either side were shops, all closed and locked for the night.

Up ahead the street forked in two. She took the narrower way, an alley between empty shops. It was the wrong choice: the alley ended in a brick wall, too high to climb. A single street lamp threw light across the path, but there was no door, no way out. She was trapped. Cassie looked about desperately for something to defend herself with. There was nothing in the alley but a rubbish bin, a broom and a stray cat. Cassie seized the broom. With her back to the wall, she stood her ground, gripping the stick in both hands as her pursuers reached her.

There were six of them. One had a nose like a tapir, another hairy, bat-like ears. Some had scales and fur, others leathery skin or tufts of feathers and long claws. All were grinning as they brandished cooking knives and nets. Their leader stepped forward, wielding an oversized fish hook tied to a rope.

'Now, dearie,' he said. 'Don't be afraid of us, we just want to have a little chat.'

'Don't come near me!' shouted Cassie, brandishing the broom at them.

The men laughed. 'Whatcha gonna do? Sweep us under the rug?'

They drew closer. She could see their beady eyes and pointed teeth and worst of all she could smell them, worse than a basket of unwashed gym socks. Cassie gagged and in that moment, a net was thrown over her. She caught it on the broom handle and tossed it aside. There was a howl of rage and a knife glanced past her shoulder and clattered off the bricks.

'Now then gents, don't want to damage the merchandise, do we?'

They were closing in around her, pushing her back against the wall. Cassie waved the broom about wildly. They leapt away with surprising agility. There were too many of them and they had her cornered.

'Get on the broom,' said a calm, cool voice.

Cassie looked about for the speaker.

'Unless you have a better plan, that is. Only, you seem at a loss for ideas.'

The grey cat was sitting on a rubbish bin, watching her with round amber eyes and the disinterested expression that is the trademark of its species.

'Excuse me?' asked Cassie.

'Those are goblin nabbers,' said the cat. 'They plan to smuggle you across the border and sell you to the gentry as a pet. Trust me when I suggest this is not a desirable fate. I'd get on the broom if I were you.'

She looked at the old broom in her hands. 'You want me to sit on this?'

'Yes, that is the general idea.'

Cassie shook her head. None of this made any sense

but she didn't have time to figure it out. The goblin leader was swinging his hook in a wide arc above his head.

She put one leg over the broom and grasped the handle. The cat leapt down from the bin and landed on the bristled end.

'Jump!' said the cat.

Cassie jumped as high as she could, clutching the broom and feeling a bit ridiculous. To her surprise, she did not come straight down again. The broom floated a few feet above the ground, Cassie's legs dangling on either side.

'Point the handle up,' instructed the cat.

Cassie did as she was told, hugging the broom tight. It began a leisurely ascent.

'Up, up!' she begged it, but the broom ignored her urgency.

'Oi! She's gettin' away!' called one of the goblins. They rushed to the spot Cassie had stood a moment before but she was above their heads and just out of reach. The broom was nearly vertical now and Cassie was wrapped around it like a monkey, her feet perched on the bristles to keep from sliding off.

The goblin leader released his rope and the hook flew towards her, catching the broom handle above her grip and yanking her violently down.

'You got her, boss!' cried the goblins with glee.

'Help me pull, you dolts!'

They gave a hard yank on the rope and the broom jerked beneath her. Still holding on with one shaky hand, Cassie reached for the hook. It had dug itself into the wood, but the goblins' efforts had righted the broom so it was horizontal once more. Cassie pushed at the hook, trying to slide it off.

'You might try reversing,' suggested the cat, who was clinging to the brush with his claws.

'How?' asked Cassie, tugging desperately at the hook.

'Think backwards.'

But at that moment the old broom gave out. The hook, which had dug itself deep into the wood, snapped off the top of the handle, sending Cassie and the cat crashing backwards into the wall. There was a nasty crunch, but Cassie kept hold of the broken broom and willed it onwards and upwards.

Now they were speeding up, leaving the shouting, angry goblins behind. They rose higher and higher, until they were above the rooftops. Cassie urged the broom to stop, but still they rose. She made the mistake of looking down. Her stomach did a somersault. Below them were the rows of houses and shops that made up Trite and the neighbouring suburbs. The goblins were tiny shapes, jumping about like crickets; they were a long, long way down.

A cool mist enveloped her. They were passing through a damp haze, the broom lifted them up and up until they popped out through the clouds into the cool night air. The rolling grey mist formed a blanket beneath them through which Cassie could no longer see the lights of Trite. She looked up. There were stars, thousands of stars, more than she'd ever seen from her dormitory window. It was as if someone had thrown a bucket of diamonds into the air and they remained suspended there, in the deep blue velvet of the sky.

Cassie looked over her shoulder at the cat who, having regained his composure, was now perched comfortably on the broom, cleaning a paw.

'Always gives me splinters.'

The broom shuddered beneath them. Cassie gripped it tight, she didn't want to think about what would happen if she fell.

'Better land soon, I don't think this old stick will hold out much longer.'

The broom quivered again.

'How do we get down?' asked Cassie.

'I suggest you find an elevated platform. I do not like our chances of making it to the ground in one piece.'

Cassie angled the broom down. She had discovered that by turning the broomstick with her hands she could change the direction it was flying in. Pushing down made it go lower, pulling up made it rise. However, the broom seemed to resist any abrupt changes in direction in favour of a gentle, curving turn.

As they descended through the cloud, Cassie saw a newly built tower block. The flat top offered her the platform she needed. Bracing herself, she angled the broom down, putting her feet out to stop them smashing into the building. It didn't help much – they hit the cement hard.

Chapter Six

The Cat, the Imp, and Egg and Cress Sandwiches

Cassie rolled off the broom while the cat made a nimble leap to the ground. Wincing, she sat up to inspect the damage. Nothing broken, but she'd grazed her arms and was pretty sure she'd have some impressive bruises in the morning.

The broom was in a bad way, its handle a mess of splinters. Cassie cradled what was left of it in her hands and wondered that it had ever held her weight. It was little more than a broken stick now, but it had saved her from the goblins.

'Shameful, to use a witch's broom, even one as old as that, as a common street sweeper,' said the cat.

'A witch's broom?' asked Cassie. It looked much like the one used by the groundskeeper at Fowell House, although far worse for wear.

'That is no wood native to the lands of Britain. This broom was a living thing, it had a name once, and a purpose.'

Cassie regarded the broken broom with a pang of pity.

'It was near the end of its life when we found it. That was its last flight and it served well,' the cat explained.

Cassie laid the broom gently on the rooftop and pulled her knees up to her chin.

She could see the suburbs spread out below her. Pinpricks of light marked out rows of houses, a few cars crawled along like beetles, their headlights snaking through the streets. On a dark hill in the distance she could just make out the shape of Fowell House. It looked flat, as though it were cut out of cardboard. The sky had turned a lighter shade of grey along the eastern horizon, promising dawn was on its way.

Another ordinary day was about to begin for the

residents of Trite. Soon they would wake up, make tea, burn toast and set out for school or work. Meanwhile, Cassie had just barely landed a flying broom, escaped a gang of goblins and was sitting next to a talking cat. As she caught her breath, Cassie wondered whether she had ever really woken up at all, perhaps she was still lying on the gazebo bench and this was all some bizarre and troubling dream. Yet the stinging scratches on her arms seemed real enough.

Cassie had a lot of questions and they all fought to come out at once. As he appeared to know rather more about the situation than she did, Cassie addressed herself to the cat. 'The goblins, why were they chasing me? What did they want?'

'Those particular goblins were nabbers, they are in the business of stealing babies to sell to the gentry of Faerie. Sometimes they leave one of their own in its place, an ugly old goblin done up in a bib and bonnet; you'd be surprised how long it takes most parents to notice the difference. Nabbing was common enough in the old days when humans left their offspring unattended. Witches were often able to recover the babe if they were called in time. Recently, however, the goblins have begun taking older children.'

'The missing children in the papers!' Cassie had a new and horrible understanding of just what had happened to Jane Wren. She shuddered. If the people of Faerie *were* real, they were nothing like she had imagined. 'I thought faeries granted wishes and helped people. In most stories they're beautiful and good.'

The cat snorted. 'Are all humans good? Or all cats, for that matter? It's hardly that simple. Why, there may even be sweet-tempered goblins, though I've yet to meet one. The folk are many and diverse in nature, some are kindly towards humans, but far more are not.'

'Are you...'

'One of them? Yes, although I was born into your world, I'm a familiar. In Faerie all beasts can speak the mortal tongues, though in Britain we are considered exceptional.' The cat smoothed his whiskers. 'You may call me Montague.'

'If you are a faery, does that mean you can do magic?' Cassie asked.

'Witches *do* magic, faery folk *are* magic. Why, it is as natural to us as breathing.'

'Please, will you show me some?'

'I am not a performing animal. If you require evidence of magic, may I suggest the events of the past hour might suffice?'

Cassie had to admit that he was right, and a talking cat *was* sort of magic in itself. Certainly none of the pigeons or mice at school had ever spoken back to her. The chance of encountering him at just the moment she needed to escape the goblins did seem unlikely though.

'If you don't mind my asking, just what were you doing in that alley?'

'I was looking for you, Cassandra Morgan.'

She stared at him in disbelief. 'Amongst the rubbish bins?'

The cat twitched. 'My navigational skills are usually flawless, however on this particular occasion I must admit to a slight miscalculation that I was in the process of correcting.'

'You were lost?'

'Temporarily,' admitted the cat, shifting from paw to paw. 'However, in the end it was most felicitous. You could say I was in the right place, simply ahead of time. These things often work out that way.'

'What things? Why were you looking for me? How do you even know my name?'

'I take it you did not receive a message from the Hedgewitch?' Montague asked.

Cassie shook her head.

'Ah, that explains your perplexed expression.' The cat made himself comfortable, wrapping his tail around his paws. 'I was sent to find you, by your aunt.'

Cassie frowned. 'Then you've got the wrong girl, I don't have an aunt. I haven't got any family at all except my mother.'

'On the contrary, you have an aunt, an uncle, a cousin and numerous other relations.'

'That's impossible. I've never heard of any of them!'

'Improbable, not impossible. Until recently, they were not aware of your existence either.'

'But why?'

'That is an excellent question and one I imagine your mother could answer if she were here.'

'Do you know where she is?' Cassie asked, hands clenched in sudden wild hope.

The cat did not move, but looked away from Cassie, over the town, where dawn was tingeing the buildings pink. 'I'm afraid not. No one has heard from Rose Morgan for over thirteen years.'

'Since before I was born.' Cassie sighed, her hope deflated.

'Quite. Your aunt Miranda received a letter from

a solicitor yesterday, informing her of your mother's presumed demise and at the same time of your existence. She sent a telegraph to the school and tasked me with collecting you and returning with you safely to Hedgely.'

'Hedgely,' Cassie repeated, liking the taste of the word. It stirred something within her, like a memory or a dream, although she could not recall having heard it before.

'I went to the school but you had already absconded. Fortunately, I am of a long line of Morgan cats, I can trace my ancestry back to Grimalkin the Third, and that brings with it certain skills. I will always be able to find a Morgan, wherever she may be.'

'Sort of like a homing pigeon?'

'Certainly not! It is a skill no half-witted bird could manage.'

'But you can't find my mother?'

'Not for want of trying. I cannot sense any trace of Rose Morgan. Perhaps she truly has left this world, or else she does not wish to be found.' They sat for a minute, watching the first stirrings of life in the streets below.

'What are they like, my family?'

'The Morgans are an old witching family. Your aunt is the current Hedgewitch, as your great-grandmother was before her. Your uncle works for Wayland Yard and Rose

68

too was quite talented before—'

'Are you saying my mother is a witch?'

'She trained as one, yes, although she never received her licence.'

Cassie frowned. Why had she been left at Fowell House when she had family she might have stayed with? At least she could have gone there for the holidays. Why had her mother never taken her to meet them, or told her they were witches, or even that there were such things as witches?

'Does that make me a witch too?' she asked, unsure if it was something you inherited, like red hair or crooked teeth.

'One is not born a witch, it is a skilled craft. There are many years of training and practical examinations involved. However, you could become one, if you so wished.'

Cassie shook her head, none of her books had prepared her for this. It was all too much to take in at once and she was at a great disadvantage, having spent the last seven years behind the bars of Fowell House, where even mentioning magic had landed her in detention. 'I don't know much about witches or goblins or faery things.'

Montague rose and stretched. 'Then you shall learn

and there is no better place for that than Hedgely.'

Cassie hesitated, she'd run away from school with one goal in mind – to find her mother. Now she knew about her family, things were a bit more complicated, but she still had no intention of giving up her search. Then again, it seemed there was a lot about Rose Morgan she did not know. Perhaps her aunt could help her; they might even look for her mother together. It wasn't as if she had anywhere else to go.

'But how do we get there?'

There was no question of using the broom again, so they took the stairs. Cassie was secretly relieved not to be doing any more flying just now. It had been exhilarating, but also terrifying and her grazed limbs still stung from the landing.

'We'd better send a message to your aunt first, to inform her you have been located,' said Montague, as they reached the small garden that surrounded the tower block.

'Should I call her?' asked Cassie, wondering if she could find a telephone box anywhere nearby.

'The Hedgewitch does not possess a telephone,' said Montague, disappearing into the bushes. Cassie heard a scuffle and a small angry screech. The cat came back with something in his mouth. As he got closer, Cassie saw that it was a bundle of arms and legs, waving wildly about and punching him on the nose. The bundle was squawking in some incomprehensible language, interspersed with rude words in English. Cassie crouched down and plucked the tiny creature from Montague's jaws. It had skin the colour of a maraschino cherry and seemed to be all bony, pointy limbs and sharp teeth. It sunk the latter into Cassie's finger.

'Oww! It bit me!' Cassie dropped the creature.

Montague leapt after it, pinning it beneath a paw.

'Of course she bit you, she's an imp. They're vicious, thieving pests. They live out of rubbish bins and steal anything that isn't tied down. London is full of them, the vermin. However, they can be useful.'

Despite her sore finger, Cassie was fascinated. The imp was no taller than a pencil and had hair that stuck up like a parrot's crest. Her small eyes flashed with fury and her tiny face was contorted with rage. She was nothing like the pretty, delicate creatures illustrated in the margins of Cassie's storybooks, sipping nectar from bluebells and wearing forget-me-not gowns.

'I thought they'd have wings,' she said.

'Some of them do, they pull them off moths, bats and

small birds and wear them as hunting trophies. They don't actually need them to fly.' Montague wrinkled his nose at the squirming creature. 'Imps are not the most reliable messengers, but they're fast. Have you got anything shiny? A button or an earring or some such bauble?'

Cassie pulled the school pin from her blazer.

'Will this do?'

'Very good, give it to the little beast.'

The pin was snatched from her fingers by the eager imp, who clutched it tightly and rubbed at it with tiny hands, polishing the surface. It squawked something at Montague.

'She has agreed to take our message,' said the cat. He addressed the imp, speaking slowly, 'Tell the Hedgewitch that Montague has found the girl and will return with her this evening.'

He repeated it twice, to make sure she got it right. The imp nodded and vanished, taking the school pin with her.

'Imps travel faster than thought,' Montague explained. 'Which is why most humans are too slow to see them. Your aunt will know of your impending arrival by the time she sits down to breakfast. Now, we need to get to Euston station.'

Montague led her, with only one wrong turn, to the nearest overground stop. The cat ceased talking once they were surrounded by strangers, so as not to draw unwanted attention. They were a source of curiosity all the same; the untidy girl in school uniform following the grey cat with his tail in the air were not the sort of passengers the people of Trite were used to seeing on a Tuesday morning.

Cassie didn't have any money and was worried about their tickets, but Montague instructed her, 'Pluck some leaves from that holly hedge.'

Cassie stripped a couple of leaves from the prickly bush, conscious that an old lady with a white dog was watching her.

'If anyone asks for your ticket, show him those,' said Montague. 'Don't worry, it's the oldest trick in the book.'

To Cassie's surprise, the leaves worked. The ticket collector on the 7:30 express to Euston barely glanced at them. Cassie turned them over in her hands, but they were still only leaves to her eyes; it seemed Montague had shown her a little faery magic after all.

Although the past night had involved more running than sleeping, Cassie spent the journey wide-eyed, staring out the window of the carriage. It was seven years since she'd seen anything beyond the Fowell House gates. They passed grand stone buildings, canals with red and blue boats, rows of elegant white houses and parks bordered with black railings, full of tall plane trees. Not everything was picturesque though, there were many rows of drab houses, black with coal dust and the dark skeletons of bombed-out buildings, surrounded by rubble in which grubby children played. London was a city of contrasts, the well-to-do in their feathered hats and fur coats avoiding the hungry gaze of men crouched in empty shopfronts. Boys with no shoes polished those of pinstriped businessmen and the street markets thronged with people from all walks of life.

At last, they reached Euston station. Cassie marvelled at the great arch, its columns towering above them.

Here, the crowds rushing about paid no attention to the girl with the grey cat. Cassie carried Montague, to his evident displeasure, so that they would not be separated in the throng.

She had to ask a baggage boy, but they found their platform just in time and climbed up into a carriage. It was the sort with doors on either side and no corridor, so once you were aboard you could not move between carriages. There were already people inside.

'Would you like the window seat, duck?' asked a large woman in a red polka-dot dress. She had a cage on the seat beside her, which housed a fat rooster. The bird watched them with beady eyes and cried in alarm when it saw Montague.

Cassie thanked the woman and took her seat. There was a rack above for luggage but she kept her satchel with her. Across from her, a man was buried in his newspaper. On the front page was another story about a missing child, a young boy from Brighton. All she could see of the man behind the paper was a pair of legs in striped trousers and shiny black shoes.

Cassie settled into her seat with Montague on her lap and felt a jolt of excitement as the whistle blew and a great puff of steam surrounded them in white fog. The conductor announced their departure and another small, sweet voice called out through the steam.

'Come on, Mummy! We'll miss the train.' A girl's head appeared through the carriage door, she was holding her hat on with one hand and clutching a large white rabbit in the other.

'I'm sure this isn't our carriage, darling, it's *third class*,' hissed the woman behind her. 'If you'd only wait a moment we could find our seats.'

The girl ignored her mother and pushed past the newspaper to take the window seat across from Cassie. The woman clambered in after her and struggled to arrange their suitcases in the luggage rack above.

The girl was terribly pretty. She had soft black curls and big dark eyes fringed with heavy lashes, just like the rabbit's. She wore a blue dress with white gloves. Her mother was beautifully dressed and made up too, with scarlet lipstick in a cupid's bow.

Cassie looked down at her own stained and crumpled uniform and touched her hair, which was doing its best to resemble a bird's nest.

The girl smiled at her and it was such a conspiratorial expression that Cassie couldn't help but smile back.

'This really is dreadfully crowded,' complained the girl's mother. 'Why you couldn't wait until we found someone to escort us, Tabitha, I simply don't understand.'

The girl gave an exasperated sigh. 'The train was leaving!'

And she was right, with a groan and shudder of wheels on rails the engine heaved itself out of Euston station and began its long journey north.

Cassie stared out the window as they hurtled through tunnels, past rows of houses and allotments. They crossed a river and soon the gardens gave way to fields and there were more cows and sheep than people. The great green blanket of England unrolled before them. Hills undulated in grassy waves and hedges frothed with blossom. Small white clouds cast shadows over the hills and birds chased the train as it sped through a valley. They dived into a tunnel of leafy green, branches scratching the windows as they flew past. Cassie's eyes and heart ached with the beauty of it. Until now, her life had been painted in greys and browns, the drab colours of Fowell House. All of a sudden her vision was flooded with green grass, blue sky and fields of golden dandelions.

No one else in the carriage seemed much concerned with what was going on outside the window. The newspaper rustled occasionally, the woman in the red dress pulled a ball of knitting from her handbag and began to clack away with her needles.

'Mummy's going to have a rest, dear, try not to bother her,' said the girl's mother, closing her eyes with a pained expression.

Cassie's stomach growled. She'd eaten nothing since the day before.

'Here, I've got some sandwiches, do you want one?' asked the girl.

'Yes, please.'

The girl opened her little handbag and produced two packages wrapped in wax paper.

'They're egg and cress, I'm afraid, but cook makes them with plenty of salt and pepper so they're quite nice really.'

She handed Cassie one of the packages, which opened to reveal perfect rectangles of white bread with the crusts cut off. Cassie wolfed hers down before she even remembered to say thank you.

'You *must* be hungry!' said the girl, laughing. 'I'm Tabitha by the way, Tabitha Blight, and this is Wyn,' she stroked the rabbit's soft fur.'

Cassie introduced herself and Montague.

'Are you heading to Oswalton?' Tabitha asked.

Cassie shook her head. 'We're going to Hedgely to meet my aunt.'

'Wonderful!' The girl clapped her hands together. 'I'm bound for Hedgely too, to stay with my grandmother. I don't know anyone else there. Oh, I'm so glad we've met!'

'Have you been to Hedgely before?' asked Cassie.

'Once, when I was much younger. It's a little frightening, don't you think? Being that close to the border. Of course, there's the Hedgewitch to keep an eye on things. That's why I'm going, to train with *her*. But tell me, why have you been banished to the country? Did you do something terrible?' asked Tabitha with mock seriousness.

'Actually, I've run away,' said Cassie, lowering her voice to a whisper. She felt she could trust Tabitha, even though Montague gave her a disapproving glare. Cassie told her about the Garm, and Burnhope's Home for Children, but she didn't mention the goblins. She wasn't sure if the other girl would believe her.

'Oh, I should have run away too!' said Tabitha. 'That school sounds horrid. You were awfully brave, though. What will you do now?'

'I'm going to find my mother. I'm sure she's still alive.'

'I'll help you! Let's think, you should start by asking the Hedgewitch, she's one of the best witches in the country, they say. I'm sure she'd know what to do.'

'Actually, the Hedgewitch is—' Cassie began.

'Tabitha, darling,' said her mother, opening one eye and looking with evident distaste at the state of Cassie's hair and uniform and the scratches on her face. 'What did I tell you about talking to strangers?'

Tabitha flushed and gave Cassie an apologetic smile. Cassie didn't mind though, there was plenty to look at outside the window. She lay back against the plush seat and let her mind wander as the fields and villages flew by. Very soon she would be in Hedgely, she would meet her aunt and together they would set out to find her mother.

Chapter Seven

The House
on the Hill

'Last call for Hedgely station! Last call!'

'Hsss! Cassandra, wake up.'

Montague jumped off her lap as Cassie started awake. Overcome by exhaustion, she'd fallen asleep during their journey and now the carriage was empty. She'd nearly missed her stop! Cassie opened the door and jumped down to the platform, still foggy with sleep. She looked about for Tabitha but the girl and her mother had gone.

A whistle blew, the train hissed steam and disappeared into a tunnel of foliage. Cassie and Montague were alone at a small station with hanging flower baskets and a painted sign that read 'HEDGELY'.

'What do we do now?'

The question died on her lips as she realised they were not alone after all.

There was a little man standing by the road. He was dressed in pea-green tweed, with a flat cap on his head from under which poked the largest ears she'd ever seen on a person. His beard was red and he wore a pair of embroidered purple boots with gold tassels. The boots did not seem to belong to the rest of him, but they were very clean and beautifully made. He was holding a sign, upside down, which read 'NⱯƆᴚOW'.

'Hello, are you waiting for me? I'm Cassandra Morgan.'

He looked her up and down and nodded. 'Name o' Brogan, Gillie Brogan.' He extended a hand, which Cassie shook. He eyed her satchel. 'That all you've brought then?'

'Yes, I was in a bit of a hurry.'

'Suit yourself. Cart's round the back.'

The cart was a simple, old-fashioned farmer's dray but it was hitched to the most beautiful horse in the world. She was grey, a silvery sort of grey that was almost white and made her appear ghostly in the fading light. She had a waterfall of mane and deep, dark eyes like wells with stars at the bottom. Cassie, who had never been a horse-mad girl, ran up to her at once and stroked her noble head.

'That's Peg,' said Brogan, by way of introduction. The horse lifted her head and whinnied.

'Wantin' 'er dinner, she is.'

He helped Cassie into the cart, while Montague leapt up behind and settled down amidst the remains of a hay bale. At the click of Brogan's tongue, Peg lifted her feathered hooves and began a slow and stately walk.

The road was unpaved and gouged with deep wheel ruts. Cassie could feel each bump and jolt as the cart meandered through the wooded valley. The trees shivered with the pale greenery of early spring and the fading light revealed glades of bluebells. The air was crisp and cool, like the first bite of an apple.

'There's a rug under the seat, if you're feelin' a chill,' said Brogan.

Cassie pulled out the red wool blanket and wrapped it about her shoulders, thanking him.

'I'm sorry, but are we related?' she asked, hoping this wouldn't offend him.

The little man grunted, which Cassie took for a laugh. 'I work up at the 'ouse – gardens, odd jobs, that sort o' thing.'

As the woods gave way to fields, a tawny owl swept down from an old oak and glided across their path. They were going uphill now. Cassie watched Peg's silver flanks ripple as she pulled them up the road. When they came to the crest of the hill the trees parted to reveal a scene from a picture postcard.

Below them, laid out in neat little squares bordered by hedgerows, was a carpet of fields and pasture dotted with the small grey shapes of sheep. Nestled at the bottom of the shallow valley was a village; a high street, surrounded by cottages with twinkling lights and threads of blue smoke rising from their chimneys. A church spire poked out behind the houses. Beyond the village there was a shining ribbon of water, snaking down the valley and disappearing behind another hill.

The sight that dominated the view, however, was to the west, where the sun had gone down, leaving a thin line of pale blue sky. It was a great dark shadow that seemed to go on forever, like the sea. Cassie had to look at it hard before she realised it was a wood. Not a dainty little wood like the one they'd come through, but a true forest, thick with tall and ancient trees. It loomed over the village, threatening to swallow it up.

'The Hedge,' said Montague, following her gaze.

'I've never seen so many trees.'

'And you're not likely to again,' said the cat. 'The Hedge is the largest wood in Britain and the oldest. All that remains of the ancient wild wood that once covered half this island.'

'It's like something from a story, I feel as though there could be bears or wolves hiding in there.'

'There be worse 'n that in the 'Edge,' said Brogan.

With a flick of the reins they were descending into the valley.

Cassie couldn't take her eyes off the wood. As they reached the village it hovered at the edge of her vision, a storm cloud of tree shadow and dense leafy green.

They passed through the heart of Hedgely, a cobbled high street lined with shops shouldering each other, like people on a crowded bus. Their doors were painted in bright colours, their signs swung in the breeze. Most were shuttered up for the night, but one establishment spilled light and laughter on to the street – a large inn with a sign that read 'THE PICKLED IMP' with a picture of a small green faery in a bottle. Someone was playing music inside, a leaping tune that made you want to dance.

'Hullo Brogan! Come 'n join us, man!' called a red-faced fellow from the doorway.

'Not t'night, Emley,' Brogan replied.

Cassie thought he looked disappointed, though it was hard to tell, her companion was not the most expressive character.

They drove out of the village, towards the river. Now Cassie could see that its source was somewhere in the Hedge. Crossing an old stone bridge that echoed with the clap of Peg's hooves, they started up another hill.

The road was lined with ancient beeches, their silvery boughs reaching overhead to form a tangled archway. At the top of the hill, it brought them between two stone gateposts topped with statues of hares, their heads lifted up to the sky.

The rough drive led up to a big house. It looked as though someone had taken bits of various buildings and cobbled them together. There were dark beamed walls with white plaster and others of red brick and golden stone, with crenelations and gargoyles perched above. Set into these were windows with stained glass, diamond panes and gothic arches, like those in old churches. They glittered from within with a yellow light. The house had two turrets, one square with arrow slits, the other round with a pointed roof. Ivy and wisteria competed in a mad race up the walls and a rowan tree grew by the door, creamy with blossom. Each part of the house seemed to belong to a different century, but somehow they all worked together to give it a comfortable, if eccentric, appearance. Cassie loved it at once.

''Ere we are then,' said Brogan as Peg pulled up, tossing her head.

'Hartwood Hall,' Montague supplied.

'Does my aunt really own all of this?' Cassie asked. The house was surrounded by rambling gardens that receded into the gloaming.

'Not strictly speaking,' said Montague. 'She's the Hedgewitch, the house comes with the position. There have been Hedgewitches at Hartwood for a thousand years.'

At that moment, the great oak door of the house burst open, ejecting a large woman who came bouncing down the stairs towards them.

'Oh, my gooses and ganders! Here she is, here she is at last!'

Before she'd even reached the ground, Cassie found herself engulfed in a great bear hug that crushed the air out of her. Her assailant smelled of gingerbread, which would have been lovely if Cassie could breathe. Finally, the woman released her, clasping her soft hands on Cassie's shoulders.

'Let me look at you! Cats and kippers, why, you're the very image of Rose when she first came here, isn't she just?'

Brogan grunted, he was busy with Peg's tack. Cassie opened her mouth to ask a question but the woman carried on.

'To think, all these years and you locked up in that awful school and us not even knowing. Rose's daughter! Why, there hasn't been a child at Hartwood since your dear mum was no bigger than you. But you're such a slip of a thing, what did they feed you at that school? Poor lamb. Well, we'll soon sort you out. Come inside, come inside, I've just put the kettle on and there's a fresh loaf in the oven, thank goodness I thought to do a second bake today. She'll be quite famished when she gets here, I said to myself, she'll be wanting her tea and stale bread simply won't do! Thank the stars. Oh, and you've Rose's hair, only without the curls...'

Cassie allowed herself to be steered towards the house, Montague trotting ahead of them. Cassie had a lot of questions at this point, however, as she'd had nothing but a sandwich since the day before, the prospect of a hot meal rather dominated her thoughts.

The woman led her through the open door and into a high-roofed hall where a winding stair wrapped itself around the trunk of a great tree with green-gold leaves shaped like hearts. Its branches reached right to the ceiling, leading off down hallways and corridors on the upper storeys and spreading out in a canopy beneath skylights that revealed the early evening stars.

Cassie stood beneath it, her head craned back and her eyes wide. There was no breeze inside the hall, they'd shut the door behind them, and yet the leaves on the lower branches quivered as she approached. Cassie reached out to touch one, it was soft as velvet.

'The Hartwood tree,' said the woman by way of explanation. 'Come along, this way.'

They went through a succession of rooms, down a short flight of stairs and into a kitchen. The floor was of smooth flagstones, each as big as a bed. Above them were heavy, dark beams from which hung bunches of drying herbs, onions, copper pots and a ham. One whole wall was taken up by the fireplace, where a cauldron simmered softly to itself over glowing coals.

Montague padded straight towards it, positioning himself before the hearth.

The woman led Cassie to a table that dominated the room, a great slab of wood hewn from a single tree, and sat her down on a bench padded with cushions. She was at the end near the fire and could feel its warmth. Delicious smells wafted to her from the cauldron.

'Now, you sit there and I'll have your supper ready faster than you can sneeze!'

Cassie watched the woman bustle about the kitchen, fetching cups and saucers, plates and knives. She was wearing a pink dress with primroses on it and a flour-dusted apron. Her silvery-blonde hair was piled on her head and fixed in place with a spoon.

Cassie found her voice again, 'Excuse me, but are you my aunt?'

The woman turned to her, eyebrows raised and a butter knife in one hand. 'Bless you child, your aunt? What a lark you are! I'm the housekeeper, you can call me Mrs Briggs.'

Cassie was a little disappointed, it would be rather nice to have Mrs Briggs for an aunt.

'Now then, no long faces in my kitchen! You'll meet the Hedgewitch soon enough and in the meantime you've supper coming. We'll have you rosy-cheeked and stuffed like a Christmas goose by the time you're done.'

Mrs Briggs brought Cassie thick slices of brown toast, oozing golden butter, cottage pie with fluffy potatoes, sweet green beans, baked apples and a pot of steaming bramble tea with honey. Cassie stared at the spread before her, unsure where to start. She'd had dreams like this at Fowell House.

Brogan came into the kitchen through the back door, wiping his boots on the mat and helping himself to a chunk of bread and cheese.

'Fetch a plate. We've company and I'll not sweep up after your crumbs again!' Mrs Briggs scolded him.

Brogan muttered to himself but did as he was told and soon the three of them were seated at the table in the warm glow of the fire.

Cassie sipped her tea and tried to imagine Rose in the house when she was a girl.

'My mother, was she happy here?' Cassie asked.

''Course she was, love,' said Mrs Briggs. 'Mind, she was even younger than you when she got here, with your aunt Miranda and uncle Elliot. That was back when your great-grandmother, Sylvia Morgan, was Hedgewitch. Those three rascals were as thick as thieves, running about the place in muddy boots, bringing home imps in jars and brewing potions in their bedrooms. Why, there's a stain on the parlour carpet, from when your mother spilt a bottle of elderberry ink, that I've never been able to get out.'

'Loved the gardens too, she did. Always a great one for flowers, was young Rose,' said Brogan.

'Then why did she leave?' asked Cassie.

Mrs Briggs and Brogan shared a silent look. Mrs Briggs put down her teacup and dabbed at her face with the corner of her apron.

'They had a row. Rose and your aunt Miranda,' she said, looking into the fire.

Brogan simply shook his head and glowered into his cheese.

'What did they argue about?' asked Cassie. 'It must have been something dreadful for her to go.'

The two Hartwood staff exchanged another meaningful glance and Cassie could see they knew more than they were going to tell her.

'It was a long time ago,' said Mrs Briggs slowly. 'I'm sure they've both regretted it since. They were always proud girls, especially your aunt Miranda, she'd never admit to being wrong about anything. And your mother, well, Rose was a free spirit, she wore her heart on her sleeve for all to see but she had her secrets too. Best to let the past lie, there's nothing that can be done about it now and your aunt won't thank you for bringing it up.'

Cassie was not satisfied with this at all. She'd come to Hedgely to find out more about her mother – if Mrs Briggs and Brogan wouldn't tell her, she'd have to ask the Hedgewitch directly.

'Where is my aunt?'

'She'll be up at the Pickerin's place,' said Brogan. 'Old Pete was sayin' as 'ow they'd lost their prize bull calf last night.'

Mrs Briggs sighed and began to clear the supper things. 'She won't be back until late then. Cassandra will have to wait until the morning to meet her.'

'What does the Hedgewitch do exactly?' Cassie asked.

They both looked at her as if she'd asked what the postman did for a living.

'Bless you dear, they really taught you nothing about us at that school, did they? Fancy, a Morgan child not knowing about the Hedgewitch.'

'She protects the village,' said Brogan, matter-of-factly.

'And the rest of England by way of it. It's one of the most important positions in the country. A great honour and a great burden,' said Mrs Briggs.

'Yes, but what does she protect people from?' asked Cassie.

'Why, from the Hedge of course,' Mrs Briggs answered, as if this were obvious.

Her aunt protected England from a wood? It didn't make sense, but Cassie was very tired and having difficulty trying to form her next question.

'Come now, let's get you upstairs to bed,' said Mrs Briggs. 'You look like a drooping daisy. You'll see your aunt in the morning and you can ask her all about it then.'

Cassie submitted to being shepherded upstairs by Mrs Briggs, Montague trailing behind them. The housekeeper carried a lamp to light their way.

'The house has never been wired for the electric,' she explained. 'They tried once, in your great-grandmother's time, but the brownie didn't like it and chewed through the wires.'

The great hall was lined with portraits of women, all dressed in black. Many wore tall pointed hats. Past Hedgewitches, Cassie supposed. She stopped before a full-length painting. It was of a woman in medieval dress, with long black hair wrapped in ribbons. There was a raven perched on her shoulder. The woman was holding a book in one hand and a cup in the other, but Cassie was drawn to her face, which was beautiful, intelligent and fierce. The painting reminded her of the pictures in *Tales of Faerie*.

'That's your ancestress, Morgana of Faerie, the first Hedgewitch. Of course, it was painted hundreds of years after she died. The artist got her nose all wrong.' The housekeeper tutted, leading Cassie to the staircase that wound about the great tree. As they climbed, Cassie reached out a hand to brush the Hartwood tree's rough bark. They were up amongst its canopy when Mrs Briggs led them off along a darkened hallway.

'Mind you follow Montague or myself until the house gets used to you. It has a mind of its own and sometimes decides you should be somewhere other than where you want to be. Why, only last Tuesday I got up in the night to use the water closet and found myself in the second pantry. Good thing I did though, there was a frid eating my damson jam!'

They went down a long corridor, past closed doors and empty passages, coming at last to a little arched doorway at the end of the hall.

'Here we are then, I thought you'd like to have Rose's old room.' Mrs Briggs opened the door for Cassie to step through.

The room was circular and Cassie realised that they must be in one of the turrets she'd seen from outside. There were two deep-set windows on opposite sides, one with a window seat which she saw immediately would be perfect for reading. Beside the other was a brass bed with a patchwork quilt. An old wardrobe with a mirror in the door stood by a small writing desk and, best of all, there was a bookshelf stuffed with books. The floor was covered with a green rag-rug that looked like moss and across from the doorway a fireplace glowed with a few orange coals. Cassie went to warm herself by it and found there were pictures on the mantelpiece. A smiling man and woman, dressed in old-fashioned clothes, and another of three children, climbing an apple tree.

'Your grandparents,' Mrs Briggs explained. 'Olive and Edward Morgan, they died in a motoring accident, that's why your mother came here. The children are Rose, Miranda and Elliot. That was taken not long after they arrived.'

Cassie touched the silver frame and smiled. Her mother must be the girl with curly red hair.

'Now, this ought to fit you, I should think,' said Mrs Briggs, holding up a long white nightgown. 'There's some frocks and blouses in the dresser too, they were your mother's when she was a girl. A bit old-fashioned, but they'll have to do until I make you something new. You certainly can't go wearing those drab things about. Here, give them to me and I'll wash them.'

Cassie surrendered her uniform gladly, not caring if she ever saw it again. Soon, she was dressed in the clean, lavender-scented nightgown which fell to her ankles. She wanted to explore the bookshelf, but Mrs Briggs insisted it was too late and she was tucked into bed with a hot water bottle. Montague curled up on a cushion beside the fire.

'Good night, sleep tight, don't let the bogles bite!' said Mrs Briggs, blowing out the lamp on her way out.

Cassie lay in bed, adjusting to the shadows of the unfamiliar room. She imagined her mother walking through the halls of Hartwood, eating Mrs Briggs' cooking, sleeping in that very bed. She thought about the village of Hedgely, the silvery river and the great dark wood. She would explore it tomorrow, she decided, after she'd met her aunt and they'd come up with a plan to find Rose.

Chapter Eight

The Hedgewitch

Cassie woke in a pool of sunlight. A bumblebee hummed in lazy circles about her room. The window was open, letting in blackbird song and the dew-green scent of the morning. She lay there for a while, looking up at the wooden beams of her ceiling, which met in the centre to form a snowflake pattern.

Cassie pulled back the covers and crossed the rug barefoot to the east window. The sun was already above the hills, though the light still had the watery quality of early morning. Through the window she could see the Hartwood gardens, bound by a mossy stone wall, and beyond them fields and rolling hills. But the west window, which was still in shadow, gazed toward the dark fringe of the Hedge.

Cassie said good morning to the photo of her grandparents and looked again at the picture of her mother as a girl. Her aunt must be the other girl in the picture, she had long dark hair and serious eyes. How odd it was to suddenly acquire a whole family.

'Wake up, sleepy-head!' she called to Montague, who was curled in a ball by the cold fireplace.

The cat muttered something and tucked his head under a paw.

Cassie washed her face and hands in the basin and dressed in a frock and cardigan from the wardrobe. The dress was a bit big but Cassie was so pleased to be out of her school uniform that she spun around, sending her skirt flying.

'Eeowwww!' wailed the cat as she trod on his tail. 'Watch where you put those great clomping feet!' He scowled at her. 'Why you should be up at this awful hour is beyond me. All those birds squawking, nasty cold air, damp grass – entirely unpleasant. I suppose you'll be wanting breakfast now too.'

Cassie's stomach growled in answer.

'Very well, come along then. Perhaps once you're fed I can have some peace.'

Without Montague as a guide, Cassie would soon have been lost trying to find her way back to the kitchen. The house was a maze of doors and hallways that twisted and turned, lined with bookcases, paintings and mirrors. Finally, Cassie and Montague came to the great hall and the Hartwood tree. From the direction of the kitchen, a delicious, savoury smell wafted up to them.

'Sausages!' cried Cassie.

Breakfast at Fowell House had consisted of a lumpy grey sludge that passed itself off as porridge. She hadn't eaten sausages in years, but she would never forget that smell. Cassie entered the kitchen and gasped in delight at what she saw.

The great table was laden with dishes: piles of bacon, soft-boiled eggs with speckled brown shells, heaps of fried mushrooms, tomatoes and beans, slabs of thick-cut toast, pots of marmalade and blackcurrant jam and the fat blue teapot with steam rising from its spout.

'Help yourself, lamb,' said Mrs Briggs. 'We don't stand on ceremony in the mornings.'

Cassie loaded her plate with more food than she could possibly hope to eat and quickly got to work on it.

'My goodness, you'll surpass Brogan if you finish that lot.' Mrs Briggs laughed. 'He'll be along for his soon, I should imagine. He's been up since the crack of dawn, working in the garden.' Mrs Briggs was stirring something in the cauldron. 'Myself, I like a bit of a lie-in when I can get it. I'll just finish this up, then I'll join you.'

'What is it?' asked Cassie, wondering what could possibly be missing from the ample spread.

'Porridge, for your aunt. She doesn't eat this sort of thing.' Mrs Briggs waved a hand over the eggs and bacon. 'Plain and simple fare, she likes. Bit too plain if you ask me, but it takes all sorts.'

Cassie loaded her fork again. What an odd person her aunt must be to choose porridge over sausages.

The back door creaked open. Cassie looked up, expecting to see Brogan come to join her at the feast.

Standing in the doorway was a woman dressed entirely in black, from collar to boots. Her skirt was spotted with mud and she clutched a pointed hat in her hand. She had a sharp face with high cheekbones and straight brows. A large black cat with a white spot on its chest brushed past her. The woman stared at Cassie as though she were a ghost.

'Good morning, Miranda,' said Mrs Briggs. 'Found the calf, I trust? You must be tired. Here's your porridge now, with a pinch of salt, just as you like it.'

Cassie stared back. Miranda looked nothing like her mother. Rose had wild red hair and pink cheeks, while the woman in the doorway had frown lines on her forehead and short, dark hair. The only thing they had in common were the eyes, the same stormy grey as Cassie's own. But while her mother's eyes were full of laughter, Miranda's intense gaze made Cassie want to melt into her seat.

'Thank you, Mabily,' said the Hedgewitch, placing her hat on the table. 'The calf was recovered – there was a broken fence and he'd wandered into the Hedge. Not stolen, I think, more likely spooked by something, although one can't be too careful at this time of year.'

Miranda took her seat at the head of the table and the black cat took the best spot by the fire. Mrs Briggs put a steaming bowl of porridge in front of her but she did not touch it.

'So, you are Cassandra.'

'Yes, miss...'

'You may call me "Aunt Miranda" when we are at home.'

'Yes, Aunt Miranda.'

'Very well, as you will be living here for the foreseeable future, we shall establish some house rules.'

'Rules?'

'Indeed. I am a very busy witch with many responsibilities. I will not be able to supervise you all the time and neither will Mrs Briggs or Brogan.'

The housekeeper smiled at Cassie and turned back to the stove.

'Therefore, I expect you to be independent, responsible and to behave in a way befitting a Morgan. We have a reputation in this village, you understand, people turn to us for help, so we must be irreproachable in our conduct.'

Cassie felt as though she were being accused of some crime she'd yet to commit. She'd only just arrived in Hedgely; she'd hardly had time to get into trouble.

'There are three rules that I expect you to follow. The first, and most important for your own safety, is this: you must not go into the Hedge alone.'

'But why not?'

'The Hedge is full of dangers, few who enter are able to find their way out again and there are things within that should not be disturbed. You are not to enter the Hedge unless I accompany you, do you understand?'

Since she'd seen the woods the night before, Cassie had a yearning to explore their depths. Perhaps she could convince her aunt to take her there, although that would rather spoil the fun of it.

'I understand,' she agreed reluctantly.

'Good. The second rule is common sense. You must not leave the Hartwood grounds after dark.'

Cassie nodded. She was used to curfew at school and with summer approaching she would still have hours of daylight to spend outside.

'Finally, you may go wherever you please within Hartwood Hall, with the exception of my study in the northern turret. It is locked when I am out and I must not be disturbed in my work.'

That must be the other turret Cassie had seen from the drive. She had no real interest in her aunt's study and would probably get lost trying to find it. At least that rule would be easy enough to follow.

Miranda seemed satisfied and turned her attention to the porridge. But now it was Cassie's turn to speak. It took her a moment to find the courage to begin.

'Please, do you have any idea what happened to my mother?'

The Hedgewitch stared at her, the spoon halfway to her mouth.

'Only, I don't believe she's dead,' Cassie continued

quickly. 'I know that's what the lawyers said, but it can't be true. I'd know if it was.'

Miranda laid down her spoon and clasped her hands together.

'I would advise you to forget about her. Wherever Rose has gone, she's not coming back.'

Cassie couldn't believe what she'd just heard. 'Forget about... my mother?'

'Rose abandons people. It's what she does. She never thinks about those she leaves behind. She has no doubt forgotten about us. We must get on with our lives.'

'No!' Cassie stood up, slamming her palms on the table. 'That's not true! How can you say that? She promised me she'd come back, if she hasn't it's because she can't. She's lost or hurt or, I don't know, but she might need our help.'

Miranda folded her arms. 'Believe that if you will, but ask yourself: why did she stay away all these years? Why did she leave you in that school and not with your family, your home, your place here in Hedgely? This is where you belong, Cassandra, and she never even told you we exist. Rose keeps secrets and she runs away when things get tough. She did the same thirteen years ago, when she left Hedgely.'

'Maybe she just couldn't stand living with you!'

Cassie pushed back the bench and ran out of the kitchen, crashing through the back door into the garden. She crossed rows of leeks and kale, stopping only to cast a furious glare back at the house.

How dare Miranda say such things? Rose hadn't abandoned her, she'd only wanted Cassie to be safe. While Cassie had to admit it was strange she'd not been told about Hedgely and her aunt, there had to be a perfectly good reason for it.

Cassie set off down one of the garden paths, not caring where it led her. She wrapped her arms about herself. Her aunt was horrid. She ought never to have come here. She'd escaped Fowell House only to be trapped in this place, with its silly rules and a woman every bit as bad as the Garm to boss her around.

However, Cassie couldn't hate Hartwood. As she followed the path away from the kitchen she passed clumps of violets and nodding golden cowslips. She came through a small orchard where the trees bore clouds of scented blossom that hummed with bees. Everywhere she looked, fresh green leaves were bursting through the soil or budding on branches. It was hard to stay angry walking through the cool, dewy grass.

At last she came upon a rose garden. There were rose hedges and standards, like lollies on sticks. Long stemmed red roses and tumbling white cabbage roses that carpeted the grass in petals. Briars climbed the high garden wall and miniature roses scrambled about at her feet. Every single rose was in full bloom, as if it were the height of June. Cassie made her way to the rose-carved bench at the centre of the garden, breathing deeply the unmistakable scent. She'd stepped from spring into midsummer.

'Impossible,' she said to herself.

'Just takes a bit o' work and a touch o' magic,' said a gruff voice from behind a bush.

Cassie walked round to find Brogan on the other side, a pair of pruning shears in hand and a pile of discarded branches beneath him. He was wearing canary-yellow wellingtons.

'It's so beautiful – and the smell!' said Cassie.

'This was your ma's garden,' he said. 'She planted most of these. I just keep an eye on 'em, when I've got the time.'

Cassie looked about her with fresh eyes. She tried to imagine her mother here, caring for the roses, but it was hard. She'd never seen Rose so much as touch a trowel.

'They're faery roses, not sure 'ow she got them. They bloom all year, even in midwinter. Makes for a lot of dead-headin', though.' He snipped another wilted bloom off the bush.

Cassie sat down on the bench, running her hand over the smooth carvings.

'Do you think she's still alive?'

'Don't know about that, 'spect you've not given up on 'er, though.'

Cassie sighed. 'Everyone seems to think I should. Aunt Miranda told me to forget all about her.'

Brogan said nothing, there was only the snip-snap of the shears.

'I don't think I like Aunt Miranda very much,' Cassie admitted. 'And I don't think she likes me.'

The gardener shrugged. 'Was a shock to 'er, findin' out about you.'

'It was a shock to me too! That's no excuse for being awful.'

'Maybe not, but the older you are the longer it takes to come round to things, if you get my meanin'.'

Cassie thought that was ridiculous. Adults ought to be able to handle changes better than young people – wasn't that the point of growing up?

'You're telling me I should give her time to get used to having me here?'

Brogan shrugged and went back to his pruning. 'These 'ere roses, they're still bloomin', even though your ma's gone. They've not withered and died without 'er. Matter of fact, they've grown bigger and stronger.'

Cassie put her feet up on the bench and hugged her knees. She pulled out her key, and twirled it between her fingers.

'She promised she'd come back. I can't give up on her yet.'

Brogan nodded. 'One thing I'll say about Miss Rose, she was never one for breakin' a promise.'

Cassie reached for the nearest bloom, pulling it down to her nose and startling a honey bee that had been hiding inside, its furry body dusted in pollen. She was not going to give up so easily. If the Hedgewitch wouldn't help her, she'd just have to find her mother on her own.

Chapter Nine

Elevenses

'I fail to see why I must chaperone you on this pointless errand,' said Montague, gingerly picking his way between muddy puddles on the road downhill to Hedgely.

Cassie wondered if the cat was always this cranky in the morning.

Feeling better after her talk with Brogan, she'd returned to the kitchen, but the Hedgewitch had vanished. Mrs Briggs explained that her aunt had gone upstairs to sleep, having been out all night. The housekeeper gave Cassie a handful of coins and a shopping list and swept her out the door. She was sent off to explore the village with the disgruntled cat, dislodged from his place by the fire.

'It's a beautiful day,' said Cassie, enjoying the sun on her face. 'And it isn't entirely pointless, there's kippers on this list.'

Montague said nothing but picked up his pace, his tail held up like a flag.

When they reached the old stone bridge that crossed the river, Cassie stopped. The river flowed down from the Hedge, under the bridge and out into the fields. She leaned over the wall and gazed into the clear water below. Lily pads were just beginning to unfurl and long strands of riverweed rippled in the current like green hair. There were shoals of minnows and stripe-backed yellow perch sunning themselves near the surface. Cassie could see her shadowy reflection in the water and, as she watched, another face appeared beneath her own, rising pale and glistening to the surface. It was a woman's face, eyes wide, mouth gaping open as if for air.

'What are we stopping for?' asked Montague.

'There's someone down there, in the water,' said Cassie. She ran across the bridge and began to slide down the bank, the wet grass staining her dress. 'She's drowning!'

To be truthful, Cassie couldn't swim, but that made her all the more worried about the woman in the river.

Perhaps she could find a large branch and drag her to safety, or a rope.

'Hullo!' she called. 'Are you all right? I'm coming!'

Bullrushes lined the bank but Cassie found a break and pushed through. She couldn't see the face any more, just the deep, dark river, flowing slowly past.

'Cassandra, keep back from the water!' called the cat.

Ignoring him, Cassie pushed her way to the river's edge. Something cold and wet grabbed her ankle and pulled.

Before she could draw breath or cry out she was underwater. Sharp, bony hands clawed at her, tugging her down. She flailed and kicked but could not escape their grip. Green weeds swirled around her, obscuring her view. The face appeared again, the woman's face; it had lidless eyes like a fish and a shark-toothed grin.

Cassie tried to scream, but her lungs filled with water. She grabbed at the river weeds but they were slimy and slipped from her grasp. The claw-like hands held her tight, pulling her deeper beneath the surface. Cassie's vision blurred, her chest ached. The water was so cold it chilled her to the bone.

With the last of her strength, Cassie kicked out. Her knee hit cold flesh and the woman stepped back. Fighting against the water, her arms flailing madly, she lunged for the surface. Cassie breached, gasping for breath, and in that second someone grabbed hold of her hand. But the river woman had caught her again; bony arms encircled her waist, pulling her once more beneath the water. She was caught in a painful tug of war between her rescuer and the creature that held her. Then, something round and white landed on the surface of the water and floated by. The woman released her and dived after it. Slowly, Cassie was dragged to the riverbank.

Lying in the mud, she coughed up brown water and pushed back streaming hair from her eyes. Hovering above her on a broomstick was her rescuer, a girl of about Cassie's own age, or a little older. She had a brown, freckled face surrounded by short frizzy hair and she was grinning.

'You all right?'

'Yes,' Cassie gasped. 'Thank you.'

'Bit brisk for a swim,' said the girl, landing her broom and giving Cassie a hand up.

'What was that thing? It tried to drown me!'

'Old Wendy Weedskin? Oh, she's a river hag, pretty harmless as far as folk go, only it's not the best place to take a dip. She lives under the bridge. If you want to go fishing, you have to feed her first.'

'Feed her?'

'Yes, speaking of which, you owe me elevenses. Had to toss my bun to distract her, it was a custard one too.'

'Is she...' Cassie paused, hoping the girl wouldn't laugh at her, '...a faery?'

"Course! There's loads of them round here, comes from being so close to the Hedge. The Nix flows down from the woods. You find all sorts of strange things in the river. Why, you've gone a funny colour. Have you never seen a faery before?'

'I have,' said Cassie. 'Only, where I'm from most people don't believe they exist.'

'Don't see what believing has to do with it, might as well not believe in baths or brothers, you have to put up with them all the same. I'm Rue, by the way, Rue Whitby – and this is Natter.'

She pointed to the toad perched on her shoulder. He was brown and lumpy, with stubby fingers that clung to Rue's shirt.

'She must be the new Morgan girl,' said the toad in a raspy voice.

Rue's eyes lit up. 'Everyone's talking about you. Just wait 'til I tell the boys I saw you first!'

'Everyone?' asked Cassie.

'Yes, everyone in the village. Emley Moor saw you come in last night, word gets around pretty quick here.'

'Especially with your mum helping it along,' said Natter. He winked at Cassie.

'That your familiar?' Rue asked, pointing at the grey cat who was making his way gingerly across the wet grass towards them.

'Certainly not,' said Montague. 'If I *were* her familiar she might actually acknowledge my counsel. Really, Cassandra, what is the point of my accompanying you on this misadventure if you ignore every word I say? You look like a drowned rat. We'll have to return to the house now and your aunt will not be impressed.'

'No need. You can dry off at my place,' Rue offered.

'And meet the rest of the clan,' said Natter.

'It's not far.'

Cassie wrung the water out of her hair and accepted the loan of Rue's pullover. The other girl tucked her broomstick under her arm and led the way.

'You'll be joining the coven then?' she asked Cassie.

'The coven? I don't know...'

'But you're a witch, aren't you? You're the old bat's— I mean, the Hedgewitch's niece. You must have witchcraft coming out your ears!'

'I've flown a broomstick once, but I've never cast a spell or anything like that. Do you think they'd let me join?'

'Sure! Any girl can learn witchcraft, even if she's not from a witch family. 'Course, some have a knack for it, not that it matters unless you're a real badge-hunter. We meet Fridays after school at the old hall,' Rue explained. 'We're going into the Hedge next week. It'll be smashing, you've got to come!'

Somehow, Cassie found herself agreeing to attend the following week. It was hard not to get swept up by Rue's enthusiasm and besides, learning a bit of witchcraft might help in finding her mother.

Hedgely sat in the cusp of the valley. Its rows of shops and houses, built of the same yellow stone, glowed softly in the morning light. The high street was bustling with people carrying shopping baskets and pushing prams. A policeman whizzed past them on a bicycle and a busker stood by the market cross, piping a cheerful tune on a penny whistle, his hat full of shiny coins.

Cassie's shoes squelched with river water as Rue

led her into the heart of the village. People turned to stare at them as they passed, whispering behind their backs. Cassie caught the words 'Hedgewitch' and 'Rose' and realised that they already knew who she was. Aunt Miranda would not be impressed by the soggy sight she made on her first appearance in town, it was hardly befitting the Morgan reputation, she would say.

They passed The Pickled Imp, a butcher, a draper and the small red post office.

'Here we are!' said Rue, opening the door of a shop with a flourish. The sign above read 'Whitby's' and had an apple painted next to it. The contents of the shop spilled out on to the street: baskets and barrels of fruit and vegetables, some still covered in earth. Bunches of daffodils and tulips filled a bucket by the door and the window was plastered with advertisements for soap powder, canned beans and cocoa.

Rue pulled her inside. The interior of the shop was lined with shelves crammed with packaged goods.

'Hi, Mum!' Rue called to the woman behind the counter as she tugged Cassie towards the stairs.

'Now hold your horses, Ruth Whitby! Who in the king's name is this poor creature you've dragged into my shop?'

'Who, this?' asked Rue with a cheeky grin. 'Just Cassie Morgan. She had a little run-in with Wendy Weedskin so I'm taking her upstairs to change.'

Mrs Whitby stepped out from behind the counter. She was a short, round woman with the same dark frizzy hair as Rue. She wore a green apron which made her resemble the apple on the shop sign. Her eyes lit up at the sight of Cassie.

'My word, so it is! I never believed it when they told me. Rose Morgan's daughter, they said, impossible, I said! But here you are and you couldn't be anyone else's.'

Cassie was dripping river water on the floor but Mrs Whitby didn't seem to notice.

'Well, that'll put a bee in Miranda's bonnet and no mistake,' she continued with a satisfied smile. 'Suppose you'll be starting at the village school, then? Rue will keep an eye on you, of course, but if you ever need anything you just pop in here of an afternoon and I'll sort you out. We got on well, your mum and me. Don't suppose you've heard from her, then?'

'Mum!' Rue complained.

'Oh, all right, no harm in asking now, is there? We're all wondering, aren't we? Anyhow, there's clean towels in the linen cupboard and mind you don't get mud on my carpets. Oh, and if you're going out after, take Oliver with you, he's getting under my feet.'

'But, Mum!'

'Off with you then, I'm a busy woman.'

Rue sighed and led Cassie upstairs. 'You ever call me Ruth and you'll regret it,' she warned.

Cassie emerged on to the street a short while later, dressed in a pair of Rue's shorts and a rather baggy jersey that belonged to one of her older brothers. Her wet hair was braided into two damp plaits. She didn't feel very presentable, but at least she was warm and mostly dry. Mrs Whitby had given her a basket full of the groceries Mrs Briggs had requested, a bunch of sweet violets tucked in beside.

Rue was holding the hand of a small boy in a white shirt. He had wispy brown curls framing a cherubic face.

'Come on, let's get something from Marchpane's. I'm starving,' she said.

'Buns!' said Oliver, tugging on his sister's arm.

'How many brothers do you have?' Cassie was feeling

a bit envious of Rue's cosy family.

'Three, which is plenty, and Oliver is more trouble than the rest of us together.'

Marchpane's was a small shop with a pink-striped awning and the smell of cinnamon, toffee and fresh bread wafting through the open door. Inside it was packed with people buying loaves, rolls and pies, and small children with their noses pressed against the glass cases. Cassie soon saw why. Lined up in neat little rows were currant buns and crumpets, gingerbread goblins and hedgehog cakes, toasted muffins and marshmallow meringues, saffron buns and swiss rolls and faery cakes with green icing.

Cassie fingered the pennies Mrs Briggs had given her to buy herself a treat and wondered how she'd ever make up her mind.

'Try a toadstool tart, they've got raspberry jam inside,' said Rue, helpfully.

Cassie and Rue finally reached the front of the queue, where a smiling woman in a pink apron awaited them.

'And what can I get for you, dears?' she asked, with one eye on Oliver who was drooling on the glass case.

'I'll have a loaf of white and two liquorice eclairs,' said a high-pitched voice from behind them. The voice belonged to a short, elderly woman in a witch's hat. With her, carrying a shopping basket heaped with turnips and cabbage, was the girl Cassie had met on the train.

'Tabitha!'

'Oh, hello,' she said, her cheeks flushed.

'Excuse *me*,' said Rue, glaring at the old woman, 'but we were next in line.'

'Tabitha, who are these insolent girls you appear to know?' asked the woman.

'This is Cassie Morgan, we met on the train and—'

'I'm Rue, Rue Whitby.'

'Well, I would expect no better from a shopkeeper's daughter, but you, Miss Morgan, should know how to show proper respect for your elders.' The old woman pushed Cassie aside with her crocodile-skin handbag. 'Wrap those in paper. I don't want flour on my dress.'

The old woman claimed her baked goods, paid in small change and pushed her way back out of the shop, leaving a line of grumbling patrons in her wake.

'Sorry!' Tabitha whispered, running after her.

While Rue stood by glowering, Cassie bought three toadstool tarts, glistening red with marshmallow spots, a sugar mouse for Montague and a squashed-fly biscuit for Natter. They found a sunny spot on the village green to sit and eat them. Oliver managed to get jam all over his white shirt within seconds and, having finished his treat, ran off to chase the ducks.

'How dare she!' said Rue, who was still fuming over the encounter. 'Shopkeeper's daughter? Everyone knows the old trow doesn't have a penny to her name, despite her airs and graces. I'd like to stuff her head in that handbag.'

'I doubt it would fit!' said Natter.

'Is she a witch too?' asked Cassie.

'Old Mrs Blight? I suppose so, though I've never seen her do any witchcraft. Mostly, she just likes to boss people about and strut around like she owns the village. She's not even from Hedgely! The Blights are a Somerset witching family.'

Mrs Blight must be Tabitha's grandmother, Cassie realised.

'Tabitha is all right though, she shared her sandwiches with me on the train.'

'I wouldn't waste your time on her, Cass. Those Blights are all the same. Oh, imp spit! Oliver's trying to pet the geese again, hold this for me, will you?'

Cassie watched Rue chase her brother around the green and wondered if she was right about Tabitha. Mrs Blight was a bad-tempered old woman, but you couldn't choose your family, as Cassie was all too aware.

'There's only one thing left on this list,' she said, as Rue returned, dragging her muddy and jam-smeared brother. Cassie peered at the scrap of paper Mrs Briggs had given her. 'It says "collect order from Widdershin's".'

'Oh, he's just down Loft Street,' said Rue. 'See the green door? Here, I'd better take Oliver home and get him cleaned up. Mum's going to kill me when she sees the state of him. Meet you here tomorrow afternoon? I'll let you have a go on my broom!'

Cassie waved goodbye to the Whitbys and turned to follow Montague towards the green door.

Chapter Ten

The Book Wyrm

Widdershin's was the last in a row of shops along Loft Street. It looked as though it had arrived late and found there wasn't quite enough room, but had squeezed itself in regardless. The three-storeyed building was leaning alarmingly to the right, its green door at such an angle that Cassie had to tilt her head to enter. A bell jingled somewhere in the dark interior.

'Hello?' she called. There was no reply. The shop was much bigger than it had seemed from outside and full of towering crooked shelves that carved the space into winding aisles.

The afternoon light came through a window high above, turning the floating dust into dancing fireflies. Cassie blinked; the shelves were stuffed with *books*! There were piles of books on the floor, stacks of books on small tables nearly collapsing from their weight and books teetering precariously in slender towers as high as the shelves themselves. Every sort of book you can imagine was there: old tomes bound in brown leather with faded gold titles, yellowing paperback novels, slim black volumes with ribbons dangling from their spines, brightly coloured picture books, stacks of old magazines and newspapers – more than Cassie could read in a lifetime!

She breathed in the scent of dust, leather and the peculiar vanilla smell of aging paper. Making her way carefully between the stacks to the nearest shelf, Cassie ran her finger along the spines and read a few titles: *Merrow and their Manners*, *The Mostly Inaccurate Prophecies of Tegwen the Recluse*, *The Gardener's Guide to Growing Gurtroot*. She was just pulling out *A Natural History of the Hedge* when something small and white scuttled across her feet. She jumped back and saw a thin scaly tail disappear under the bookshelf.

Getting down on her hands and knees, Cassie peered

into the gap, but the thing was gone. From the stack of books behind her came a scuffle and the unmistakable sound of tearing paper. Cassie crept towards it. There, in a nest of dictionaries, was a small white lizard with two stubby horns and a ridge of spines down its back. Scraps of printed paper lay about it. It held a torn page and was munching on a corner. Cassie saw that it was missing a claw on its right foreleg. The lizard stopped munching and looked up at her with beady eyes, for all the world like a child who'd been caught with his hand in the biscuit tin.

'This dust is working horrors on my allergies,' said Montague, brushing past her legs.

The cat and the lizard caught sight of each other and froze, motionless for a long second. The creature dropped its dinner and scarpered, Montague leapt after it. The lizard dashed under a shelf and down another aisle, pursued by the grey cat who knocked over a stack of books, causing a small explosion that released a cloud of dust into the air.

'Montague!' Cassie called, losing sight of him between the shelves but able to follow the chase by the sound of falling books. She hurried after him.

Turning a corner she ran into a little old man wielding

a butterfly net.

'Which way did he go?'

Cassie pointed in the general direction of the commotion. The man leapt over a stack of fallen books with surprising agility and joined the chase. There was a resounding crash and a cry of victory from somewhere at the back of the shop.

'Aha! I've got you now, you little beastie!'

Worried about Montague, Cassie hurried towards the voice. But when she arrived, the cat was cleaning himself, calm as you like.

The little old man was grinning with glee. He had a pointy white beard and eyebrows that curled like moth's antennae, and his long, drooping ears ended in tufts of hair. He was wearing four pairs of glasses, two on his head, one on his nose and another dangling from a chain round his neck. He held the butterfly net aloft; in it, the white lizard thrashed back and forth.

'You'll not escape me this time! Been into my Archimellius again, have you? Well, that was your last meal!'

He scurried over to what must have been a desk, although it was buried under a mountain of books. From a drawer somewhere he produced a potato sack and thrust the lizard inside with a look of satisfaction. Behind him, coals burned in a pot-belly stove.

'What are you going to do with him?'

'Fire! Only way to deal with book wyrms is fire. They burn nicely with all that paper inside them.'

Cassie rushed over to stand between the man and the stove. 'You can't! I won't let you!'

The little man frowned at her. 'What else am I to do with this vermin? Let him go? He'll be back before you can wink, devouring my stock. This is a bookshop, not a buffet!'

'Let me take him then,' offered Cassie.

'You can't be serious,' Montague interjected. 'Your aunt—'

'She doesn't need to know, does she?' Cassie whispered.

The bookseller sighed and handed over the squirming sack. 'Very well, but if I catch him in here again he'll go straight in the furnace!'

'Do they only eat books?' asked Cassie, wondering if she might keep it as a pet.

'Books, scrolls, pamphlets, newspapers... anything with words on it. Had one munch through an entire encyclopaedia overnight, "Abbey Lubber" through to "Zennor Mermaid". Now, I presume you have some business here, besides this ill-advised rescue mission?'

'Oh, yes, I'm here to collect an order for Mrs Briggs, something called *The Violet Mist*?'

'Ah, another of those gentry romances she goes through, no doubt this one will feature a handsome lord with flashing eyes and a voice like velvet.' The old man sniffed. 'Let me give you a piece of advice, girl, you ever run into a faery prince, throw a horseshoe at him and run as fast as you can in the opposite direction! The new books are out the back, wait here while I fetch it –and keep a tight hold of that sack!'

Cassie's eyes wandered and came to rest on Widdershin's desk. It was cluttered with papers, receipts, pens and bottles of ink, but on top of all of this rested a large book bound in ivory leather. Checking that Widdershin was not coming back right away, Cassie went to have a closer look.

The book was attached to the desk by a thick chain, as if it might escape otherwise. Its worn, yellowed cover was embossed with a strange pattern and a series of symbols she did not recognise. At its centre was a raised bump with a slit in it. She stroked the cover with a finger; it gave her a strange tingling sensation up her arm. Slowly, the slit opened and a glassy eye stared out at her from the cover. She snatched her hand away. The eye regarded her, blinked once and then shut again.

Cassie approached the book once more. Carefully, she opened to a page at random. The book was written in an ornate script in a language she did not know. Despite its apparent age, the writing looked fresh and clear. While she could not read it, she found it had wonderful pictures. All around the margins of the text vines curled and trees grew, animals crawled and birds flew and tiny people went about their work ploughing fields and building houses.

She turned the page. There was an image of a dark forest, through it rode a train of beautiful people on horseback. A young man followed on foot, his armour was black and his head bowed. The facing page showed a city on the edge of the sea, with a silver palace and delicate towers, reaching into the clouds. Cassie turned the page again.

Two flaming eyes looked out at her from a bone mask, the skull of a stag with branching antlers, woven through with thorny vines and yew leaves. The picture sent a cold dagger of fear through her. It was just an illustration, but those bright eyes, set deep in bony sockets, were terribly alive. She stared at the skull and felt it staring back at her, piercing her mind. Beneath the image were three words and she found that she could read them: 'The Erl King'.

'What are you doing?' cried Widdershin. He rushed over and slammed the book shut, nearly crushing her fingers.

'I'm sorry, I was just looking.' The image of the stag skull was burned into her mind. She shook her head, attempting to dislodge it.

'Humans! I will never understand your confounded curiosity, always prying into things that don't concern you. You're worse than cats!'

Montague shot him a look.

'It's a beautiful book. What is it about? I couldn't read it.'

The bookseller sighed. 'Well, count yourself fortunate in that. It's a history of sorts, I'm sure you would find it very dull. Here, take this.' He handed Cassie a book wrapped in brown paper. 'Now, you'll be needing your handbook too, I assume.'

'My what?'

'*The Witch's Handbook* of course! I've got the latest edition here, there's a new chapter on elfshot – you'll find that useful.'

Widdershin scrambled up a stepladder and retrieved a

slim black book with a swirling silver symbol on the cover and offered it to Cassie. She opened the book to the table of contents and read: 'A Practical System for the Training of Young Witches... How to Track a Hytersprite... Simple Wards made from Household Goods... The Nine Signs of Enchantment...'

'I'll put it on the Hedgewitch's account,' said Widdershin, shooing her out of the shop. 'Now, off with you! I've got to do something about this mess. Book wyrms, they'll be the ruin of me, one of these days!'

'Widdershin – is he a goblin?' Cassie asked Montague once they'd left the shop. There had been something distinctly goblinish about the little old man, but he'd seemed harmless enough, unless you were a book wyrm.

'Not a goblin, a hob.'

'What's the difference?'

'Dental hygiene and a rudimentary moral compass,' Montague explained. 'They are two sides of the same coin, you might say, only, the hobs owe their allegiance to the queen. Now what, pray, do you intend to do with that thing?'

Cassie considered taking the book wyrm home with

her but knew she would have to hide him from her aunt, confining the creature to her bedroom. That seemed unfair on the book wyrm and besides, she'd rather not sacrifice her mother's books to his appetite. She decided instead to release him, somewhere far enough from Widdershin's that he wouldn't find his way back.

'I'll return him to the Hedge.'

'But your aunt said—'

'I know, I won't go into the woods, just up to the tree line. It will only take a minute.'

Montague muttered something about the technicalities of her aunt's prohibition but followed all the same. They turned off Loft Street just before they came to the bridge, following the river at a safe distance; Cassie wasn't eager for a second swim that day.

Together, they climbed the long grassy slope towards the dark shadow of the Hedge. The sun was going down behind the trees, casting them in silhouette, a line of tall, dark sentinels against the sky. Their shadows reached towards Cassie like fingers.

The forest began at the top of the hill with hawthorn and twisted elder and a few spindly ash saplings. Behind them, the solid trunks of oak and beech rose up in a haze of twilight. The air tasted of leaf mould and hyacinth.

Cassie peered into the shadows. The Hedge fascinated and unsettled her. Since the night before, when they'd driven past it on the way to Hartwood, she'd been constantly aware of its presence. Whether she was walking through the village with Rue or lying in her room at night, she could sense the Hedge, lingering at the edge of her mind, waiting. Now she had the eerie feeling that the wood, or something in it, was looking back at her.

'Montague, just how big is the Hedge?'

'No one can be certain. The wood plays tricks on travellers; paths appear and vanish, or lead one in circles. There are no maps and ordinary compasses fail once one is inside. Why, you might walk for days or weeks and finally come out where you started. Some say that at night the trees pull up their roots and change places.'

There was no light between the pillars of wood, only deepening shades of green. A shiver ran up Cassie's spine. Something was bothering her, something Tabitha had said about Hedgely being close to the 'border'; Brogan's matter-of-fact description of the Hedgewitch's role in protecting the village; Miranda's own rule against Cassie ever entering the wood alone.

'But if you *did* go all the way through, if you came out the other side...'

The cat looked up at her with his amber gaze. 'Then you would find yourself in Faerie.'

Cassie stared at him, wide-eyed. It made an impossible sort of sense and explained why Hedgely was so very different from London; why a hob could run a bookshop, why Rue had taken the existence of faeries for granted, why the village was full of witches. The Hedge was the frontier between England and Faerie. The Hedgewitch wasn't protecting them from the wood itself, but what lay beyond it. Faerie was real, it was somewhere you could visit, if you could find a way through the forest.

'Don't go getting any ideas,' said Montague, watching her. 'The way to Faerie is paved with thorns, or so they say. One can only pass through on the Crossing Nights and even if you managed to reach the other side, you'd never find your way back again.'

Despite his warnings, Cassie was seized with the sudden wild thought that she might, someday, enter another world.

'But surely people do come back, sometimes?'

'No human has returned from Faerie for hundreds of years. Even the Hedgewitch does not cross the border.'

The sack wriggled violently. Cassie kneeled down and loosened the string that bound it. The book wyrm writhed free, tumbled over her hands with a chirp and scurried off into the undergrowth. She watched it disappear through the ferns, hoping it would not find its way back to Widdershin's any time soon.

Cassie shivered again. The temperature had dropped and her hair was still damp from the river. Within the woods, a shadow detached itself from a darker clump of trees. It was hard to make out, but Cassie thought it was a person, wrapped in a cloak. The figure was moving slowly, it paused before another shadowy shape, a tree stump perhaps? Cassie couldn't tell at this distance.

There was an ear-splitting crack, like a gunshot. Cassie ducked. Wood pigeons took off from the trees in a confusion of grey wings. When she looked back, the figure was gone.

'What was that?' she asked.

'I do not know, but we shouldn't be here,' Montague replied, and he set off towards the village.

Cassie rose to her feet and followed, turning now and then to look back at the darkening wood.

Chapter Eleven

1st Hedgely Coven

Cassie saw little of her aunt during her first week at Hedgely. Miranda was often out on Hedgewitch business, returning to the house long after Cassie had eaten supper and gone to bed. When they crossed paths, on the stairs or in the kitchen, they said little and avoided eye contact.

Cassie had not completely forgiven her aunt for their argument and it seemed neither had any intention of apologising for the scene, so they continued in uncomfortable silence. Cassie told herself she didn't mind, that she could find her mother without her aunt's help and in doing so, would prove her wrong.

Besides, she was busy baking scones with Mrs Briggs and helping Brogan plant out the strawberry runners. They made a cheerful, hungry crowd at the kitchen table and Cassie soon began to feel as though she'd lived at Hartwood for years.

The afternoons she spent with Rue. Her new friend was Hedgely born and bred. She knew every house, field and farm – and everyone who lived in them. Together, they explored the village and surrounding hills. They climbed Mr Scrump's apple trees and searched for the nests of fridi, who have a penchant for ripe fruit. Rue gave her a tour of the overgrown churchyard at St Aelfwig's, reading the gravestones and keeping an eye out for ghosts in the yew grove.

When Friday arrived, Cassie was equal parts excited and nervous about the prospect of going to coven and meeting the other young witches from Hedgely and the surrounding villages. It was never easy to be the new girl and Cassie worried what they'd think of her. Despite being the Hedgewitch's niece, she had a lot of catching up to do when it came to witchcraft and faery things.

The Hedgley Coven hall was on the west side of the village, beyond the last of the houses and in the shadow of the Hedge. It had a pointed slate roof like a witch's hat, spotted with moss and lichen. A cloud of purple smoke rose from the chimney and laughter could be heard from the open doorway. Cassie followed two girls dressed in smart black uniform. They wore cloaks that fell to their knees and wide brimmed hats and each carried her broomstick.

The uniformed girls raced each other up the path but Cassie lingered outside. She wished she'd arranged to meet Rue at the bridge so they could arrive together.

The hall was surrounded by a garden of flowering herbs. Wrens and blackbirds hopped about, searching for insects and ignoring the scarecrow in the faded witch's hat.

'Who are you?'

A girl with bobbed black hair was standing in the doorway, staring at her. Her cloak was covered in badges and on her shoulder perched a brown stoat, its long body wrapped around her neck like a fur collar.

'I'm meeting my friend here,' Cassie began to explain.

The girl's frown melted into a honeyed smile. 'Oh, you're new! Well, don't worry about not having a uniform, I'm sure your people can arrange something by the next meeting. Who *are* your people, anyway?'

'I live at Hartwood, with my aunt.'

'It's her!' hissed the stoat.

The girl's eyes widened. 'You're Cassandra Morgan? Whyever didn't you say? I'm Ivy Harrington. Come inside, you can sit with us in Thorn. We're by far the best patrol, everybody says so.'

Cassie found herself shepherded through the door. Inside, the hall was lit and warmed by a circular fire set in the centre, supporting a large black cauldron. The floorboards creaked beneath Cassie's feet and above her hung drying herbs and small black shapes, like folded handkerchiefs – they were bats! Along the wall was a rack of brooms. The hall hummed with the laughter and chatter of a dozen girls. Two younger girls chased each other around the cauldron while the pair she'd seen outside shared a bar of chocolate. There was no sign of Rue.

Ivy grabbed Cassie's hand and dragged her over to one side of the hall, decorated with branches of blackthorn and purple bunting. Four girls were seated there on violet cushions and a faded sofa, talking amongst themselves. They cast withering glances at the noisy ones running about the hall.

'This,' said Ivy, pushing Cassie forward, 'is Cassandra Morgan. The Hedgewitch's niece.'

143

'Just Cassie is fine.'

They looked her up and down. Cassie began to wish she'd brushed her hair.

'This is Anika Kalra, she only joined last month,' Ivy introduced her. 'Susan and Phyllis Drake and our patrol leader, Eliza Pepper.'

They offered Cassie a cushion and made it very clear the great honour they were doing her. Ivy began to show Cassie each of her badges and explain how she'd earned them.

'This one is for wearing uniform correctly and this is my Chantress badge. We had to learn three chants and perform them at a home for retired witches. I was the only girl in the coven given a solo.'

Cassie kept an eye on the door and at last she saw a familiar frizzy head come through, this time with a crooked black hat jammed on top.

'Sorry, my friend is here,' said Cassie, interrupting Ivy's tale.

Rue was flushed from running. 'Phew! Oliver ran off and it took me ages to find him – he was scoffing cream cakes in the kitchen at Bramble's! I thought I'd never get here in time. Was that Ivy Harrington you were talking to? Right bore, isn't she? Thinks she's going to be the next

Hedgewitch or something. Did she show you her Camp Monitor badge?' Rue enacted a dramatic yawn. 'Come on, I'll introduce you to my lot.'

Rue's patrol were sitting in a circle, playing a game with flat, smooth pebbles. Each was marked with a strange symbol which clearly meant something to them as they laughed and called out to each other over wins and losses. It was an altogether different atmosphere to Thorn Patrol.

'Hullo there! Playing Blinkers without me, are you? You must be afraid of losing. Oh, this is Cassie by the way!'

The girls welcomed Cassie to the group. There were six of them, including Rue.

'Good to have you here, I'm Harriet Webb, Ash Patrol leader,' said a tall girl with short blonde hair. 'This is Nancy Kemp, my second. Over there's Lucy Watercress, Heather Shuttle and Alice Wong, who's currently winning.'

Cassie tried to memorise their names and faces. The girls seemed genuinely interested in her and asked lots of questions. Alice was just explaining the rules of Blinkers when a hush fell over the hall.

Cassie felt a prickling sensation on the back of her neck, she turned around. There, in the doorway, was the Hedgewitch.

'What's my aunt doing here?' she whispered.

Rue raised her eyebrows. 'She's the Coven Mistress. Thought you knew?'

'Form the circle, quickly now!' Miranda commanded, sweeping into the room and taking up position opposite the cauldron.

The girls rushed to form a ring around her, joining hands. Cassie fell in between Rue and Lucy, who gave her a shy smile.

'Heather, where is your hat?' asked Miranda. 'Alice, put down those runestones and straighten your cloak, that's better. Ivy, you may lead the chant today.'

Ivy looked very smug about this and began to sing in a clear, high voice while the others scrambled to join in.

'The sky is clear as we fly on
Beneath the dazzling stars.
We know their names and stories,
Their wisdom, it is ours.

The cauldron boils and bubbles,
A sweet and healing brew.
We gather herbs and flowers
To make our potions true.

146

The night is calm and peaceful,
The lamb bleats in his stall.
We guard the village and the home
From dangers great and small.

For we are witches, one and all,
And we are not afraid
Of goblins, grigs and gwyllions,
Our wards and charms are laid.

For we are witches, one and all,
A coven of the best.
Good friends who stand together
Through any threat or test.

For we are witches, one and all,
We know, protect and heal,
With noble hearts, loyal and kind,
And courage true as steel.'

'Very good. Thank you Ivy. Now, I have some important news.'

Cassie held her breath. Would her aunt introduce her to the coven?

'This year our coven camp will be held in July. Mr Bellwether has generously agreed to let us pitch tents in his field.'

The circle burst into excited chatter.

'Quiet! Any girl wishing to attend the camp must perform well in her craft and earn no black marks before that day. As you have the entire summer to get through, I imagine some of you will find this challenging. I want no repeat of last year's hijinks and tomfoolery at Midsummer. Hopefully, the camp will provide some incentive.'

Rue sighed.

Miranda looked directly at Cassie. 'Furthermore, only girls who have passed their Fledgling Test will be allowed to join the camp.'

Muttered comments on this announcement passed around the circle.

'Today, we will continue our work on the identification and uses of various fungi for your Mushroomer badges. Although we usually collect mushrooms in the autumn, there has been plenty of rain overnight and you will find several species that fruit in spring. Patrol leaders, please organise the baskets, we will all meet outside the hall in five minutes.'

The circle broke apart into knots of excited girls, eagerly discussing the news.

'Coven camp! We have to go, Cassie! Even if it does mean staying out of trouble, although it's an *awfully* long time to be good,' said Rue, biting her lip.

'What is the Fledgling Test?'

'Oh, that! There's different grades of witch in the coven, you see: fledgling, sapling and sterling. You can't truly join a patrol until you pass the Fledgling Test and get your hat. It's easy enough though, we'll sort you out. Never fear, you'll be coming to camp with the rest of us, I'll make sure of it!'

Cassie was somewhat reassured by this, although she hadn't liked the way her aunt had looked at her.

'Come on, you lot!' called Harriet. 'Enough jaw, we've got mushrooms to find!'

'I need not remind you that the Hedge is a dangerous place, even in the light of day and the company of friends,' said the Hedgewitch, as they huddled together on the grassy slope, facing the edge of the wood. 'Remain on the path and in sight of your patrol leader at all times. Do not go so far in that you cannot see the sky through the trees. If you encounter anything, or anyone, blow your whistle three times. We will meet back here in an hour.'

Cassie looked past her aunt into the cool leaf-shade of the wood. A cold thrill ran through her at the thought of finally stepping across that boundary into the Hedge.

They were to collect samples of mushrooms and toadstools with magical properties, as illustrated in *The Witch's Handbook*. These, Harriet explained, would be dried and powdered for later use in potions. Each girl had a basket and was paired off, although the patrol as a whole planned to stick together.

There were two paths that opened out from the wood on to the grassy hill. One was broad and well-trodden, the other narrow and overgrown. Thorn Patrol were already starting down the wider path, but Harriet pulled her patrol aside.

'Right, it's a bit of a risk, but I say we take the other path. If we trail after Thorn, all we'll find is their leftovers. I've been this way before, it joins the main path later on, or at least, it used to. If we stick together and keep our eyes peeled we might just come up trumps. Got your baskets and books? Good. Holler if you find anything interesting.'

The wood was full of bluebells, a carpet of purple that dipped and bowed, filling the air with perfume. Cassie followed Rue up the narrow path, bracken fern brushing her legs and catching on her stockings. She lifted her face to the gold-green light that filtered through the canopy. Somewhere in the treetops, a cuckoo was calling.

'Head down, Cassie,' said Harriet. 'You're not going to find any mushrooms up there.'

The leaf litter at their feet was still damp from the previous night's showers. Cassie and Rue examined rotting tree stumps and peered beneath fern fronds. It would be a great win if they could find one of the rarer fungi in the book.

'Over here!' called Lucy. 'I've found something!'

The rest hurried to see what she was pointing at. On a fallen log there perched a row of bright-red bowls and saucers, like a child's tea set.

'Scarlet elfcups! Well done, Luce, pick a nice one and we can cross that off the list,' said Harriet.

The rest of Ash Patrol soon made finds of their own: knobbly black dead-man's fingers, grey candlesnuff fungus, inkcaps, both common and shaggy, and even a stinkhorn. Rue discovered this accidentally by treading on it and releasing an awful stench that had the whole patrol pinching their noses in disgust while the culprit herself grinned with glee.

However hard she looked, Cassie couldn't find a single mushroom that hadn't already been spotted by the other girls. They were getting deeper into the Hedge now. There was only a glimmer of blue and green between the trees to the east, marking the edge of the woods and the safety of the village.

The path they had taken veered to the right where it joined up with a broader track. Standing in a huddle ahead of them were Thorn Patrol.

'Hullo!' Harriet greeted them. 'Found something good?'

The Thorn girls turned with self-satisfied smirks. 'Oh yes,' said Eliza, 'Ivy's found a golden earthstar. Come and see!'

Ivy was crouched beside the path, beaming with pride. At her feet bloomed a tiny yellow mushroom. It looked like a chestnut, ringed with six points like the petals of a flower or the rays of a star.

'Glory!' said Heather. 'That's not even in the handbook.'

'I know,' Ivy said. She carefully plucked the earthstar and added it to her basket which was already overflowing with brightly coloured fungi.

'Good work, girls,' Eliza addressed her patrol. 'That'll do for today. We'll be the first back at the hall.'

Ash Patrol watched them leave. Although no one wanted to admit it, Thorn Patrol had triumphed this time.

'Oh, well,' said Harriet. 'We'd best head back too. The sun's gone down a fair way and we won't be able to see our boots soon enough.'

Cassie and Rue trailed behind the rest of the patrol. Cassie's basket was still empty.

'Don't worry, it's your first day. No one expects you to find a golden earthstar or anything like that,' said Rue.

Cassie smiled, but it didn't help. Even Rue had managed to find the stinkhorn. No one would want her in their patrol at this rate.

Harriet led them in a cheerful marching chant as they tramped back – something about a toad who fell down a well, but Cassie didn't feel like joining in the chorus. She fell behind the others, still looking half-heartedly to either side of the path, then something caught her eye. The tree shadows were lengthening and the undergrowth was thrown into darkness, so she may not have seen it at all except that it glowed very faintly against the brown leaf mould, just a few feet from the path.

153

The patrol had gone on ahead, if she were quick, she could investigate and rejoin them before anyone noticed she was gone. It was probably only a common puffball, but it would be good to have something to show for the afternoon and, if by chance, it was a rarer specimen, even Aunt Miranda might be impressed.

Cassie pushed through the bracken, determined to reach the toadstool. It was further from the path than it had first appeared. She pulled out her handbook and tried, in the fading light, to identify it. The toadstool was about the size of a grapefruit and snowy white, with faint blue gills. There was another one a little further off, and another. Cassie stood up and realised she was in a clearing. She could see the purple and orange sky above her through a circular hole in the canopy and at her feet was a perfect ring of white toadstools. She had to show them this.

'Rue!' she called. 'Harriet! Come look!' She waited, but nobody came. They must be too far off to hear her, she would have to pick one and hurry back to the others. Whatever the toadstools were, they were more impressive than Ivy's tiny mushroom. But which should she pick? The one at her feet was in good shape, but there were some larger ones on the other side of the clearing. She stepped over the toadstool into the ring.

Chapter Twelve

Glashtyn

As Cassie stepped into the clearing, the air changed. There was a soft sigh, as if the earth were releasing a long-held breath. A scent rose from the grass, thick and sweet, like wildflowers drowned in honey. The toadstools began to glow softly against the forest floor. Cassie's skin turned to gooseflesh. She shouldn't be there, she saw that now, she should never have left the path.

Cassie retraced her steps. As she reached the edge of the toadstool circle her feet turned of their own accord, leading her back into the ring. She tried again, heading in a different direction this time, but once more her feet twisted under her. She could walk around the inside of the ring, but as soon as she tried to leave she lost control of her legs. She could feel nothing there, no invisible wall, no barrier, and yet she could not cross, her own body would not let her.

Cassie sat down on the grass, wrapping her arms about her knees, it was growing cold. Surely they'd notice she was missing soon and come back for her?

'Rue!' she called, her voice sounding hollow. 'Aunt Miranda?'

There was no reply, only a rustling in the leaves at the edge of the circle. Probably a blackbird, she told herself, or a squirrel. There were worse things in the Hedge, Brogan had said. Cassie tried not to imagine what they might be.

'Cass-sandra.'

She started at the voice.

'Do not be afraid, Cass-sandra.'

It came from behind and above her. Something long, dark and lithe moved amongst the branches of an old hornbeam tree. It blurred, shifted and landed on the grass at the edge of the toadstool ring. Between a ferret and a cat in size, the creature was pitch black apart from its yellow throat and amber eyes. It had a blunt head, round ears and small, sharp teeth. She had only seen pictures in books, but Cassie thought it might be a pine marten.

'If you don't want me to be afraid, let me out.'

'I'm here to help you Cass-sandra. To help you find what you are seeking.'

'I was just looking for a mushroom and I've found plenty, thank you.'

'What you *truly* want, your heart's desire,' hissed the marten. It paced slowly around the ring. Cassie kept it in her line of sight.

'What do you know about my heart's desire?'

'I know all about you, Cass-sandra Morgan. I have been watching you. I know what you fear and what you hope for, your nightmares and your dreams. I can make them come true.'

'The dreams or the nightmares?'

'That is up to you.' The marten stopped and looked over its shoulder into the dark woods. 'We do not have much time. Follow me Cass-sandra, I will take you to your mother.'

'My mother? What do you know about my mother?'

'I know where she is hiding, she is waiting for you. Come with me and I will show you.'

'I don't trust you.'

'I do not seek your trust but I can prove my claim, if you will only follow me; we must go deeper into the woods.'

They were interrupted by a crashing in the bushes, it was Rue. She tried to enter the circle but could not. Rue shouted something, but although Cassie could see her open mouth, no sound reached her.

'Rue!' Cassie called back.

'She cannot hear you and she cannot see me,' said the shadowy creature.

'Let me go!'

'You must listen, Cass-sandra. I am the only one who can help you. The others will fail you. Only I can lead you to your mother. Remember that.'

Cassie ran towards Rue, but once again her feet failed her. Rue was digging for something in her pocket.

'When you decide to take up my offer, call me by my name – call for *Glashtyn*,' said the pine marten. 'But don't wait too long.'

Three sharp whistle blasts broke the night air. A minute later, the Hedgewitch was there on her broom. She reached for a bag at her waist and threw a handful of powder on to the toadstools, turning them brown and shrivelled. Cassie leapt out of the circle into Rue's outstretched arms. The spell was broken.

'You all right?' asked Rue.

'I think so,' said Cassie, still shaking, but then she saw the look on her aunt's face.

The Hedgewitch said nothing on the way back to the coven hall, where both patrols were waiting, anxious and excited over Cassie's fate. She said nothing on the long, cold walk through the village and up the hill. She said nothing when they returned to Hartwood, where Mrs Briggs fussed over Cassie and gave her supper. She said nothing until they were alone in the great hall, beneath the Hartwood tree.

Miranda paused before the portrait of Morgana. Cassie could see the resemblance, although the woman in the painting had a warm, wise smile, which was not reflected on her aunt's face at that moment.

'What were you *thinking*? Wandering off like that?'

'I didn't mean to—' Cassie began.

'Do you have any comprehension of the danger you were in? Of what could have happened to you, to your coven mates? The Hedge is not a playground for your amusement. You are not immune to its threats.'

'I know—' Cassie wanted to tell her about the pine marten, but her aunt cut her off.

'Leaving the path, wandering off alone, entering faery rings, for stars' sake, Cassandra. This is exactly the sort of foolhardy behaviour that got your mother into trouble in the first place!'

Cassie gasped. 'What trouble? What sort of trouble is my mother in?'

The Hedgewitch averted her gaze, ignoring Cassie's desperate questions. 'I ought to forbid you from attending coven, but somehow I doubt that would prevent you from getting into these situations. Better that you should gain an understanding of the dangers and how to avoid them. Tomorrow afternoon you will come with me as I make my rounds of the village and see first-hand the damage faery folk cause and the responsibilities of the Hedgewitch. Hopefully that will inspire you to take my warnings seriously.'

'But I was going to practice flying with Rue, Mrs Briggs said she'd pack us a picnic.'

'You will meet me on the drive at one o'clock. Good night, Cassandra.'

Cassie watched her aunt climb the stairs towards her study. The thought of spending her Saturday afternoon with that icicle of a woman was far from thrilling.

Cassie struggled under the weight of the Hedgewitch's great carpet bag. It was crammed with jars and bottles containing various potions, powders and preparations Miranda might need in her work. Cassie was pretty sure there were some stones in there too – it weighed a tonne. Montague had elected to stay at Hartwood and so Cassie left the house with Miranda and her familiar, Malkin. Like his witch, the lean black cat was silent and aloof.

They had a dozen or so visits ahead of them. Cassie had come down to the hall at midday to find a swarm of imps buzzing about the Hartwood tree. They dived at her, screeching in high-pitched voices, eager to convey their messages. Cassie was saved by the arrival of Miranda, who commanded silence and received them one at a time. Each imp was carrying a small card on which was written a name and address. Miranda collected these and flicked through them quickly. The creatures were rewarded with marbles from a bowl on the table, vanishing with the shiny glass orbs clutched in their arms.

Their first stop was Mr Bellwether's farm. Cassie was curious to see the field where the coven camp would be held, although her chances of attending were not looking too good just now. Mr Bellwether was a large, balding man who wore a wax jacket and chewed the end of a clay pipe. After shaking Miranda's hand, the farmer led them to his chicken coop.

'You see, 'edgewitch, they just won't lay. I've changed their feed, given 'em fresh straw for nesting, sat out 'ere of an evening, stealthy like, to see if there's any foxes about, giving 'em the quivers, but there's been naught. As a rule we get a good dozen eggs out of them a day, this time of year.' Mr Bellwether lowered his voice. 'I think them's been hexed – goblin spit or some such!'

'We'll take a look,' the Hedgewitch assured him.

Cassie followed her aunt around the coop, stumbling under the weight of the bag while Miranda inspected the wire. There was no sign of a break and nothing had tried to dig underneath. The structure was entirely sound.

Mr Bellwether's hens were running about in mad circles, clearly spooked by the close proximity of Malkin. The large black cat sat outside the wire, watching them.

'Cassandra, fetch me one of the hens please.'

Cassie stared at her aunt. The only chicken she'd encountered before now had been in coronation salad.

'How?'

'With your hands. I'm sure it won't prove too difficult.'

The Hedgewitch was *definitely* punishing her, Cassie decided as she chased the squawking hens around the coop. The silly birds scattered whenever she got near them, leaving her sprawled in the straw.

Finally, she managed to separate one speckled hen from the flock and, with a flying leap, wrestle her to the ground. Cassie came out of the coop covered in straw, feathers and what she hoped was mud, with the fat hen struggling in her grasp.

Miranda took the bird from her with firm hands and looked it over. The hen calmed immediately and seemed content to have its legs and beak inspected.

'There is nothing wrong with this hen, Mr Bellwether. She is in fine fettle.'

The bird was released to join her companions.

'Cassandra, I need you to take a look in the nesting boxes.'

Cassie sighed and crawled back into the coop.

The boxes were dry and full of straw squashed against the sides. They'd been used recently, but there was no sign of any eggs. She put her hand in each box and felt about. In the third she found a small red cap, no bigger than a thimble. Cassie took it to her aunt who held it up to the farmer.

'I'm afraid Mr Bellwether, that you have grigs. Your hens have been laying plenty of eggs, but grigs have been stealing them before you get to the coop. They're particularly fond of a tansy omelette. As I'm sure you're aware, they can also shrink to the size of a grasshopper, allowing them to climb through your chicken wire easily.'

'The filthy thieving pests! You tell me where they're nesting, 'edgewitch, and I'll set my dog, Bess, on them. She's a good ratter.'

'That is quite unnecessary. We will place wards around your chicken coop and the grigs will be unable to enter. Deprived of their food source, they'll move on of their own accord. Cassandra, find me four wardstones if you please.'

So there were stones in the carpet bag! Cassie put her arm inside and felt around amidst the bottles and pouches until she found them. They were cold to the touch and heavy, although each fitted snugly in the palm of her hand. Holding them up, she could see they were inscribed with runes.

'They are ironstone and will deter faery folk. Place one at each corner of the chicken coop,' Miranda instructed.

Once this was done, Cassie stood back to watch her aunt work. The Hedgewitch walked around the perimeter of the coop three times clockwise, muttering a spell. As she reached each stone she bent down to touch it, tracing one rune with a finger.

'The ward is complete. Mr Bellwether, make sure no one moves those stones and your hens will be safe. You should have eggs for your breakfast tomorrow. I would also recommend leaving a small bowl of cream on your doorstep overnight to appease the grigs, you don't want them raiding your dairy next.'

From the farm, they returned to the village where the Hedgewitch made a series of deliveries. At her instruction, Cassie handed out small bottles of cough syrup and soothing ointments, amulets for protecting children and wards for the home. The carpet bag grew lighter as Cassie found herself introduced to half the village. Wherever they went, her aunt was welcomed, offered tea and biscuits and given the best seat in the house while her advice was sought on finding lost jewellery, healing cradle cap and dealing with bogles. Sometimes her aunt would make practical suggestions such as 'have you looked under the bed?' or, 'try rubbing his head with oil'. However, other visits required more magical intervention – a carefully placed ward, a healing charm or a short consultation with the brownie, the household sprite who knew everything that went on in the home.

Their last call was to a large house in the newer part of the village. It was rather grand, with big windows and a stretch of green lawn spread before it, surrounded by neatly trimmed bushes.

Cassie was about to lift the knocker when the door swung open to reveal Ivy Harrington.

'Oh, Hedgewitch, thank you for coming—' the young witch began, before noticing exactly who was standing in the doorway. 'You!' she said, her welcoming smile vanishing. 'What are you doing here?'

'Cassandra is helping me today,' Miranda explained. 'Have there been any changes?'

Ivy shot Cassie a furious glare as she held the door to let them in. 'No, she's just the same as always.'

The Hedgewitch led them upstairs, evidently familiar with the house.

They entered a large bedroom, decorated in robin's-egg blue. The canopied bed was occupied by a sleeping woman, her long dark hair spread across the pillow.

Ivy's stoat familiar, Kastor, lay beside her. The woman's expression was calm and vacant, only the gentle rise and fall of her chest suggested life. She did not stir as they approached.

Miranda checked the woman's pulse and felt her forehead with the back of her hand. Taking out a small brass pendulum, she held it suspended over the woman's chest; it did not move. Miranda frowned and pocketed the pendulum. 'Ivy, bring me a glass of water.'

Ivy nodded and dashed off down the hall.

'Cassandra, the bag.'

Cassie dragged the carpet bag over to her aunt.

'What is the matter with her?'

'Mrs Harrington has the faery sickness, the *esane*. For offending one of the gentry, the great lords and ladies of Faerie, she was blasted with a curse. She is in no pain, but neither will she wake and it is beyond my abilities to heal her.'

Cassie looked at the woman's sleeping face. 'A part of her is missing,' she said.

Miranda nodded. 'Indeed. Some witches believe that the esane cannot be cured because the spirit has been separated from the body and taken by the faery who cast the curse.'

Ivy returned with a glass of water and offered it to Miranda.

The Hedgewitch reached into the carpet bag and withdrew a small glass vial. It contained a bright golden liquid. Miranda removed the stopper and placed three drops in the water where it swirled in milky clouds. She held the glass to the woman's mouth.

'The sap of the Hartwood tree. It keeps her body alive, although she does not eat or drink. It is all I can do for now—'

'Hedgewitch, I've been reading about curses,' Ivy interrupted. 'If we could find the faery who cast it, I'm sure we could get them to take it off!'

'What have I told you, Ivy? It is too dangerous. The faery who did this to your mother was one of the gentry, far more powerful than any sprite or bogle you have encountered. How would your father feel to lose you too?'

Ivy sniffed. 'Daddy doesn't believe she was faery-cursed. But the doctors can't explain it at all.'

'She should go to Convall Abbey,' said Miranda. 'There are many skilled Menders there who could care for her better. I will talk with your father but, in the meantime, look after her, keep her comfortable. She is a strong woman and we must not give up hope, but nor must you place yourself in danger attempting to save her.'

Cassie understood how Ivy felt. She too would do just about anything to have her mother back. It was infuriating to be told there was nothing you could do.

Ivy saw them to the door. 'Hedgewitch, if you need an assistant I could help you. Cassandra hasn't even passed her Fledgling Test.'

Then again, Cassie thought, it wouldn't be so bad if the faeries took Ivy after all.

'Thank you, however, that will not be necessary,' said the Hedgewitch. 'This afternoon is a lesson and not a reward. Come, Cassandra, we have one last task today.'

Chapter Thirteen

The Weirstone and the Warlock

The Hedge was bathed in warm afternoon light. Small emerald moths rose from the ferns and cow parsley as they made their way along the narrow path. It was little more than a deer track, but the Hedgewitch led Cassie and Malkin along it, deeper into the woods. Miranda moved like a faery herself; so light and silent were her steps that she never broke a twig or disturbed a bird. In her dark cloak she merged into the tree shadows as if she were part of the forest. Years spent patrolling the Hedge showed in the calm alertness of her bearing and the sureness of her stride. In contrast, Cassie tripped over tree roots and startled wood pigeons as she crashed through the undergrowth.

Cassie was surprised that her aunt had brought her back to the Hedge so soon after the incident with the faery ring. Her skin prickled at the memory and she found herself searching each tree for a lithe black shadow. The pine marten was out there somewhere, waiting for her.

The Hedgewitch stopped suddenly and Cassie crashed into her, dropping the carpet bag; its contents spilled on to the ground. She stooped to gather them up.

'Leave that,' said Miranda. 'Look here.'

It was a stone, as tall as Cassie and standing alone in a circle of dead grass. Its granite surface was weathered by the years and yet it sparkled with flecks of mica.

'This is a weirstone, one of many within the Hedge. They form a ward, a great chain that protects the border.'

'Oh, like the stones we placed around Mr Bellwether's chicken coop?' Cassie asked.

'Yes, something like that, but much older and stronger.' Miranda raised an eyebrow. 'What do you know of the Treaty of Rosehill, Cassandra?'

Cassie thought back to her history lesson with Mr

Hastings. 'It means the faery folk have no claim to Britain, that they can't cross the border.'

The shadow of a smile flickered across her aunt's face. 'Indeed, the treaty was signed by the Queen of Faerie and binds all her people. However, the goblins did not sign and that is why they may come and go as they please. And, of course, there are wild creatures in Faerie that know no laws or treaties. The weirstones were created to keep them out and to limit the passage of the goblins. No faery creature can touch the stones, they form a frontier between our lands – a border only passable on the Crossing Nights, when the magic of Faerie is strongest and all wards are weakened.'

Looking closer, Cassie saw the stone was engraved faintly with faery runes. They ran in a circle, so that you had to walk around to read them all. Cassie recognised some of the runes from the ironstones, but there were many more she did not know.

'But this one is broken,' said Cassie. The top of the rough stone column was shattered, the remains lay in fragments beneath. The ring of runes was interrupted by a jagged line where it had parted. She traced the line with a finger. 'The damage is new. There's no moss growing on the broken side.'

'Indeed. It is the third shattered weirstone I have found this year. I fear it is deliberate.'

'But if the faery folk can't touch the stones, how can they be broken?'

'Only a warlock could do this,' Miranda explained. 'A witch in league with Faerie, a traitor to the Witches' Assembly. One who seeks to use magic to harm and destroy rather than heal and protect.'

'But why would anyone want to break the stones?'

'The Hedge is already a dangerous place, without the weirstones it is more so. With each stone broken, the ward is weakened. If enough are destroyed, the goblins will be able to smuggle stolen goods across the border whenever they wish and those in league with them will profit.'

The stolen children, Cassie realised. Someone was helping the goblins take the children away to Faerie.

'On my first day in Hedgely, I came up to the edge of the woods. I didn't go in' – Cassie added quickly – 'but I saw someone alone in the Hedge.'

Miranda fixed Cassie with the full intensity of her gaze. 'Can you describe this person?'

Cassie shook her head. 'It was dark and they were too far away, I think they were wearing a cloak.'

'I fear that someone in the village is in the pay of the goblins. We must be vigilant – until the warlock is found, we are all in danger.'

As May ripened into June, the meadows were glazed golden with buttercups and Cassie joined Rue at the village school. To her great relief, it was nothing like Fowell House. The Hedgely schoolhouse was a small, cosy building with just two classrooms, one for the infants and another for the older students. Cassie sat with Rue, Alice Wong and Lucy Watercress. They studied together under Miss Featherstone, a soft-spoken, bright young woman who loaned Cassie a book on famous witches throughout history.

Now that Cassie had to balance her schoolwork with coven activities, broom practice and helping around Hartwood, she barely had a moment to herself. When she did find an hour or two, she liked nothing better than to take a book and sit in the rose garden to read. There, amidst the petals and thorns, she could almost feel her mother's presence and soon enough she would find her mind wandering from the words on the page to the mysteries surrounding Rose Morgan. Cassie had a feeling that the goblins, the warlock and the missing children were wrapped up in it somehow, but she knew too little to figure out the answers on her own. If only her aunt would help, but the Hedgewitch still refused to talk about her sister.

As mistress of the coven, Miranda treated Cassie with the same cool regard as the other young witches, showing her niece no preferential treatment. If anything, she was even more critical of Cassie's progress. When Cassie burned pine resin on to the cauldron, she was scolded in front of the other girls and made to scrub it out. When she recited the incantation for harvesting clubmoss, she received no praise, just a curt nod, as if it were expected of a Morgan. Nothing she did impressed the Hedgewitch and Ivy gave Cassie a smug smile every time Miranda praised *her* work.

Nevertheless, Cassie persisted in training for the Fledgling Test. She'd been unofficially adopted into Ash Patrol and they were eager to help her learn the skills she would need to pass.

First, she had to memorise the Witch's Oath:

I swear, by the seven stars,
To stir my cauldron in healing,

To weave my wards in defence,
To fly by the light of wisdom,
Standing with my sisters
In service of this land.

Cassie repeated it to herself every night before bed and was soon word-perfect.

The Ash Patrol witches schooled her in their own particular skills. Heather Shuttle taught her about the various herbs and flowers growing in the coven garden while her hedgehog familiar, Igil, rooted for snails at their feet.

'Rowan, vervain, and solwort are the three most powerful warding herbs,' Heather explained. 'If you hang them over your door, nothing bad can enter.'

Nancy Kemp, patrol second, drew pictures of the night sky with coloured pencils and hung them up in the patrol corner, to help her learn the stars.

'That's Polaris, the North Star. It's the brightest star in Ursa Minor – the little bear,' she told Cassie, pointing it out on the chart. 'If you can find Polaris, you'll never lose your way at night.'

The Ash Patrol leader, Harriet Webb, took them out tracking and showed Cassie how to recognise the difference between human and faery footprints, which were much lighter and slightly pointed.

Cassie learned to tie witch knots to prevent things being stolen by imps and goblins and to make the secret witch signs – hand signals for moving through dangerous territory silently.

Alice Wong gave Cassie a set of rune stones she'd made herself, smooth river pebbles painted with the faery runes. Each had a name and its own secret magic – it was a whole new language to learn.

The only problem was that Cassie did not know which of her new skills would be tested, for the Hedgewitch would change the Fledgling Test for each new contender. But she would certainly have to prove her ability on the broom and this troubled her. Rue said she was getting better at flying but she still fell off during sharp turns and she couldn't fly any higher than the potting shed roof without feeling queasy. It was a miracle that she'd ever escaped the goblin nabbers on a broken broom. Her beginner's luck had clearly deserted her.

On a sunny afternoon when bumblebees dozed in the towering purple foxglove spires, Cassie and Rue entered the hall to find the rest of the coven in an excited huddle.

'Cassie!' called a cheerful voice. A girl with shiny black curls broke through the group and rushed to meet them. 'Oh, I had hoped you'd be here.'

It was Tabitha Blight. She took Cassie's hands.

'What's *she* doing here?' hissed Rue.

'I've come to join the coven of course. Isn't it wonderful?'

The look on Rue's face showed she thought it far from wonderful. She stalked off to the Ash Patrol corner.

Tabitha's cloak and hat were spotless, inky black. She wore the fledgling pin and a row of badges embroidered with cobwebs, leaves and cauldrons.

'How do you have so many badges already?' Cassie asked.

'Oh, I was in a coven back home in Somerset, but I'm still just a fledgling. Everyone here seems so nice. Ivy said I can join their patrol!'

That would not win her any points with Rue, Cassie thought.

Ivy came to retrieve Tabitha, pulling her away to the Thorn corner. She was clearly keen to have someone from an important witching family like the Blights in her patrol.

They were making faery traps that day, circles of bindweed and willow wrapped with protective herbs and woven through with witch knots in red thread. They would only catch smaller, weaker faery folk, the Hedgewitch explained, but could be placed in children's bedrooms to keep away bogles.

Miranda paired them off. To Ivy's evident annoyance, Cassie and Tabitha were put together as the newest members of the coven.

It was the first time they'd had a chance to talk since the train journey. Tabitha was going to school in the next valley at Clematis Academy, which sounded almost as bad as Fowell House. After school and on weekends she had to help her grandmother. The cantankerous old witch treated Tabitha like a servant, expecting her to do all the household chores, cooking and shopping.

'But it's only because she has a bad back and struggles with the stairs, I don't mind really,' said Tabitha.

Mrs Blight didn't think much of the Hedgewitch and wanted to train Tabitha herself, in the old-fashioned style of mistress and apprentice. Tabitha wrote to her mother, who put her foot down and insisted that she be allowed to join the coven.

'That's the reason I was sent here in the first place. The oldest girl in our family is always sent away to learn witchcraft from one of the Border Wardens. Mummy was furious when she heard I hadn't been allowed to come to coven. You'll have to tell me everything I've missed! Have you found out any more about your mother?'

'Girls,' said the Hedgewitch, addressing the coven. 'Yes, Ivy, that's very good knotwork. Now, I want your undivided attention. In three weeks' time, at the Midsummer Fair, we will stage a witchcraft demonstration for the village.'

The girls chattered excitedly.

'You shall each select a spell, craft or skill to display. You may work in pairs. I expect only serious demonstrations of the witch's craft, no nonsense. The most accomplished will be rewarded with a prize. This is an opportunity to show your families and neighbours what 1st Hedgely Coven is made of. You have the rest of the afternoon to plan your projects.'

Before Cassie could blink, Ivy was there, entwining her arm through Tabitha's.

'I know exactly what we should do, come on, we don't want to be overheard.' She led Tabitha away rather forcefully.

Rue came over with two currant buns to help them think.

'Well, I was going to suggest flying, but we've only got the one broom.'

'And I'm likely to fall off it,' said Cassie. 'I'd understand if you wanted to work with someone else. I'm not even a fledgling yet.'

'You can stop that, we're in this together and I won't hear a word otherwise!'

They sat on the hall steps in the afternoon light and flipped through their handbooks with sticky fingers.

'We could learn some of these chants?' suggested Cassie. 'The Lambton Wyrm, Skillywidden...'

Rue screwed up her face. 'Sing? In front of everyone in the village? No thanks! Besides, if we want to win the prize we should pick a warding skill. Here, what about this? Witch salt – a deterrent to all but the most powerful faery folk.'

'Eggshells, charcoal, salt – we could get most of these ingredients from the kitchen at Hartwood,' Cassie offered. 'I'm sure Mrs Briggs would let us have them.'

'That's settled then, pity we haven't got any goblins to test it out on! Do you think we could catch an imp?'

'I'm not sure that's a good idea,' said Tabitha, returning with buns for herself and Ivy.

Rue leapt up. 'What do you want? Spying on us, are you?'

'No, I just meant you might hurt the poor creature,' said Tabitha. 'Witch salt is strong stuff.'

Rue scowled. 'You shouldn't have been listening in the first place. If you tell Ivy what we're doing, I'll—'

'I'm sure Tabitha wouldn't do that, she was just trying to help,' Cassie interrupted.

Rue rolled her eyes and Tabitha fled back to Thorn Patrol.

'Steady on,' said Cassie. 'You didn't have to upset her like that.' She wished the two of them would get along but Rue had stubbornly hated Tabitha from first sight, just because she was a Blight.

Rue sniffed. 'Serves her right for snooping about. Our project is going to be much better than theirs. Where do you think we can get juniper berries?'

Chapter Fourteen

The Erl King

The next week it grew so hot that Cassie had to sleep with the windows open at night. The scent of honeysuckle and her mother's roses came in through the east window, but from the west there drifted strange breezes tasting of silver and spice. They gave her odd dreams, of giant bats and golden trees and herds of white deer. Sometimes her mother appeared, calling to her, and Cassie would wake up in a tangle of sheets.

During the day she had little time to ponder their meaning. There were school examinations coming up, on top of which she had to study for her Fledgling Test and practise on the broom with Rue. On Sundays, she helped Brogan in the garden, weeding and watering. Some animal had taken a fancy to his radishes and was nibbling them in the night.

'Rabbits or an 'are, most like,' he said. 'Could be them pesky urchens, though. Don't usually go in for vegetables, but I wouldn't put it past 'em.'

Cassie practised her wards on the radishes, drawing faery runes in the soil. Most of Brogan's attention was devoted to a tuft of feathery leaves growing under a protective awning.

'My gurtroot,' he explained, with pride. 'Emley Moor's got another thing comin' if 'e thinks to win the red at the fair this year!'

The days flew by and, before Cassie knew it, June 12th had arrived, which was her birthday.

Cassie's past seven birthdays had been unremarkable. She'd kept the date a secret from the other girls at school, fearing an unwanted 'birthday present' from the hockey team. Cassie had yet to mention it to her friends in Hedgely either, so it was without any sense of anticipation that she entered the kitchen that morning, followed by a sleepy Montague.

'Happy birthday, dove!' said Mrs Briggs, enveloping her in a floury hug. 'Thirteen years old! And you've grown an inch since you arrived, if I'm not mistaken.'

'Many 'appy returns,' said Brogan, shaking her hand.

Her aunt even gave her a small smile before returning to the copy of the *Hedgely Herald* she was reading. Best of all, Rue was there.

'How did you know?' asked Cassie.

'My mum found out, she's good at that sort of thing,' said Rue, dragging Cassie over to the kitchen table where vases of poppies and sweet peas were surrounded by plates piled high with pancakes, strawberries and cream. There was even ice cream and lemonade.

'Hardly breakfast food,' said Miranda.

'Well, it's no ordinary breakfast,' said Mrs Briggs. 'Don't you want to open your presents first, duck?'

At the end of the table was a small pile of packages wrapped in brown paper with bright ribbons. Rue pushed a roughly wrapped parcel into her hands.

Cassie opened it to reveal a small brass lantern with a candle inside and a loop on the top.

'My brother made it,' said Rue. 'It's for your broom, when you get one, so you can fly at night without crashing into things.'

'I can hardly fly during the day without crashing into things, but thank you, it's splendid!'

The pink-ribboned parcel from Mrs Briggs contained a witch's cloak, sewn by hand from the softest black wool. Now she would match the other girls in coven.

'Plenty of room to sew on all those badges you've been earning,' said the housekeeper.

Brogan gave her a pair of new boots with purple laces and thick soles for broom landings. Cassie put them on at once and the old gardener turned red at her thanks.

Finally and quite unexpectedly, Miranda pushed a neat rectangular parcel across the table. Inside was a book bound in soft green leather, it was *A Natural History of the Hedge*.

'Widdershin said you'd been reading it in his shop,' her aunt explained. 'He asked me to remind you that he does not run a library.'

Cassie thanked her, opening it to examine a detailed drawing of a royal fern.

'I hope someone's saved me some pancakes!' called a new voice, rich with laughter.

A man came in through the kitchen door, wearing a neat grey suit and a wide grin. He had to duck beneath the lintel, removing his bowler hat to reveal a head of red hair. Under his arm he carried a long lumpy parcel tied up with red string.

'Elliot!' said Miranda and Mrs Briggs in unison.

The man laughed. 'Don't sound so surprised! I wouldn't miss seeing my newly discovered niece on her birthday now, would I?'

Miranda stood up. 'Cassandra, this is your uncle Elliot. He works for Wayland Yard and is generally too busy for social calls.'

'But I do make exceptions for special occasions.' He beamed at Cassie. 'It's a great pleasure to meet you at last, Cassandra, or do you prefer Cassie? I was thrilled to hear you'd be coming to stay at Hartwood. This place needs a bit of shaking up. I'll have to bring your cousin Sebastian to visit, you two will get up to no end of trouble, I'm sure!'

Cassie wasn't sure what to say. Elliot was in the picture on her mantelpiece, a little boy with rosy cheeks and chubby hands who reminded her of Rue's brother, Oliver, but she could not reconcile that image with the tall, smartly dressed man in front of her. Like her mother, Elliot had an easy smile and laughing eyes and couldn't be more different from her stiff and serious aunt.

'Have a seat over there and I'll whip up some more pancakes! There's raspberries and elderflower cream on the table, all your favourites,' said Mrs Briggs, fussing over him. 'Why, it's just like old times!'

'Thank you, Mrs Briggs,' he said. 'I nearly forgot! Here, Cassie, this is for you.'

Cassie took the parcel and untied the string. The paper fell away to reveal a slender, twiggy broom. The wooden handle was polished to a high sheen, it had a soft leather grip and amulets for speed and safety tied to the brush.

'Whoa!' said Rue, leaning in to inspect it.

'It was your mother's broom, she called it Tantivy. I've been looking after it in her absence. Had one of our broomsmen at the Yard polish it up for you. That's Grade A whifflewood, with Scotch heather and Scandinavian birch in the brush,' Elliot explained. 'It was made by one of the best broomsquires in England.'

The broom was light in Cassie's hands. 'It was my mother's?'

'Indeed! She was a whizz on the broom, our Rose. Used to knock the chimney pots off the roof!'

'She was a careless flyer and that broom is far too wilful for a novice witch,' said her aunt.

'Nonsense, I'm sure Cassie can handle it!'

Rue was tugging at Cassie's sleeve. 'Come on, you've got to let me have a ride after you!'

Elliot laughed. 'Go on then, it's a glorious day out there and I want to have a chat with your aunt about dull, witch-business things.'

Cassie wanted to ask her uncle more questions about her mother, but not with Aunt Miranda there. Perhaps she would have a chance later on. She thanked him for the gift and allowed Rue to pull her through the door.

There was a narrow, grassy path running between the vegetable garden and the orchard. Brogan trundled his wheelbarrow down it daily and the girls had co-opted it for a broom course. It was there they headed to try out Cassie's new broom. Previously, they'd been taking turns on Rue's, but now they would be able to fly together and run races like the other girls did after coven meetings. That is, if Cassie could stay on.

Learning to ride a broom is a bit like learning to ride a bicycle, in that you have to find your balance and lean into your turns. However, unlike a bicycle, a witch's broom has opinions of its own and doesn't always respond to instructions. Rue's broom, Blaze, was a battered but sturdy old thing with a messy brush that shed twigs. It went very fast on the downhill but liked to pull to a sudden stop without warning. Cassie had often wondered if it would be easier to learn on a different broom. Now was her chance to find out.

They mounted at the start of the course, in front of the potting shed. The new broom was surprisingly comfortable and had excellent balance. Cassie was starting to feel confident.

'Come on!' said Rue. 'Last one to the rose garden is a warty toad!'

'I resent that!' grumbled Natter from her pocket.

Rue shot off. Tantivy needed no encouragement to fly after her. Its handle cut through the air, smooth as a knife through butter. Cassie glided past rows of cabbages and onions. She took the first turn neatly, holding tight with her legs as Rue had shown her. She was pleased to find the broom responsive to her lightest touch. It was at the next turn, behind the orchard, that Cassie usually fell off. Tantivy made an elegant arc of it and sped up, gaining on Rue. Cassie was flying beautifully and wished her aunt would come out to see her. On this broom she'd pass her Fledgling Test with triumph.

Ahead was the rose garden. The course ended in an archway of white blossom. Cassie flashed past Rue, shot through the arch and let out a whoop of delight. She'd never flown this fast before, it was exhilarating and a little scary. She pulled up on the broom handle, urging it to halt. The broom ignored her, carrying on through the garden.

'Stop!' Cassie begged, but the broom was no longer responding to her signals. It did a loop around the fountain and dragged her straight through the nearest hedge. Cassie was scratched and pricked by thorns, but the broom was still going at top speed.

'Rue! Help!'

Rue dived after her but couldn't catch up on her old broom.

Clinging to the out-of-control broomstick, Cassie flew through the orchard, over flower beds, past the bee skeps and straight towards the big kitchen window. Cassie shut her eyes and braced for impact but, at the last second, the broom made a ninety-degree turn and flew straight up, parallel to the wall of the house. It was all she could do to hold on as she reached the third storey.

Having passed the roof, the broom turned again, flying back over the garden, but now it was upside down! Cassie clung underneath with both arms and legs. Tantivy bucked and twisted and flew loops in the air, as if it were trying to throw her off. Cassie's stomach lurched. She was getting dizzy. The broom twisted free of her grasp and she fell, straight down into Brogan's compost heap.

Frowning at the broom, which came to a leisurely rest against the wall, Cassie lifted a wilted cabbage leaf from her head. Then she heard her aunt's voice.

'So, the Yard have been unable to trace their route?'

Cassie couldn't see Miranda, as the compost heap was piled up against the walled garden and the Hedgewitch's voice was coming from within.

'Oh, I'm confident they soon will. We have one of our best wardens on it.' That was her uncle's voice. 'Cassie looks well, settling in nicely, is she?'

The walled garden was always kept locked, Cassie had never seen what lay inside. Her aunt must have taken Elliot there for a private conversation.

'Don't change the subject. A girl from Oswalton went missing last month. She hasn't been found. They're not only nabbing from the cities, but towns and villages too. They must be taking the children through the Hedge – I've found traces of their camps in its depths. In the past they stole the odd baby, but never older children, and never this many. And what's more, someone is deliberately destroying the weirstones, I've found three broken already. The ward is holding, but for how long?'

'I've always said the Hedge was too big for one witch to manage. Why don't I send some of my people out to help you?'

'I don't need more witches, I need more information. What do you know about His recent movements?'

Rue came running towards Cassie, who held a finger to her lips and gestured to the wall. They crouched there together, listening.

'I don't know who you're referring to, Miranda,' said Elliot.

The Hedgewitch lowered her voice, 'You most certainly do, but if I must spell it out for you, I am referring to the only one who has ever been able to control the goblins, the Lord of Rags and Tatters.'

'The Erl King? You really mustn't listen to such nonsense, Miranda. I don't know what sort of stories are circulating out here in the country, but I can assure you, no one at the Yard takes the idea of a goblin king seriously. I very much doubt he even exists.'

There was a heavy silence.

'I know you were young at the time, Elliot, but you cannot have forgotten what happened to Rose. We did not imagine that.'

'Rose made her own choices. What happened then has

nothing to do with the missing children. I thank you to leave our sister out of this. Look, if I hear anything else you will be the first to know.'

'The Erl King, that's the name I read in Widdershin's book,' said Cassie. She shuddered at the memory of the awful image, the antlered skull with its burning eyes.

They were sitting in Cassie's bedroom eating birthday cake. Montague was half-asleep in the sun and Natter was perched on the windowsill, watching the flies buzz and butt against the glass. Elliot had left after lunch, promising to visit again soon. Unfortunately, there had been no chance for Cassie to question him further.

'When I was little, Mum used to tell us the king of the goblins would get us if we didn't eat all our sprouts, but I thought she made him up to scare us,' said Rue.

'Aunt Miranda seems to think he's real enough and that he had something to do with the missing children – and my mother.'

'Can't we just ask the Hedgewitch about the Erl King?' Rue suggested.

'And admit we were eavesdropping? No, whenever I

ask her about my mother, she changes the subject and if I push it, she gets cross.'

'You might find answers in Widdershin's book,' Montague suggested.

Cassie shook her head. 'I could read those three words, but the rest of it was in some strange language. Even if I could understand it, Widdershin was furious at me for touching the book, he won't let me near it again.' Cassie sighed. 'Wait a moment, what else did Aunt Miranda call him?'

Rue thought for a moment. 'The Lord of Rags—'

'—and Tatters! I've seen that name before.' Cassie leapt up to fetch *Tales of Faerie* from her bookshelf.

'Here it is, "The Lonely Tower". I remember reading this, it's about a poor woman who gets lost in the woods; she's starving and cold when she stumbles upon a mysterious tower. Inside there's a table set for two, heaped with delicious food, and a fine dress of green velvet. She puts on the dress and sits down to eat, but when she raises her glass there's a shadowy figure sat across from her, in the other chair. The story calls him the Lord of Rags and Tatters.'

'What happens to her?'

'Since she's drunk his wine and eaten his food, he requests payment – her first-born child.'

'What does he want with a baby?' asked Rue.

'The story doesn't say, but it's probably the same thing the Erl King has planned for the missing children. Aunt Miranda thinks he's behind it, that's why she was asking uncle Elliot about him. What if he has my mother too?'

'I don't know, Cass.' Rue frowned. 'Even if this Erl King exists, what can we do about it?'

'You heard what my aunt said about the weirstones. Someone is breaking them – faery folk can't touch the stones, so it has to be a witch.'

'A witch is helping the nabbers? Why would anyone do that?'

'I don't know, maybe the Erl King is paying them or maybe they don't have a choice, like the woman in the story.'

'If we can figure out who it is and stop them, that'd be real witchcraft,' said Rue, her eyes bright. 'Why, they'd have to give us the Argent Star!'

'More than that, whoever is breaking the weirstones and helping the goblins is working for the Erl King – they might know something about my mother.'

'We'll start a full investigation right away,' said Rue, making the witches' salute. 'Let's call it "Operation Grass Snake".'

Chapter Fifteen

By Mirrored Moon and Shining Flower

That Friday it rained. The steady drizzle kept 1st Hedgely Coven indoors around the hall fire, their brooms steaming gently against the wall. Cassie had not brought Tantivy, deciding she needed a little more practice on her new broom before she embarrassed herself in front of the whole coven. The Hedgewitch was away on urgent business and so Mrs Briggs watched over them while they worked on activities in their patrols. The Hartwood housekeeper was eagerly welcomed, as was the swiss roll she'd baked for their afternoon tea.

In Thorn Patrol, Ivy, Tabitha and the others were practicing magical first aid. Surrounded by piles of bandages and pots of ointment, they recited healing charms over one another.

Meanwhile, Ash Patrol were carving amulets from slices of rowan and juniper wood, inscribing them with protective runes and threading them on braided cord.

'What should we do next?' asked Alice, sweeping up a pile of wood shavings.

Nancy reached for the patrol's log book. 'We haven't revised the nine signs of enchantment in a while.'

Rue groaned.

'You'll need to know them if you want to get into Wayland Yard,' said Harriet.

'Wayland Yard?' asked Cassie. 'Isn't that where my uncle works?'

'It's in London,' said Rue. 'The headquarters of the wardens. That's where I'm going when I get my licence!'

'*You*, a warden?' interrupted Ivy, on her way to fetch more bandages. 'They only take the best witches.'

'Oh, go stick your head in the cauldron, Ivy!' said Rue.

Cassie frowned. So that was why Renata Rawlins had shown up at the school, looking into the missing children. The wardens were *witches*. And Miranda was one of them, Tabitha had called her a Border Warden.

Mrs Briggs chose that moment to announce that cake and orangeade were served and the coven rushed to claim their tea.

Rue pulled Cassie aside. 'I've been thinking about Operation Grass Snake. I know who the warlock is!'

Cassie glanced over her shoulder to make sure no one was listening, but both patrols were preoccupied with cake.

'It came to me last night,' said Rue. 'Who would like to see the Hedgewitch fail? Who needs money so badly they'd take goblin gold? Who hates children and wouldn't mind a few going missing? It has to be old Mrs Blight!'

Cassie frowned. 'Tabitha's grandmother?'

'Yes, my mum heard her say to the postmistress that Miranda wasn't anything like as good a Hedgewitch as the previous one, that she was letting things slip around Hedgely and soon we'd be overrun with hordes of goblins. I bet the old wyrm would like that, and that's why she's breaking the weirstones.'

'I don't know, Rue. Mrs Blight is pretty horrid, I'll give you that, but I don't think she's strong enough to split the stones. Tabitha said she can't even get upstairs without help.'

Rue scoffed. 'That's probably just an act, or perhaps she takes a fortifying elixir, or maybe Tabitha is in on it!'

'Shhh!' Cassie whispered urgently.

Tabitha was coming over with two generous slices of swiss roll, oozing strawberry jam.

'Here, I thought I'd better bring you some before it was all gone. Thorn Patrol are already on seconds. Didn't you hear Mrs Briggs calling?'

Rue sighed and took the cake as if it were a great burden.

'I'm sorry, I didn't mean to interrupt,' said Tabitha, backing away.

'We were just talking about my mother,' said Cassie. It was a half-truth – Rose was involved in all of this, somehow.

'Oh! I've had an idea about that. What you need is a seeking spell,' said Tabitha, licking jam off her finger.

Cassie looked blank. Rue sniffed.

'A seeking spell. My grandmother has one for finding her gloves, she's always putting them down somewhere and forgetting where. It goes like this:

'Under rug or over hearth,
Whether hidden, lost or taken,
Guide me to the secret place
Where my missing gloves are waiting.'

'Somehow I don't think that'll work for Cass's mum,' said Rue.

'No, probably not, but I'm sure the Hedgewitch will know a better one. I bet there's loads of powerful spells in her grimoire.'

'Her grim-waar?' asked Cassie.

'A grimoire is a witch's personal spell book,' Tabitha explained. 'Where they write down potion recipes and incantations. Some of the older girls in coven have started their own.'

'They're top secret though, I doubt the Hedgewitch would let us see hers,' said Rue.

'Not likely,' Cassie agreed. 'But I bet I know where she keeps it.'

Cassie decided to look for the grimoire the very next day. It would mean breaking one of Miranda's house rules, but if she could find a spell to lead her to her mother, it would be worth the risk of getting caught. All she had to do was wait for the Hedgewitch to go out.

Unfortunately, her aunt was in no hurry to leave Hartwood that morning. Cassie sat at the breakfast table, watching Miranda eat porridge and sip nettle tea for what felt like hours.

Even when the Hedgewitch finally scraped the bottom of her bowl and drank the last sip of tea, she did not leave the kitchen, but had a long, dull conversation with Mrs Briggs about household supplies. Just when Cassie thought that was over, Brogan came in, wearing embroidered velvet slippers. Miranda asked him about the moonwort he was growing for her and whether it would be ready for the potion she wanted to teach the coven the following Friday, and this led to another long discussion of the merits of various magical fertilizers. Finally, the Hedgewitch rose from her chair, dusted a crumb from her sleeve and announced that she would be in her study for the rest of the day.

Cassie sighed and dragged herself back up to her room.

'This is an imprudent course of action, you know,' said Montague, watching her pace up and down. 'However, if you are determined to go through with it you'll just have to hope she is called away this afternoon.'

'But what if she stays in all weekend?' Cassie frowned. 'No, what we need is an emergency, something she'd have to leave the house to deal with.'

'We *are* out of pickled herring,' suggested the cat.

'A *real* emergency, you know – fire, flood, goblins. Wait a moment, I have an idea, do you remember the nest of urchens we found under the potting shed last week?'

'Indeed, but I do not like the direction you appear to be heading in with this line of enquiry.'

'I need you to stir them up a bit.'

'Out of the question, urchens have a nasty bite and aren't afraid of cats. My great uncle lost the tip of his tail to an aggravated urchen.'

'I could always tell Mrs Briggs who ate the last of the Hedgely Blue cheese?'

Scowling at her and muttering under his breath, the cat slunk off downstairs.

Cassie perched on the window seat, flipping through her handbook but not reading a word. Through the open window she could hear Brogan whistling as he planted out pumpkin seedlings. This peaceful scene was shattered by a loud crash. Cassie stuck her head out the window – down below, she could make out the form of Brogan, his cap blown off and his red hair sticking up like dandelion fluff. At his feet were a lot of broken terracotta pots. He was brandishing a rake at a pack of urchens scurrying out from beneath the potting shed. They had spines down their back and long, whiskery noses. They hissed at him and dodged the rake. Cassie laughed.

She ran to the staircase. 'Aunt Miranda! Aunt Miranda!'

A moment later the Hedgewitch appeared. 'What is all this noise, Cassandra? I told you not to disturb me.'

'But I think Brogan needs your help in the garden!' The squealing urchens and Brogan's shouting could be heard throughout the house.

With a sigh, Miranda hurried down the stairs.

Cassie ran to the nearest window. Snatches of their voices drifted up to her.

'Built a nest under my pottin' shed – ruined my seedlin's – pinched my readin' glasses!' wailed Brogan.

'They're quite harmless,' said Miranda.

'You call this 'armless? It's them's been eating my radishes. They'll be after my gurtroot next! Little thievin' vandals. I'll show 'em ' armless!'

Cassie would have liked to stay and watch, but she didn't have much time if she was going to find the grimoire. Leaving them to it, she raced down the hallway to Miranda's study.

The door was locked. Of course it would be locked, why hadn't she thought of that? Frustrated, Cassie gave the handle another sharp tug. The spell she needed to find her mother might be on the other side of that door and she had only a few minutes before Aunt Miranda returned to catch her in the act.

She pushed against the door with her shoulder, her hand on the lock. There was a fluttering sensation over her chest. She'd felt it before, at the gates of Fowell House. Cassie pulled the key out from beneath her shirt. It was warm to the touch. She tried it in the keyhole but it didn't fit. Turning the handle again, she was about to give up when the door swung open, as easily as if it had never been locked in the first place.

Had the door just been stuck? Or did her key have some magic of its own? Cassie didn't have time to figure it out, she had to find the grimoire before her aunt came back.

That was not going to be easy. For all Aunt Miranda's talk of rules and order, her study was complete chaos.

There were jars and boxes of ingredients strewn across the work table, books lay open with leaves and hair pins to mark the pages. A scattering of purple crystals spilled from the table on to the floor and every surface was covered in pools of candle wax and scraps of parchment with runes scrawled on them. Clearly this was one room that never saw the benefit of Mrs Briggs' feather duster.

Cassie stepped around a stack of rusty cauldrons. The study was lit only by a high window and a single candle burning on the desk. Cassie took the candle and began to examine the open books, none of which looked promising.

'If I were Aunt Miranda, where would I keep my grimoire?' she whispered.

'Probably somewhere young and inexperienced witches cannot access it,' said Montague, slinking in through the door. 'They're still at it down there, but you'd better be quick, the Hedgewitch could return at any minute.'

There were plenty of books stacked in piles about the room. The grimoire could be any one of them, she didn't even know what it looked like. Cassie crouched down, tilting her head on the side to examine their spines: *The Crossing Nights*: *A Year in the Hedge*; *A Magical Miscellany*;

The Dialects of Faerie – it was difficult to read in the murky darkness of the room. There was a fat blue volume on the bottom of the stack, it had no writing on the cover but was spangled with stars. As Cassie freed the book, the rest of the stack fell down with a loud thud. She flinched, her heart racing, but the house was quiet.

Cassie carried the book to her aunt's desk to inspect it by the light of the candle.

It wasn't the grimoire but an old copy of *Earwig's Ephemeris*, from years before Cassie was born. The pages were covered in tables, densely packed with numbers and symbols that had no obvious meaning. As she shut it, a slip of yellowed paper fell out. It was a cutting from the *Hedgely Herald*, a picture of a group of girls in witch uniform. In the first row was a face she recognised from the photo on her mantelpiece: a young girl with a toothy grin and curly red hair – her mother.

'What is taking so long?' asked Montague. 'We'll both be discovered if you don't make haste!'

Cassie stuffed the clipping in her pocket to read later and replaced the book.

'I'm still looking. Just keep watch.'

The grimoire was her aunt's spell book, her constant reference. It had to be somewhere she could easily access it. Cassie's eyes fell on the high mantelpiece. There were no books there, just bottles of coloured liquids and jars containing snakeskin and dried seedpods. Between these was a large, flat wooden box. Cassie dragged a stool to the fireplace and clambered up. The lid of the box was carved with faery runes for protection and secrecy, but there was no lock. The lid lifted silently on its hinges; Cassie peeked inside.

It was a book!

She lifted it from the box and laid it carefully on the desk, needing both hands to manage. The book was bound in yew-green leather, tooled with a pattern of leaves and thorny vines. The design was worn smooth in places from years of handling. Cassie brought the candle closer and opened the cover.

The first pages were written in faded brown ink in a language that looked like English, but was full of strange words. Unlike the white book at Widdershin's, it was not accompanied by beautiful pictures, but rather a messy scrawl of notes and diagrams in the margins, some of which had been crossed out. As she turned the pages, the handwriting changed and the words grew more familiar. Towards the end of the book she found notes in her aunt's own hand. This wasn't just Miranda's grimoire, it must have belonged to all the Hedgewitches who came before her. The accumulated knowledge of generations of witches was in her hands and she had no idea where to start.

'I can hear footsteps!' called Montague from the doorway.

The book was full of spells and recipes, chants and charms, but there was no index to help Cassie find what she wanted. She turned a page and read:

To Reveal What is Hidden by Faery Glamour

Walk in a clockwise direction about the glamoured place, person or object while repeating the following charm:

> *Glamour glowing, glamour fading*
> *Through the veil of shifting mist.*
> *Shine the light of witching power,*
> *All enchantments are dismissed.*

> *By the candle of my art,*
> *With witching sight I see anew.*
> *Shades and phantoms must depart,*
> *Banish the false, reveal the true.*

No, that wouldn't help, not unless her mother was disguised as a post box or something. Cassie flipped frantically through the pages: 'Cure for the Elf-Sneezing', 'To Catch a Cowlug', 'Portents for the Death of a Monarch' – there was nothing that looked like a seeking spell.

'She's coming up the stairs!' hissed Montague.

Cassie shut the book. Placing both hands on the worn leather she closed her eyes and thought hard. *Please, I need to find my mother, please help me, Hedgewitches!*

She might have imagined it but her fingers began to tingle slightly. Cassie gripped the book with both hands and let it fall open on the table.

To View One's Friend or Foe at a Distance

On a clear night when the moon is full, place an article belonging to the person in a silver bowl. On to this pour water gathered from a living stream and add the flowers of the lanthorn. Stir nine times clockwise with a birch wand and repeat the incantation:

By mirrored moon and shining flower,
Over sea or mountain peak,
Reveal to me this item's keeper
For I would glimpse the one I seek.

Over Montague's frantic hissing Cassie could hear her aunt's footsteps echoing up the corridor. She read the incantation again and shut the book, dropping it back into the wooden box. Her heart beating like a drum, she pulled the door shut behind her and raced across the hall to the nearest empty room, with Montague at her heels. Hiding behind the door, Cassie peered through the narrow opening. She was sure her aunt would hear her breathing, but the Hedgewitch swept past them, clutching a small, spiky person in her hand. They heard the door of the study open and shut.

'All this subterfuge has absolutely shattered my nerves,' said Montague. 'I'm going to need a very long nap.'

Cassie whispered the incantation to herself: *by mirrored moon and shining flower...* She had to remember it, word for word – the spell that would lead her to her mother.

Chapter Sixteen

Saltash & Son

Two days later, Cassie and Rue met up after school to work on their witch salt. They'd found most of the ingredients in Mrs Briggs' pantry and the rest in the cupboard at the coven hall. They now had everything they needed except angelica root. The herb grew in the coven garden but it would not be ready to harvest until autumn, so they would have to visit the apothecary.

Cassie told Rue about the grimoire on the walk into town.

'I can't believe you broke into the Hedgewitch's study. You're pluckier than you look, Cass!'

'Oh, and I found this.' She passed Rue the newspaper

clipping. 'There's my mother, when she was our age. Her patrol won some sort of award for bravery, the Argent Star, for saving a boy who got lost in the Hedge.'

'Ivy would eat her hat to get that badge!'

'Do you think we should ask Tabitha for help with the seeking spell? It was her idea, after all.'

'Here, let me see,' said Rue.

Cassie passed over her *Witch's Handbook*, she'd written the spell in the back as soon as she returned to her room, afraid she would forget something.

'Looks pretty simple, my mum's got a silver fruit bowl we can use. We don't need Tabitha. Besides, what if she told your aunt? Or one of the girls in Thorn? Not to mention her grandmother is likely in league with the Erl King. You can't trust the Blights, Cass.'

Cassie thought Tabitha could probably keep a secret as well as either of them, but she supposed it was safer if fewer people were involved.

'When's the next full moon?' asked Rue.

'I looked that up in *Astaroth's Almanack*, it falls on the same night as the Midsummer Fair. We can get water from the Nix, but I don't know about the lanthorn flower. I couldn't find it in the handbook.'

'Never heard of it, but I bet old Saltash has!'

'Saltash & Son, Apothecary – est. 1582', read the peeling letters over the shop, beside a picture of a snake curled around a goblet. In the window were round-bellied bottles of blue and red liquid, a branch of bright orange coral, a stuffed hoopoe and a large jar of yellow stones that looked suspiciously like teeth.

They entered a dimly lit room lined with shelves bearing even more jars, filled with dried leaves, flowers, seeds, roots and powders. The cabinets beneath had hundreds of little drawers, each labelled in spidery calligraphy. On the display counter were curious fossils, crystals, shells and feathers. The air was full of spices and the balsamic odour of exotic resins. Above their heads a crocodile skeleton hung from the rafters.

A tall, thin man with grey hair looked up from the counter and glanced briefly at Cassie and Rue. He was serving an elderly customer – it was none other than Mrs Blight.

'I'm sorry, ma'am, but that item is restricted and has been for thirty years.'

The old woman had not noticed the girls yet. 'I am

well aware of that, only I have heard that you have ways of getting ahold of these more... delicate ingredients. Contacts across the border? Certain boxes beneath the counter? I can pay – in *gold*.'

Cassie and Rue exchanged a meaningful look.

The shopkeeper cleared his throat. 'My apologies, ma'am, but this is a reputable establishment. I do not know where you have heard such rumours, but I can assure you they are entirely unfounded. Here is the coltsfoot you requested, if the cough lingers I can make up some horehound pastilles. Now, if there is nothing else, it would appear I have other customers to see to.'

Mrs Blight looked over her shoulder and glared at the girls. She grabbed the herbs with one clawed hand and hurried out the door, knocking Cassie with her bag. A small scrap of notepaper fluttered down and Cassie scooped it up.

'Wait, you dropped this...!' she called, but Mrs Blight was already scurrying down the street, so Cassie put the paper in her pocket.

Rue was toying with a set of brass scales on the counter; it overbalanced and sent a cascade of aniseed balls rolling across the floor.

'Tchhh! How many times do I have to tell you children not to touch? I ought to make you pay for those!' Saltash turned to Cassie. 'Who is this?'

'Cassie Morgan,' said Rue, chasing an aniseed ball.

Saltash scowled at her.

'We need eight ounces of angelica root,' said Cassie.

'What for? This isn't one of your pranks, I hope—'

'We're making witch salt,' said Rue. 'Have you got any or not?'

The old man grunted and went off to fill a paper bag from one of the tall jars. He tossed it on the counter.

'That'll be sixpence.'

'Oh, and some lanthorn,' Rue added, trying to look innocent, which wasn't her speciality.

'Some *what*?' snapped Saltash, fixing them with his pale eyes. Cassie wished she could disappear but she needed this if she was going to find her mother.

'Lanthorn, it's a flower,' she said.

'I know what it is.' His lip curled as he spoke. 'The question is, what would two little girls want with such a thing?'

'We're not little girls, we're witches and if you haven't got any, just say so and we'll be off,' said Rue.

Saltash sneered. 'You won't find lanthorn in any

apothecary in England. It's of absolutely no use dried, loses all of its potency, you need to pick it fresh. You could find lanthorn in the Hedge when I was a boy, but it's very rare now, nearly extinct.'

Rue sighed and tugged Cassie's sleeve to go, but she resisted. She needed to find out more, but without raising the shopkeeper's suspicions. She smiled up at him. 'That must have been wonderful, to see it growing in the wild. Is it very beautiful?'

The apothecary sniffed. 'Well, there's a picture in Grieve's *Herbaria Magica*, if you're genuinely interested.' He pulled a heavy book from beneath the counter and began to turn its stained and yellowed pages. 'Here: *Lucidus indago*, the lanthorn flower.'

He showed them an old woodcut print of a star-like flower with seven petals and feathery leaves.

Cassie took a closer look. 'What colour is the flower?'

'Bright white, like fresh snow,' said Saltash.

The shop door opened to admit two men in work clothes. Saltash returned to his senses and shut the book, waving a hand at the girls.

'Now, off with you! And don't let me catch you meddling with my stock again!'

'Is he always so rude?' asked Cassie, once they were safely out on the street.

'Saltash is an old grump, but he's harmless.'

'Here, Mrs Blight dropped this when she left.' Cassie pulled the scrap of paper from her pocket to show Rue. It was a shopping list: butter, bread, cabbage – these items were all crossed out. The last item was not.

'What is *selumbine*?' asked Cassie.

Rue shrugged. 'Never heard of it.'

'It must be the herb Saltash said was restricted. What do you think she wants it for?'

'Probably going to poison us all. What I want to know is how she can afford to pay in gold when she can't even fix her roof. My dad delivered her groceries last week and said the hallway was full of buckets to catch the water. It must be goblin gold, money she got from selling the stolen children.'

'Perhaps, but it's not enough proof to take to my aunt.' Cassie sighed. 'And we didn't even get the lanthorn flower, although at least we know what it looks like now.'

Rue tossed the bag of angelica in the air and caught it.

'Do you think the spell would work without it?'

'No, it's in the charm, remember? *Mirrored moon and hidden flower.*' Cassie frowned. 'Saltash said *nearly* extinct, didn't he? That means there could still be some growing in the Hedge. If only Aunt Miranda would take us there again, we could look.'

Rue grinned. 'What are you doing tomorrow?'

Chapter Seventeen

Ignis Fatuus

'This is a terrible idea,' croaked Natter.

'For once, I am in agreement with the frog,' said Montague.

'*Toad*, but look, you can't just go wandering about in there on your own.'

It was a glorious, sunny afternoon and the grassy hill that led up to the Hedge was spotted with buttercups and daisies. The sun was warm on their backs and they were well provisioned for the journey with ham sandwiches, bottles of Mrs Brigg's homemade ginger beer and a packet of digestive biscuits.

'But we won't be on our own, we'll stay together and we have our brooms if we get into any trouble,' said Cassie. She only hoped that Tantivy would behave itself in an emergency.

'And our first batch of witch salt,' said Rue. 'I hope we *do* meet some goblins so we can try it out!'

They'd wrapped the witch salt in cheesecloth bundles, which smelled sharply of protective herbs; Rue called them 'goblin bombs'. Cassie had a few stuffed in her satchel, and although she wasn't sure they'd work, it made her feel slightly more confident about going into the Hedge.

'We'll be back before nightfall, and if we're not, you can find the Hedgewitch and tell her everything.'

The Hedge was less threatening in the afternoon light, with rays of golden green filtering through the thick canopy. At first, they followed a wide path – it may have been the same one that Thorn Patrol had taken on their mushroom hunting expedition, but then, it may have lead somewhere else entirely. You never could tell with the Hedge.

'We need to look out for the lanthorn flower,' said Cassie. 'Remember, it's small and white and has seven petals.'

It wasn't difficult to find flowers in the Hedge,

everywhere they looked were the lace umbrellas of cow parsley, climbing tendrils of honeysuckle, waterfalls of wild roses, spotted orchids and purple columbine, but none of these matched the picture they'd seen in Saltash's book. Rue got very excited over a patch of small white flowers beneath a willow tree, but they only had six petals and smelled strongly of garlic.

As they wandered deeper into the wood, the path narrowed and the trees grew thick and tall, congregating in dense clumps. The leaf mould muffled their footsteps and the birdsong, which had filled the outer limits of the wood, was distant now, leaving only the sound of the wind in the leaves high above and the creaking of branches. Occasionally, they heard a rustle in the undergrowth and froze, but it was only ever a thrush or a rabbit.

The air was cooler and there were fewer flowers in the darker groves of the wood so Cassie was relieved when the path brought them to a clearing. It was roughly circular and in its centre was a tall grey stone, carved with faery runes.

'It's a weirstone!' said Cassie. The moss-covered monolith was unbroken, offering a small sphere of safety in the depths of the wood.

'Let's stop here for a bit, I'm famished,' said Rue.

They sat with their backs against the stone, soaking up the stored warmth of the sun, and shared the sandwiches and ginger beer.

'How long have we been out here?' Cassie asked.

Rue looked at her wristwatch. 'Hard to tell, it was four o'clock when we went in, but this thing says it's five past four now – which can't be right, because the sun's got lower. The Hedge must have meddled with it.'

'It feels like we've been walking for hours, but it's not getting dark yet,' Cassie said.

'We can fly our brooms back and save time that way,' Rue offered.

But it was so warm and comfortable, sitting with their backs to the stone and nibbling biscuits, that neither of them were keen to re-enter the cool, dark shade of the wood. Cassie sipped her ginger beer and watched brimstone and holly blue butterflies hover over the clover. There was something else fluttering at the edge of the clearing, between the trees. It was pale violet and glowed softly. Some sort of moth, perhaps?

'*Cassie*,' called a soft voice.

Her first thought was of the pine marten, the creature that had trapped her in the faery ring. Was this another trap? She looked at Rue. Her friend was lying in the grass, arms crossed behind her head and eyes closed. They should be safe here, with the weirstone to guard them.

'*Cassie!*' called the voice again. '*Where are you?*'

She sat up. It was not the pine marten, with his cold sibilant tone. This voice was warm, female and achingly familiar; it tugged at her memories, taunting her with hope.

'Rue, wake up! Did you hear that?'

'Hear what?' asked Rue. She sat up and sniffed the air. 'Wow! What is that smell?'

Cassie couldn't smell anything other than the sun-warmed grass and the cool green of leaves and moss.

'*Cassie!*' The voice was more urgent now.

She leapt up. 'There it is again! You must have heard? I could have sworn—'

'Baked apple,' said Rue. 'No, wait, it's hot cocoa with cinnamon... and roast chicken and fish and chips...'

'What are you talking about? You just ate two sandwiches and half a packet of biscuits. Can't you hear that voice?'

'What voice?'

Cassie ran to the edge of the clearing, listening

intently. When it came again it was fainter.

'*Cassie, help me!*'

She'd ached to hear that voice for seven long years, but it had only ever come to her in dreams. There could be no doubt, it was her mother.

Cassie ran into the woods. There was no path so she had to push through the undergrowth, scratching her legs on brambles and crunching through bracken. Whenever she stopped she heard the voice again, always just a little further off. The pale violet light was ahead of her now, a small twist of fire that flickered and danced.

'*Cassie...*'

'I'm coming!' she cried. The light led her to a little stream that laughed as she leapt across it. The pale flame winked and went out and she was left alone amongst the alder trees.

Cassie waited, straining her ears for the sound of her mother's voice. She waited and waited, but the voice did not come. All she could hear was the distant hammering of a woodpecker.

'Mother!' she called. There was no answer.

Cassie sat down on a mossy log and rested her head in her hands. She was completely and utterly lost.

The most important thing, Cassie decided, was not to panic. If she set off again, without any sense of direction, she'd end up even further from Rue and the clearing. Besides, some faery folk could smell fear and she might attract unwanted attention.

Unfortunately, she'd left her broom behind with Rue, but Cassie still had her satchel. She rifled through it for her Witch's Handbook and flipped to the chapter titled '46 Common Folk of Faery'. In it were listed the faery creatures and people they were most likely to encounter in Britain, along with a rating of how dangerous they were, from Mostly Harmless to R. F. Y. L. (Run For Your Life).

Will-o'-the-Wisp
Ignis fatuus

Also known as: Hinky-punk, Spunky, Jack-o'-the-Lantern
Rating: Mischievous

The will-o'-the-wisp appears as a small flame or glowing orb. It lures humans into following it by projecting the sight, sound or smell of their heart's desire. The wisp then vanishes, leaving its victim lost and disorientated. The variety found in marshland, sometimes called the Bog Wisp, is more dangerous as travellers will find themselves sinking into unstable ground. No particular warding is necessary against wisps as the experienced witch will learn to recognise their simple illusions and ignore the temptation to follow them. However, a common method to avoid being wisp-led is to wear an item of one's clothing inside out.

Well, that explained why Rue hadn't heard Rose's voice – clearly her heart's desire had rather more to do with her stomach. Cassie turned her socks inside out for good measure.

After Cassie's encounter with the faery ring, the Hedgewitch had talked to the coven about what to do if they got lost in the Hedge. There were two options, the first was to walk due east, but this was difficult if you couldn't see the sun. The second was to find a stream and follow the water. All the streams in the Hedge were said to flow into the Nix and the river ran straight through the village. Although some faery folk, like Wendy Weedskin, lived in running water, most avoided it, so it offered some small protection as long as you were wary.

Cassie returned to the stream she'd crossed before the will-o'-the-wisp went out. It was no wider than her boot. She set off in the direction it was flowing.

The stream led her through the alders, downhill into a grove of young willows, where it widened into a pool. Cassie realised just how thirsty she was and crouched down at the water's edge. It was clear as a windowpane, though rippled by the falling stream. She could see pebbles at the bottom and a layer of old leaves, like tarnished coins. Was it safe to drink? This was the Hedge after all; it looked clean but there could be some invisible enchantment.

'Drink. It will not hurt you,' said a voice.

Cassie looked up to find a large cat regarding her from across the water. It crouched on long, powerful legs, claws sunk into the soft moss. It was a lynx but entirely black, from the tufts on its ears to the stub of its tail. Its eyes were like yellow lamps.

'That is the stream called Gnost, the water of remembering,' said the lynx. 'With each sip you will recall something you have forgotten. It flows from Faerie into mortal lands, where it is diluted by the Lastor, the water of forgetting, which runs beneath the earth.'

She eyed the Lynx warily. Miranda had told them not to trust any creature they met in the Hedge. But then, she was so thirsty, a memory would be a small price to pay for a sip of that clear water.

Cassie scooped up a handful in her palm, it was icy but tasted fresh and sweet. She drank deeply.

She was sitting on a green lawn, in the shade of a fruit tree. She could smell cut grass and something salty; a sea breeze. In her hand she held a soft ball, no, it was an orange. She could feel the tiny indentations on its surface. Above her, something was flapping in the breeze, a line of washing hung out to dry. A woman was singing in a soft, lilting voice. It was a sad song, and yet she seemed happy:

'Nine years have come, nine years have gone,
And yet still I remember thee,

Think of the throne you sit upon,
Beside the Queen of Faerie.

Your own true self, your face so fair
I'd give a purse of gold to see,
And from the shadows call you forth,
Oh, when will you return to me?'

The woman turned round, looked down at Cassie and laughed. Reaching up, she picked another orange from the tree and rolled it to her across the grass. Cassie reached out to catch it.

'That was my mother.' Cassie rubbed her eyes with a sleeve. 'I remembered my mother, her face, her voice.' Eagerly, she reached for the water again.

'It was just a memory, but you could see her once more, in this world,' said the lynx.

'How?'

'Follow me, Cass-sandra, and I will bring you to her.'

'It's you!' said Cassie, leaping up. 'Glashtyn.'

'I can give you what you desire, Cass-sandra. Not mere memories or wisp-illusions, but flesh and blood. I can reunite you with your mother.'

This time, the memory still fresh in her mind, Cassie was sorely tempted. She did not know who or what this shape-shifting creature was, but if he could fulfill his promise then perhaps she should go with him. She was lost anyway and had no guide but the stream. Yet, in the pit of her stomach, something felt wrong. Glashtyn had trapped her once, what if he sought to lead her into another trap, or worse, into the hands of the Erl King himself?

'No, I won't go with you. If you really know where she is then tell me.'

The wild cat leapt across the stream and came towards her. He was the size of a labrador but moved with feline fluidity.

'You will change your mind, you will come to me, when all hope is lost. I am the only one who can help you, Cass-sandra.'

'Just leave me alone!'

Cassie reached into her satchel for one of Rue's goblin bombs and threw it at the lynx; it exploded in a cloud of pungent powder. Without waiting to see the result, she dashed off into the trees. At first, she thought Glashtyn was following her, a black shadow in the corner of her vision, but when she finally stopped, breathless and bent double with a stitch, she was alone. She could hear nothing but the creaking of branches and the rustle of leaves.

Cassie looked back the way she had come, but there was no sign of her passage. The trees closed behind her, forming a fence of slender trunks. She'd left behind the lynx, but also the stream, and without it to guide her she was hopelessly lost once more.

Chapter Eighteen

The Lanthorn Flower

Cassie found herself in a forest of birch trees with silvery-white bark peeling from their trunks. There were no paths to choose from, so she wandered aimlessly, through the bracken and foxgloves. The slender birches were endless, repeating their grey and white columns into the distance. No matter how far she walked, in every direction the birches went on and on.

Stopping to catch her breath, Cassie pulled her handbook out again, hoping for some inspiration, and as she opened it she heard a rustling above her.

Cassie did not see it at first, so well did its white scales camouflage against the birch bark. If it had not moved, she would never have seen it at all. A small, serpentine head peeled away from the trunk, sniffing the air and inspecting her with beady black eyes. It was a book wyrm.

Cassie laughed with relief. 'Hullo, what are you doing here?' She took a step towards the creature. Was this its natural habitat? What could it be living off, the papery bark of the birches?

The wyrm cocked its head and she saw that it was missing a claw on its right foreleg. It was the very same wyrm she had rescued from Widdershin's.

Cassie held out the handbook and the wyrm scurried down the tree towards her.

'Is this what you're after then? A bit tastier than bark, I imagine.'

She flipped to the introduction and tore a corner from the page, holding it out towards the wyrm. He looked at her for a moment, then snatched the paper, swallowing it whole and coughing as it stuck in his throat.

'A bit dry, isn't it?' She tore another sliver of printed paper and fed it to him. 'I wish you could help me, I've lost my way.'

The book wyrm was at her feet now, begging for more paper. She fed it another scrap.

'These trees go on forever. I don't suppose you know the way out?'

The wyrm cocked its head, regarded her for a moment and scurried away. Cassie sighed. The wyrm stopped, sitting up on its hind legs , it gave a short, sharp bark.

'What is it?'

The wyrm barked again; Cassie laughed. 'Anyone would think you wanted me to follow you.'

Could it really be trying to help her? She'd not thought the wyrm that intelligent, but then it had eaten a whole encyclopaedia.

The creature scurried back and looked up at her, before running off again in the same direction.

'All right, I'm coming.' Getting to her feet, Cassie followed. Whether or not the creature knew the way, she could hardly become more lost than she already was.

The wyrm leapt ahead of her, guiding her between the pale, slender trunks and through the green ferns that filled the undergrowth.

At last the birches thinned and changed to the reassuring solidity of oaks, their bark rough and cracked like dry earth. Somewhere, a wren was singing.

Cassie bent down to thank the book wyrm, feeding him the last page of the introduction.

'There you are, you've earned it.'

The wyrm waited to see if any more was forthcoming but as it was not, he gave one final chirrup and disappeared back into the birch grove.

'Well,' Cassie said to herself. 'At least this is a change of scenery.'

The oaks were ancient, some of them had trunks so wide that it would take all of Ash Patrol to encircle them, their arms outstretched. Cassie walked on, stepping over gnarled roots and ducking low branches. At the heart of the oak wood was a tree so old that its crown had died away, leaving only the lower boughs which dragged along the ground as if too heavy for the tree to sustain. Yet its leaves were as fresh and green as the youngest sapling and made a curtain that brushed Cassie's face as she stepped beneath it. She stood before the old tree and felt the dangers of the Hedge recede. Here, she was safe, unseen from the outside and protected by the solid presence of the oak. Cassie traced her fingers on the bark, wondering just how old the tree was. Hundreds of years? Thousands?

It was curious the way the bark twisted and bulged.

There was a knot of wood that almost looked like a face, an old man's face with a bulbous nose, bushy brows and whiskers. The cracks in the bark formed laughter lines around the mouth and eyes. It was a kindly face, she thought. Cassie reached out to touch it and felt a warm, fluttering sensation at her chest – her key, it was growing warm again.

The tree sneezed.

Cassie stepped back and tripped over a root, falling with a thud in the leaf mould. She pulled herself up again and brushed her skirt. The tree was still, the wooden face remained inert. Perhaps she had been in the Hedge for too long and it was doing strange things to her mind. Trees often looked like they had faces, the way clouds sometimes looked like fish or birds. She was letting her imagination run away with her.

Two slits in the wood opened to reveal deep brown eyes, bleary and glazed with sleep.

'Nimue?' asked the tree.

Cassie fought the urge to run. The tree was talking, that was unusual, but she supposed there were a lot of unusual things in the Hedge. If there were talking cats and toads then why not trees as well?

She cleared her throat. 'I'm sorry?'

The wood rippled, as if there were muscles beneath the bark-skin, and the face came to life.

'Ah, not she, I see that now, but one of her kin perhaps.' The tree yawned. 'Tell me child, which century is this?'

'The twentieth.'

'It seems I have had a few more than forty winks.' It chuckled to itself.

'Who are you?'

The tree smiled, its wrinkled face creasing up like a crumpled paper bag.

'I am no one of great importance, at least, not any more. You may call me Ambrose. And what is your name, young witch?'

'I'm Cassie, Cassie Morgan, and I'm not a witch yet, not really. I still have to pass my Fledgling Test. I didn't know that trees in the Hedge could talk.'

'They cannot, as a general rule, not in a language most humans understand. However, I am not a tree, but rather a man *in* a tree.'

'Like the man in the moon?'

'Yes, although he's been there a good deal longer, poor fellow.'

'How did you end up inside a tree?'

'I was put here by a witch, many many years ago.'

'How awful!'

'Upon reflection, I rather think I deserved it.' Ambrose smiled.

'But can't we get you out? There has to be some way to break the spell!'

The face squinted at her. 'What is that you wear around your neck, witchling?'

Cassie pulled out the key and showed it to him.

'Ah, many are the times I have longed to see the gift you bear, yet even the golden key cannot free me, only waken me from my slumber. No, I must await the bearer of another treasure. Never mind, it is not such a bad resting place, this tree. The earth is sweet and the silence sweeter. I no longer require anything else.' Ambrose closed his eyes for a moment. 'However, I take it you were looking for something when you entered the Great Western Wood, and I doubt very much that it was me.'

'Well, I was trying to find a lanthorn flower. It's for a spell, you see, to find my mother, but now I'm rather lost myself.'

'And you have been looking on the ground I imagine? And you have not found it?'

Cassie admitted that this was so.

'The lanthorn grows only in the clefts of old oaks, it does not like to be too close to the earth. Hmm, now let me think, it is rather late in the season for the flowers, but yes, I believe there is a small patch of lanthorn growing amongst my branches, up there, second limb to the left. It itches sometimes. Worst thing about this tree business, one cannot scratch.'

Cassie craned her neck and caught a glimpse of feathery leaves, entirely unlike those of the oak.

'I think I can see it, but I'll have to climb up to reach it. That won't hurt you, will it?'

'Not at all, just mind where you put your feet.'

Cassie took her boots off and climbed barefoot. It was easier than scaling the plane tree at Fowell House because the branches began much lower and swept down towards the ground under their great weight. She walked up the first one, needing her hands only when she reached the trunk. Bracing her feet against the rough bark, she pulled herself up into the crook of the next branch. In a cleft, just above her, she could make out a cluster of ferny leaves. Standing on tip-toe she found a single, delicate white bloom in their midst. Cassie counted the petals – seven, with a golden heart at the centre. She plucked it with great care and climbed back down.

'Found what you needed? Excellent. I imagine you'll be waiting for the full moon to illuminate your spell.'

'Yes, at Midsummer.'

'Very good. I wish you great success, only, be wary, the lanthorn will show the truth, but the truth can be difficult to accept. It is a great burden to have knowledge without the power to act upon it.'

'I'll be careful. Thank you for the flower!'

'I hope we meet again, witchling. It does an old soul good to see such determined youth. I had all but forgotten what it is to want something and strive for it. Trees do not leave home to seek their fortunes, they are content with their chosen place. It is a peaceful existence, but time passes slowly, softly, and I grow forgetful. It is good to be reminded of the quick lives of humankind.'

'I'll come back again, if I can find you,' Cassie offered. 'Only, I'm still not sure how to get home.'

'The lanthorn flower will guide you. That is one of its powers. Hold it in your right hand and think of home.'

She lifted the delicate blossom and closed her eyes, picturing in her mind the road leading up the hill to Hartwood. The front door, the warm fire in the kitchen with Mrs Briggs stirring the cauldron, Brogan reading the seed catalogue and even her aunt, sipping nettle tea. She pictured her turret room with the moss-green rug and Montague asleep by the fire.

Cassie opened her eyes again and saw the flower was emitting a faint white glow.

'Follow the light, it will grow stronger when you are headed towards home,' Ambrose explained.

Cassie thanked him again and set off through the woods, following the pale light of the lanthorn.

Rue was waiting at the edge of the wood with Montague and Natter, holding both their brooms. She had a worried frown on her freckled face.

'Cass! What happened to you? You were babbling about a voice and then you dashed off into the trees. I called after you but you didn't seem to hear me. I waited in the clearing until it was starting to get dark, but then I thought I'd better leave the Hedge while I still could. Montague wanted to go straight for the Hedgewitch, but I thought we should wait just a bit longer, in case you found your own way out. No point getting in a row over nothing. What's that?'

'It's a lanthorn flower, it led me back. We can do the seeking spell now!'

Rue admired the fragile flower, which was shining bright as a candle flame. Cassie told her about following the wisp and meeting Ambrose.

'But you weren't tricked,' said Cassie. 'Even though the wisp was tempting you with all those delicious scents.'

'Rue has her shirt on inside out,' said Natter. 'She's always in a rush to get dressed in the morning.'

'Shhh! I hear something, there, in the elder bushes,' said Montague.

Cassie and Rue peered into the foliage, it was twilight now and the Hedge was a haze of green and purple shadow. There was indeed a rustling sound, a branch of elder quivered.

Cassie hid the lanthorn flower behind her back and clutched her broom, ready to fly if need be.

A pointed black hat appeared, followed by the slender form of Ivy Harrington.

'You!' said Rue.

Ivy glared at them. She had a basket full of wilted herbs tucked under one arm.

'You've been in the Hedge!' said Rue.

'So what if I have? You're hardly one to scold, Ruth Whitby. From the state of your clothes I can tell you've spent all afternoon in the woods as well. Just what were you two up to?'

'That's none of your business,' hissed Rue.

'Well, maybe I'll tell the Hedgewitch, then you'll have to answer *her* questions.'

'You can't,' Cassie pointed out. 'Not without revealing you were there too.'

Ivy shrugged. 'It's not like I care about your silly errand anyway. These herbs are for our Midsummer project, we have everything we need now and we're bound to win.'

She tossed her hair and set off in the direction of the village.

Rue sighed. 'Of course, we can't snitch on her either.'

Cassie watched Ivy descend the hill, her black cloak brushing the waist-high grasses. 'Rue, what if she wasn't only after the herbs?'

'I don't follow?'

'Maybe it was Ivy I saw that day, breaking the weirstone – she could be the warlock.' If anyone in their coven had the skill to do so, it was Ivy.

'Ivy's a rotter, I'll grant you that much, but I don't know she'd go so far as to help the goblins. What would she get out of it?'

But Rue hadn't seen Ivy's mother. Cassie was willing to bet Ivy would do just about anything to save her, even if that meant breaking the Witch's Oath. They'd have to keep a closer eye on the Thorn Patrol witch to be sure.

They said their goodbyes and Rue flew off towards the Whitbys' shop, the toad clinging to her shoulder.

Montague lectured Cassie all the way back to Hartwood, but she had eyes only for the glowing, translucent blossom cradled in her hand, still leading her home. If the lanthorn could bring her to Hartwood then surely it would help her find her mother.

Chapter Nineteen

The Bungled
Burglary

Cassie was late for supper, but luck was on her side. The Hedgewitch had been called away by Widdershin, who was having trouble with a cursed dictionary that kept making up words.

Cassie went straight upstairs to put the lanthorn flower somewhere safe. Opening her bedroom door, she gasped – books and papers were strewn across bed and floor, some of them torn and crumpled. The wardrobe was open, her clothes and pyjamas pulled out and heaped in messy piles. The photos of her family had been knocked off the mantelpiece. She hurried to pick them up and was relieved to find the glass unbroken. She had only just cleaned her room, at Mrs Briggs' insistence, but now it looked as though a hurricane had blown through.

Montague hissed, dropped low and began stalking towards the bed.

'What is it?' Cassie reached for the poker that hung by the fireplace. She knew that all faery folk feared the touch of iron.

Kneeling down, she peered under the bed. There, in the shadows, was her faery trap – she'd tossed it there after coven and forgotten about it. Crouched over it was a hunched, bony shape. It looked out at her with shining eyes.

There was a screech, a yowl from Montague, and the bed jumped a foot into the air. A small figure scuttled out and shot towards the window. Cassie stepped between the figure and the window, blocking its escape. Montague leapt and sunk his teeth into the creature's bare foot.

'Owwowww!' it wailed. 'Lemme go! Get it off me!'

It was a goblin, smaller than the nabbers who'd chased her in Trite, but equally odd-looking. He had a long, pointy nose and was wearing what appeared to be a rather dirty nightcap.

Cassie held the poker to his throat, she wasn't taking any chances. The goblin froze, his bulging eyes fixed on the black iron.

Montague let go of his foot and spat. 'Disgusting! Don't you ever wash?'

'Who are you and what are you doing in my room?' Cassie demanded.

The goblin's eyes filled with tears. 'Pleeeease don't hurt me! I didn't take nothing, I swear!'

Keeping one eye on the miserable creature, Cassie surveyed the wreck of her room.

'You were looking for something, what was it?'

The goblin squirmed to get further from the iron point of the poker, but Montague circled behind him. The goblin broke down in a fit of loud, wet blubbing. Tears the colour of pond water rolled from his eyes and he hiccoughed.

'Oh, ohhhh... Make it quick, that's all I ask, don't make me suffer!'

He really was a pathetic creature and seemed genuinely terrified of her. Despite the mess she almost felt sorry for him.

'Look, I'm not going to hurt you,' said Cassie, crouching down beside him.

'The key!' gasped the goblin. He leapt for her throat, grabbing at the dangling necklace. Cassie jumped back.

'So that's what you're after, is it? What do you want with my key?'

A wily look came over the goblin's features and she realised that all the tears and wailing had been an act.

'It belongs to my Master,' said the goblin. 'It was stolen, long ago, he wants it back. Very sentimental it is, family hair-loom. Not worth nothing, but he wants it back all the same. You're a nice girl, aren't you? You'll give it to me, won't you?'

Cassie tucked the key back into her shirt. 'That's nonsense, the key belongs to my mother. You can't have it.'

The goblin's face crumpled once more. 'Oh, you must give it to me! It's me last chance. You don't get it, he'll kill me!'

'Enough of that!' said Cassie, brandishing the poker at him. She didn't actually plan to use it, but she wanted him to think she might. 'Either you tell me the truth or I'll call my aunt, the Hedgewitch.' Of course, Miranda was not in the house, but the creature didn't know that.

The goblin looked at her, then at Montague and sighed. 'Oh, all right. Promise you'll let me go after I tell you?'

'Witch's Honour, but first tell me who sent you and why they want my key.'

'Nobody sent me, I come on me own. As if His High and Horribleness'd send small fry like me after his precious key. He'd kill me if he knew I'd come 'ere! But, thinks I, it can't be too hard, just slip in while you was out and take a look. I'm good at that, finding stuff people have hid. If I'd got the key and brought it back, well, that'd show 'em. I'd get a promotion at the very least. Just think – me, Burdock, head filcher!' The goblin started to bite his dirty yellow fingernails. 'But if he finds I was here and I've not got the key, he's going to kill me for sure!'

'Who's going to kill you? Who are you afraid of?' asked Cassie.

'Him!' said Burdock, quivering. 'You mean you don't know? The big guy! His dreadfulness, the Prince of Goblins! Do I really have to spell it out for you?'

'The Erl King,' said Cassie.

'Cassandra, if this is true then we really must wait for the Hedgewitch,' said Montague.

'No, I promised I'd let him go if he spoke the truth. I want to know more. Why does the Erl King want my key?'

'Not likely he'd tell me, is it? All I know is he wants it bad and he'll kill anyone who gets in the way, so you

251

might as well give it to me and save yourself a peck of trouble.'

'How did you gain entry to Hartwood?' asked Montague. 'There are wards surrounding the house.'

'There's a hole, an old rabbit warren under the western wall. Your precious witch-wards only guard above ground, not beneath.'

Cassie made a mental note to tell her aunt about that.

'Just lemme go, will you? I told you everything I knows.'

'He's merely a filcher, a thief. It is unlikely the goblin is privy to the Erl King's secrets.' said Montague. 'However, if you release him, he'll go straight to his master and report everything he has learned. The only advantage we have now is that the Erl King presumes your ignorance of his desire for the key.'

Cassie bit her lip. 'I'll set you free on two conditions,' she said to the goblin. 'First, you're not to tell the Erl King, or anyone else about this. You've never spoken with me, understand?'

'Spoken to who? Who's speaking?' said Burdock.

'Promise,' Cassie insisted.

'Oh all right, I won't tell a soul. Hardly my proudest moment, is it? Not gonna go bragging about that time

I got caught by a little girl and her cat.'

'Second, you owe me a favour.' Cassie had read about deals with faery folk in her storybooks and knew she could demand a reward for his freedom. 'Next time I need something of you and call your name, you must come.'

Burdock grumbled but agreed to that too.

'Cassie, we really should wait for the Hedgewitch, she'll have further questions,' Montague hissed.

'No. The key might have something to do with my mother's disappearance – it could help me find her. If I tell my aunt she'll take it off me and then I'll never find out why the Erl King wants it. Besides, he answered our questions and I have to keep my word too.'

She lifted the poker and stepped back. 'All right, you can go.'

Freed from the threat of iron, the goblin leapt for the window. Cassie watched him clamber down the ivy like a hairless monkey. She tried to see where he went when he reached the bottom, but he vanished into the shadows.

'This is serious, Cassandra,' said Montague.

Cassie sighed. 'I know, it's going to take me all night to clean up this mess.'

It was less than a week until the full moon and the Midsummer Fair but Cassie found the wait excruciating. They had everything they needed for the seeking spell now. Rue had borrowed her mum's silver fruit bowl and Cassie had the precious lanthorn flower in her tooth-glass on the bedside table. It glowed softly at night and she only hoped it would last until the appointed day. After school she met with Rue and they planned how they would get away from the fair and perform the spell. She decided it was time to tell her friend about the key, and how it had helped her escape Fowell House and enter the Hedgewitch's study.

'Well, if it can unlock doors and gates, maybe the Erl King wants it to steal something?' Rue suggested.

'I think it can do more than that. It woke Ambrose, the man in the tree, perhaps it can unlock enchantments too? Once we do the spell and find my mother, I'll ask her.'

If the spell worked, Rose could explain everything.

On the Friday before Midsummer, the coven were working on their Potioner badges. The badge came in three stages: white, red and black. Cassie had to earn the white badge first, by successfully brewing three common healing preparations. Ash Patrol hung camping cauldrons from tripods in the field behind the coven hall. Rue helped Cassie light the fire, showing her how to pile the dry tindergrass and strike a light from her spark stone. Cassie was supposed to be brewing up a pot of yarrow salve for minor wounds, but she was distracted and put in too much marigold, turning the pot of liquid bright orange. Even Harriet, the Ash Patrol leader who was usually so patient, told her off for not paying attention.

When they stopped for lemonade and lavender shortbread, Tabitha came over. She'd already finished her own salve which was a lovely pale green, giving off a faint scent of peppermint and sun-dried sheets. Tabitha had poured it into an old jam jar to cool and set.

'What's the matter, Cassie?'

'The beeswax won't melt.'

Tabitha peered into the small copper cauldron. 'Oh, you need to chop it up first. It'll take forever if you put it in all at once. Here, scoop it out. I've got some left over you can use.'

'Thanks.'

'You've been quiet lately, is something wrong?'

Cassie wished she could tell Tabitha everything, all about the Erl King and the key and the spell to find her mother, but she'd agreed with Rue not to say a word. Tabitha meant well, but she might tell the Hedgewitch in a misguided attempt to protect them, or say something to Mrs Blight or Ivy, either of whom could be in league with the goblins.

'I'm just worried about the Fledgling Test,' she said. It was sort of true, she had been neglecting her broom practice and the other skills she should be studying. It just didn't seem as important right now.

'I passed *my* Fledgling Test on the very first attempt,' said Ivy, coming over. 'The Hedgewitch said I flew gracefully and my runes were very neat.'

'Don't worry,' said Tabitha, beaming at Cassie. 'You've been working hard, you'll pass for sure. Then we can all go to camp together.'

Ivy peered into Cassie's cauldron and pulled a face. 'I wouldn't be too confident if I were you. Being the Hedgewitch's niece doesn't make up for natural talent.'

'Cassie has more talent in her little toe than you have in that inflated head of yours!' said Rue, returning with two large slices of shortbread.

'You're just jealous because you know we're going to win the contest at the Midsummer Fair,' said Ivy. 'Come on Tabitha, as we've both finished our salves, the

Hedgewitch said we can spend the rest of the afternoon working on our project.'

Cassie and Rue watched them go.

'That's looking better,' said Rue, peering into Cassie's cauldron. 'It's almost green now.'

'Tabitha helped me. Do you think we should test out the witch salt before the fair?'

'No need, we followed all the instructions, it looks great. All we have to do is find an imp for the demonstration.'

'Who do you think will be judging?'

Rue shrugged. 'The Hedgewitch, I guess.'

Cassie sighed. 'In that case we've got no chance of winning.'

Chapter Twenty

The Midsummer Fair

'Ere, lend a hand,' said Brogan, trundling towards Cassie with a wheelbarrow full of oversized vegetables. He was wearing his Sunday best paired with bright red bucket-top boots and looked like a gentleman farmer with aspirations towards piracy. It was early on Midsummer's Eve, the air was still crisp and cool but Mrs Briggs predicted it would warm up later. The lime trees were in full bloom, droning with bees, and the garden was golden with solwort.

Cassie helped Brogan lift enormous marrows and turnips, carrots the length of her arm and a cabbage twice the size of her head into the waiting cart. They were nestled into fresh, dry straw while Peg stamped a hoof with impatience.

'And 'ere she is, my beauty. Been fed on nothin' but spring water and kelpie manure these three months. Just wait 'til Emley catches sight of 'er!' Brogan cradled an object the size of a two-year-old child wrapped in a blanket and passed it carefully to Cassie. She went to put it in the cart.

'Whoa there! My gurtroot rides up front, 'old on to 'er. She's precious cargo, goin' to win me the red ribbon this year!'

'Don't forget my fruitcake!' said Mrs Briggs, hurrying down the stairs towards them. The housekeeper gave Cassie a large tin, which she struggled to balance along with the two-foot vegetable in her lap.

'Take it to the judging tent for me, there's a dove, I'll be down later once my pies are out of the oven.'

There was no sign of the Hedgewitch – most likely she'd gone on ahead by broom, so Cassie and Brogan set off together for the fair.

The village green had been transformed overnight;

colourful pavilions crowded together on the grass, decorated with garlands of oak leaves and bunches of sunflowers, bunting strung between them. The trees were bedecked with ribbons and hung with brass suns and bells which flashed in the sunshine and chimed in the breeze. Even the duck pond had been tidied up.

Oliver Whitby ran past them, wielding an ice cream and giggling, his chubby legs going at astounding speed. Rue waved as she chased after her brother, shouting threats.

Cassie helped Brogan carry his vegetables into the produce tent and left him arranging them under the eye of Emley Moor, the owner of The Pickled Imp, who had his own stand of oversized crops, including a fat purple root nearly as big as Brogan's.

She took Mrs Briggs' fruitcake to the next pavillion and handed it to Miss Marchpane, who would be judging home baking. There she found Tabitha with her familiar, Wyn. The white rabbit wore pink bows over her ears and a disgruntled expression.

'I'm going to enter her in the pet show, what do you think?'

Cassie had never heard Wyn talk, although she assumed the rabbit could complain if she wanted to.

'She looks... lovely. Where do we go for the witchcraft contest?' Cassie asked, the jar of salt was heavy in her satchel.

Tabitha led Cassie to a black tent painted with white stars and faery runes. The banners of the 1st Hedgely Coven and Ash and Thorn Patrols fluttered in the breeze. Susan and Phyllis Drake were leading small children on broomstick rides while Harriet and Nancy sold amulets and jars of ointment to raise money for the hospital at Convall Abbey. Within the tent, members of both patrols fussed over their entries for the competition. Rue was nowhere to be seen, but Cassie found an empty space to display their jar of witch salt, carefully arranging a label she'd written for it. On the opposite table was Ivy and Tabitha's project, a glass oil lamp full of purple liquid.

'Come on,' said Tabitha. 'The judging's not until this afternoon and I saw a man selling ice cream.'

Cassie got two scoops, wild cherry and chocolate, while Tabitha chose honey-rose. They had to lick it up quickly before it dribbled all over their hands.

The fair had everything you could wish for: donkey rides and an archery range, musicians and jugglers. The best of Mr Bellwether's Hedgely Blue sheep were on display, alongside pigs and ponies and mischievous goats.

You could have your face painted like a goblin, buy a balloon shaped like a wyrm and watch the conjurer pull a weasel out of his hat.

The day grew warmer as Cassie and Tabitha tried their luck at fairground games, throwing coconuts through the wailing mouths of wooden banshees and fishing for paper merrow with lodestone hooks. Tabitha won a knitted bat.

At noon they gathered with the other villagers to watch the presentation of coloured ribbons for everything from goose eggs to giant moonflowers. Brogan's gurtroot won a red ribbon, as did Mrs Briggs' fruitcake.

As they clapped and cheered Cassie felt someone tug at her elbow. It was Rue.

'Come quick.'

Cassie followed her to the black tent, which was hot as a furnace in the afternoon sun. They were alone, the rest of the coven were still watching the prize-giving. The potions and enchanted items lay in neatly labelled rows, all except Rue and Cassie's jar, which had been knocked to the ground, the witch salt strewn across the grass.

Cassie tried to gather a handful of the salt, it prickled her fingers to touch.

'Don't bother, I've already tried. There's not enough,' said Rue.

'I've got more back at Hartwood,' said Cassie. 'If we went on your broom.'

'Our imp's gone too. I caught it this morning and put it in a cage there. Someone let it out.'

The copper cage stood empty, its door ajar.

'But who would...?'

'Tabitha said it was cruel to use an imp,' Rue pointed out.

'She was with me all day.'

'It must have been Ivy then. I haven't seen her around, have you? She didn't want us to stand a chance of winning the contest and Tabitha helped by keeping you away from the tent.'

'She wouldn't do that! I'm sure.'

'It doesn't matter now, we're out of the game. We'll just have to hope they lose to Alice and Lucy's contraption, whatever it's meant to do.'

Their fellow Ash Patrol witches had put together a strange little box with wheels and gears. No one in the coven had been told its secret purpose.

There wasn't time to catch another imp *and* fetch the rest of the witch salt from Hartwood, the coven presentations would begin as soon as the livestock prizes were over. The project they'd spent weeks planning and preparing would go to waste. Cassie didn't mind sitting it out, really, her hopes for the day were focused on the seeking spell. Rue was clearly disappointed, however, and the Hedgewitch would see it as another example of Cassie's general incompetence. There had to be something they could do.

Cassie clutched her key. Perhaps there was.

'Rue, your broomstick chain, the one with the padlock. Can you get it in time? And any other chains and locks you have in the shop.'

'Brilliant idea! We'll chain Ivy to a tree until after the contest, that'll teach her!'

'No, not Ivy. Just hurry, I'll meet you behind the stage.'

The rest of the coven were coming back to the tent to collect their projects.

'Aunt Miranda?'

'What is it Cassandra? We're about to begin.'

'Could Rue and I go last? We need a few more minutes to prepare.'

'A witch should always be prepared,' said the Hedgewitch. 'Very well, Ivy, Tabitha, change places with them. I see you are better organised.'

'What's the matter? Lost something?' asked Ivy, appearing at Cassie's elbow with a smug smile.

Tabitha frowned. 'Is everything all right, Cassie? I saw Rue running back to the shop.'

'We've just had a slight change of plan, that's all. I'll see you up there.'

'Good luck!' said Tabitha.

'You'll need it,' Ivy hissed.

The sun scorched the green as 1st Hedgely coven prepared to show the village their skills. The young witches huddled behind the stage, tinkering with their projects and rehearsing chants. Rue wasn't back yet and Cassie hovered anxiously, twisting the string that held the key around her finger.

'You'll do fine, Cassie.' A hand clasped her shoulder.

'Uncle Elliot!'

Her uncle beamed. 'Thought I'd drop by for the day, needed a break from the old office and I used to love the fair as a boy. One year, your mother and I drank a whole bottle of Emley Moor's Giddyflower Fizz between us. We were laughing silly for an hour after and left the gate open to the livestock pen. The next morning they were still herding sheep out of Mrs Blight's flower beds!'

Renata Rawlins, the warden from Fowell House, was with him too.

'Hello! Didn't expect to see my tree-climbing friend here, and in witch's uniform no less.'

'Miss Rawlins had the day off, so I asked her to accompany me. All ready with your project, then?'

'Almost, it was a bit of a last-minute idea.'

'Those are often the best.' He winked. 'Well, I'll see you up there. Your aunt asked me to judge the contest!'

'Good luck, Cassie!' said Renata. 'I'll be cheering for you.'

The Hedgewitch was already on the stage addressing the gathered villagers. All of Hedgely was there, shopkeepers, farmers and families, Mrs Briggs and Brogan, Cassie's teacher, Miss Featherstone, Mr and Mrs Whitby – but where was Rue?

Chapter Twenty One

Escapology

'Midsummer has always been a day of celebration in Hedgely,' the Hedgewitch addressed the crowd from the stage. She wore her black cloak and hat and seemed untouched by the sweltering heat. 'It is the pinnacle of the year, the height of summer and an important date in the witches' calendar, when we gather protective herbs, renew warding spells and stay awake throughout the night, vigilant against the dangers of Faerie. For all the ice cream and games, it must not be forgotten that this is one of the four nights of the year when the old roads are open and the border may be crossed. At sunset we will light the wakefire, which will burn through the night, protecting the village, but you should also keep candles lit in your windows and your children indoors. There is no need to be afraid, but we must always be vigilant.'

Cassie was watching the crowd, most had cups of tea or lemonade in their hands and a few were red from the sun. They seemed unconcerned by the Hedgewitch's warnings.

'But aren't we lucky to have these young witches of 1st Hedgely Coven here to protect us?' said Elliot, joining her centre stage. 'I'm sure they won't let any bogles or banshees bother us – let's see what they can do!'

The crowd cheered. Cassie clutched her key, watching for any sign of Rue.

'First we have Susan and Phyllis Drake, with a traditional Midsummer chant.'

The Thorn Patrol sisters climbed up to the stage and began to sing in high, clear voices:

'At midday on the longest day,
We gather in the wildwood green,
Where witches of the ages past,
Have sought to thwart the folk of Fae.

270

At midnight on the shortest night,
We search amongst the grasses tall,
For solwort, golden as the sun,
To put the wicked sprites to flight.'

There was Rue at last! Running across the grass to join Cassie behind the stage, her arms full of chain and rope. 'I still don't know why you want the chain, but I thought we could tie some witch knots in the rope and—'

'Witch knots? That's your great plan?' whispered Ivy. 'It's the very first thing we learn. No one is going to be impressed by that.'

'I'll tie your tongue in a knot if it keeps wagging, Ivy,' said Rue. 'It's your fault we've not got anything better.'

'When I was little my mother took me to a conjuring show,' whispered Cassie, steering Rue away from the rest of the coven. 'I know it wasn't real magic, just tricks and illusions, but there was one act that I thought we could try. Here, I'll explain.'

'At midnight on Midsummer's Eve,
We set the wakefire blazing bright,
With oak and ash and thornywood,
To keep us safe throughout the night.'

The Drake sisters finished their chant to a round of applause.

Harriet Webb, Nancy Kemp and Heather Shuttle climbed up to the stage. Heather was twisting a handkerchief between her fingers and sweating rather a lot.

'For our demonstration, we've brewed Mythriac, a general antidote,' announced Harriet.

'Mythriac contains thirty-six ingredients and is a simplified form of Theriadatum, which contains four hundred and seventy-two,' said Nancy.

'And takes eight years to brew – we only had a month.'

'Heather, our brave volunteer, is going to consume a handful of mildly toxic queaseberries.'

Heather had turned the colour of cement and was looking at the mushy purple fruit in her hand with wide eyes.

'As any child in Hedgely knows, queaseberries won't kill you but they will give you a nasty stomach ache. The Mythriac should cure most poisons, but for demonstrative purposes we thought this would be safer.'

Nancy prodded Heather gently. The poor young witch looked at her audience, took a deep breath and swallowed the berries.

First, her face screwed up like a prune, then she turned a delicate shade of violet. Finally, Heather clutched her stomach and groaned. Nancy produced a bucket, just in case.

Harriet ran to Heather with a spoon and the bottle of dark liquid, giving her a generous dose.

A nervous minute passed in which Heather twitched and groaned on the stage while her patrol leader and second exchanged worried glances. At last, the young witch stood up straight, her skin returned to a healthy colour, and let out a great belch.

The audience cheered and the three witches bowed. Nancy helped Heather off the stage.

Next up were Eliza Pepper and Anika Kalra from Thorn Patrol. They demonstrated aerial manoeuvres on their brooms, turning loops and making dives and doing a stunt in which Anika appeared to fall from her broom – to gasps from the crowd – only to be caught deftly by Eliza. The Thorn Patrol leader was easily the best flier in the coven and Cassie found herself wishing for even a tenth of her skill. She was quite sure Eliza would be able to handle her mother's wayward broom.

Lucy Watercress and Alice Wong followed them, setting their strange contraption on a stool. The small machine was made of polished brass, copper wires and what looked like the horn of a gramophone. There was a lightbulb on top.

'This is a device of our own invention,' Lucy announced. 'It is designed to detect the presence of wicked faery folk and let out a warning alarm.'

'It's called the Hexodetector,' said Alice.

'Easily installed in the average home, it runs on pineapple juice. Tinned or fresh.'

Alice held up a pineapple with two wires sticking out of it.

'This instrument can pick up even the taint of bad magic.' Lucy flicked a red switch on the side.

The Hexodetector let out an almighty squeal, like a terrified piglet. The light bulb flashed red and it shuddered and fell off the stool, still wailing.

'As I was saying,' shouted Lucy, picking it up. The alarm changed pitch and started squawking like a rooster. Everyone in the crowd had their hands pressed over their ears.

At last, Alice removed the pineapple and the Hexodetector fell silent. 'It still needs some fine tuning.'

The Hedgewitch ushered them off the stage to be replaced by Ivy and Tabitha.

Ivy cleared her throat. 'Our project offers a more traditional approach to the presence of faery threats. The Sprite Lamp is an ancient witches' device, used by our forebears to travel safely through the Hedge. An ordinary lamp is filled with a special oil infused with star sapphire, owl feathers and eyebright. It is inscribed with the runes Glaem and Hyd, for brightness to reveal hidden things. The lamp will ignite in the presence of the faery folk, as Tabitha will demonstrate.'

Tabitha came forward. Perched on her wrist was an apple-green imp, it appeared calm and content and was not even trying to bite her. As she drew closer to Ivy, a tiny purple flame flickered to life inside the lamp.

'The size and brightness of the flame indicates the power of the faery person. The imp is creating only a small glow, and only when it gets closer. More dangerous beings will cause it to burn bright, even at a distance. The Sprite Lamp can even detect folk who are glamoured or invisible.'

The audience clapped politely.

'I hate to admit it but so far Thorn Patrol has us licked,' said Rue.

'Help me get these ropes on stage,' said Cassie.

'And last, but certainly not least, we have my niece Cassandra Morgan and her friend Rue Whitby. I can't wait to see what they have for us today,' announced Elliot.

'I hope this works,' Cassie whispered. She placed herself in the centre of the stage and let Rue tie the ropes and chains around her – not so tight as to hurt, but tight enough that she couldn't move her arms and legs. Rue was not skilled at witch knots, but managed to tie great fists of rope that would have taken Cassie hours to unravel, even if she could reach them. The broom chain went on last, the padlock closed with a click.

'We are demonstrating a worst-case scenario,' said Rue to the crowd. 'In which one of us is caught by goblins or worse. As you can see, Cassie can hardly move. She cannot reach for her whistle to summon help or her knife to cut the ropes. She has no potions or powders on her, and yet—'

The crowd of villagers were watching attentively. Cassie could see the kindly eyes of Mrs Briggs, the hard stare of Saltash and the bespectacled squint of Widdershin's gaze. From behind, she could feel her aunt watching her too.

Cassie closed her eyes, she couldn't afford to be distracted. She needed to focus on escaping. The key had helped her when she was in danger or distress, when she needed to get through a door or a gate. She only hoped it could manage ropes.

Cassie concentrated on the sensation of the key against her skin. She focused all her thoughts upon it, willing it to work. She begged it silently to set her free but nothing happened. The villagers were waiting, she could hear restless shuffling, someone coughed.

It had to work, she couldn't embarrass her aunt and uncle and let Rue down, she didn't need to win, just to show she could do some small magic.

Cassie scrunched her eyes tight and thought about the knots, instead of the key. She imagined them loosening, unravelling, falling to her feet. She tried to move her arms, but they were still bound tight. It was hopeless, perhaps the key couldn't manage the ropes, or maybe it only worked when she genuinely needed it.

Why had her mother given her the key, after all? If the Erl King had her mother locked away somewhere, then surely Rose needed the key more than Cassie ever had.

She opened her eyes. The sky was cornflower blue. In just a few hours it would be time to fetch the lanthorn flower and perform the seeking spell. Soon she would see her mother's face in the silver bowl and learn where she was, but first she had to get out of these ropes.

The key warmed on her chest, the fluttering sensation returned, like moth's wings beating against her skin. Slowly, one by one, the ropes began to untie themselves, twisting apart of their own accord, like snakes waking from sleep. Once loosened, they fell to the ground until Cassie was bound only by the chain. She took a deep breath as she heard the tumblers in the lock click. It sprang open and she stepped free.

The crowd roared with applause, Rue took her hand and they bowed. Ash Patrol climbed on to the stage, they were clapping too; Thorn Patrol looked rather less pleased.

'A display of great skill and ingenuity. I can't even guess how they did it!' said Elliot. 'This young witch shows great promise. I hope to see you at Wayland Yard someday, Cassie, when you have your licence.'

'I couldn't have done it without Rue,' she said, and they grinned at each other, the only ones who knew the secret of Cassie's escape.

'Thank you all for supporting these young witches,' said Elliot to the crowd. 'I would like to award the prize to our final pair, Rue Whitby and Cassandra Morgan, please give them another round of applause!'

The wakefire, a great mound of dry branches mixed with magical herbs, was waiting on the low grassy hill behind The Pickled Imp. The Hedgewitch kindled the fire and soon it was a roaring blaze, sending curling blue smoke and orange sparks up to the darkening sky. The people of Hedgely gathered around the fire, eating, drinking and talking over the day's events.

'Do you think fire *really* scares away faery folk?' asked Cassie.

Rue shook her head. 'If it were that simple we wouldn't have to bother with wards and traps and things like that. It makes people feel safe, though and I suppose there's some magic in that.'

They were sitting on the grass admiring their prize. Renata Rawlins had awarded them a small pouch of carbuncles, translucent stones which glittered red in the firelight. All the girls in the coven had also been given Sunburst badges for attending the fair.

Ivy appeared, standing over them, arms crossed and eyes narrowed. 'How did you do it? Tell me.'

'Do what?' asked Rue. 'Win the contest? By being

better witches than you, obviously.'

'You must have cheated, those were slip knots, weren't they? Tell me or I'll speak to the Hedgewitch.'

In a sense, they had cheated. No one but Rue knew Cassie had the key, so it must have looked like some marvellous spell, but really she'd had an unfair advantage. Then again, if Ivy hadn't ruined their witch salt, she'd never have needed to use it.

'Oh, shove off Ivy, you're a sore loser,' said Rue. 'Tell the Hedgewitch whatever you like, you can't prove anything.'

Ivy tossed her head. 'I *will* find out what you're up to!' She stomped off towards the Hedge as other witches from the coven, including Tabitha, came forward to congratulate them.

'What I want to know,' said Cassie, once they were alone again. 'Is what set off Lucy and Alice's Hexodetector.'

Rue shrugged. 'Maybe Ivy meddled with that too?'

'Perhaps, but what if it really was picking up on the taint of bad magic? What if the warlock was nearby?'

'That doesn't help us much, the whole village was watching.'

Cassie sighed. That question would have to wait. They had more urgent business. 'How long until moonrise?'

Rue checked her watch. 'Two hours.'

The Hedgewitch blew three short, sharp blasts on her whistle. They were being called to join the coven in Midsummer chants, to sing for the safety of the village.

'We should go now,' said Rue.

Cassie nodded. 'I'll fetch the lanthorn flower from Hartwood and meet you at the bridge!'

Chapter Twenty Two

The Stolen Child

The lanthorn flower was starting to wilt, its bright glow faded to a soft glimmer. Cassie hoped it would still be strong enough for the spell. She waited on the bridge, the night was mild and she could hear music and laughter coming from The Pickled Imp. Below her the water of the Nix darkened and the moon rose silvery over the hills. The fair was coming to a close; small groups of villagers broke away, heading home for the night. Cassie had to hide behind a tree to avoid being seen.

Finally, Rue came hurtling towards the bridge on her broomstick. Her wide eyes were ringed with red and her face was blotchy, as though she'd been crying.

'It's Oliver,' she said. 'He's gone missing.'

Cassie made her sit down on the grass and the whole story came out. Rue had been asked to watch Oliver during the fair. Mr and Mrs Whitby were both preoccupied, running their stall at the fair and keeping the shop open for anyone who needed milk or bread during the day. At midday, she'd left Oliver with her brother, Angus, but Angus was meeting his sweetheart and had passed Oliver on to Bran. Bran, Rue's second oldest brother, was working for Stanley Darnwright who'd set up a stall at the fair selling iron elf-crosses, candlesticks and horseshoes. Stanley misplaced a pair of tongs and sent Bran to the smithy for another. When Bran returned, Oliver was gone.

'But it's my fault, because I was the one supposed to be looking after him,' Rue explained. 'I've searched everywhere! I was sure he'd be at Marchpane's stall, or eating ice cream or trying to catch fish with his hands in the pond, but no one has seen him for hours. I even ran into the Hedge and called for him, though he knows he's not meant to go there. In the end I had to tell Mum, she's in hysterics and the Hedgewitch was called. Your uncle came too, he tried to calm everyone down, but Mum is terrified. Cassie, what if something bad has happened to him?'

'Don't worry, I'm sure Aunt Miranda will find him.'

'She hasn't found any of the other missing children!' Rue burst out.

'You think he was taken by goblins? Right here in Hedgely, under all our noses?'

'We were distracted by the contest – and it's Midsummer's Eve, that makes them bolder. Cassie, I have to find Oliver. It's my fault he's gone, I should have been watching him. I know he's a pain and always getting into trouble – but he's my brother!'

Cassie nodded. 'We'll go into the Hedge together and look for him, as soon as we've done the spell.'

Rue hesitated. 'We could use the seeking spell to find him.'

Cassie clutched the lanthorn flower to her chest. 'But it's the only chance I have to find my mother.'

'We can get another flower.'

'They only bloom once a year, this was the last one.'

'Please, Cassie.'

'There's got to be another way.'

'He's just a kid, he can't look after himself.'

'My mother's been gone for seven years!'

'I know, and we're not going to give up on her. We'll find another spell, another way, but right now I need to find Oliver.'

Cassie cradled the fragile blossom in her hands. The petals were starting to wilt. She'd have to wait a whole year to find another flower, to gain a second chance to see her mother.

Yet Rue would never forgive herself for losing Oliver unless they got him back, and quickly, before the goblin nabbers had a chance to whisk him through the Hedge to Faerie. It gave Cassie a horrible, empty feeling in the pit of her stomach but she had to accept it. Right now, Rue's need was greater.

'All right, have you got the bowl? We'd better start.'

'You're a brick!'

Rue hugged her, but the empty feeling was still there.

The waters of the Nix shimmered in the moonlight, their rushy banks casting shadows, edging the path of silvery light in ragged black. Cassie threw a penny bun into the water to appease Wendy Weedskin but the river hag was nowhere to be seen. Carefully, kneeling in the mud at the river's edge, Rue filled the silver fruit bowl. They carried it together, keeping it steady between them and placed it on a low stone. It was the same stone Cassie had sat on after Rue pulled her from the river the first time they met, but Rue was not that laughing, carefree girl tonight. She was deadly serious and intent on the task at hand.

'All right, what do we do now?'

'Have you got something of Oliver's?'

Rue produced a baby's spoon from her pocket. The handle was shaped like a rabbit. 'Used to be his favourite,' her voice quavered.

'Now we add the lanthorn.'

Cassie dropped the white flower into the bowl. As it hit the water's surface the petals came away, floating off on their own like tiny paper boats. Cassie felt a sharp pang in her chest. She knew this was the right thing to do, but it didn't make it any easier.

Rue produced a stick she'd cut from a birch tree the day before. It was as long as her forearm and shedding papery bark. A cloud passed over the moon.

'You stir, nine times clockwise, while I recite the incantation,' Cassie instructed. She'd memorised the charm and spoke it softly over the water.

'By mirrored moon and shining flower,

Over sea or mountain peak,

Reveal to me this item's keeper

For I would glimpse the one I seek.'

They waited.

'What's happening? Did it work?'

'I don't know.'

'Did you say it right? We should try again.'

'I said it just like it was written in the grimoire, maybe the flower was too old...'

As they peered into the bowl, the moon came out once more and lit the green field in which they stood. The water shone with white light, then dimmed a little. Vague shapes began to coalesce on its surface.

'What's that? Do you see it?' asked Rue.

'I think it's a face.'

'Is it Oliver?'

'I can't tell, wait no – it's Ivy!'

'What? Let me see!'

Heads together, Cassie and Rue watched as the image became clearer, revealing the young witch with her short black hair, wearing her badge-encrusted cloak. Her face was smeared with dirt and she had her arm around something, or someone, but it was hard to see as her cloak was covering them.

'Why is it showing us Ivy? We didn't cast the spell for her.'

'Wait a moment,' said Cassie. 'The picture's moving. I can see other shapes behind her – children, Rue, there's more children!'

It was like watching a very old film. There was no sound and the faintly coloured images went in and out of focus. They saw Ivy's mouth move and her cloak withdraw to reveal a familiar, pudgy face.

'It's Oliver! He looks like he's been crying. If she's hurt him...!'

'I don't think Ivy is the one who took Oliver. Look there! That's not a child, it's a goblin. Rue, you were right, they have been nabbed. The goblins have got them.'

'But where are they?'

'I can't see, somewhere in the Hedge I think. It's dark but there are leaves on the ground, and green lights, lanterns maybe?'

'The picture is fading,' Rue complained. The details of Ivy's cloak and Oliver's face were merging into grey and black blobs. Another cloud passed across the moon and the water grew darkly transparent; they could see through it to the spoon lying at the bottom of the bowl.

Rue sighed and sat down, burying her face in her arms.

'What's wrong? The spell worked! We saw Oliver.'

'Yes, but we still have no idea where he is, or how to find him.'

'We know he's with Ivy, that's something. The goblins have both of them and they're probably in the Hedge, that's a lot more than we knew before. We can tell my aunt and she can—'

'She can do what? If the Hedgewitch knew where the goblins were keeping him, she'd have rescued all those other kids who were taken. We have to find Oliver *now*, before they can smuggle him across the border.'

Cassie frowned, it was one thing going into the Hedge on a bright sunny day, but another altogether to enter the woods after dark on one of the Crossing Nights. They would be at risk of getting nabbed themselves, and what's more, somewhere in there, Glashtyn was waiting for her. Yet Cassie still had one card up her sleeve. 'My aunt may not know where they're being kept, but I know someone who will. Come on.'

They tracked up the grassy hill towards the dark line of trees, the full moon casting their shadows before them. Cassie put out a hand to halt Rue at the top of the hill.

'BURDOCK!' she called. 'Burdock! I command you to appear!'

'What are you doing?' asked Rue.

'The goblin who broke into my room, looking for the key. He owes me a favour.'

'Do you think he'll come, though? I mean, he's a goblin.'

'He's coming now.' Cassie pointed at the creature who was scurrying up the hill towards them. The goblin was running as fast as his short legs would carry him. Every third or fourth step he went down on all fours. His face was set in a grimace and Cassie could feel the effect of his name and the promise she had extracted from him. It was as if she held a rope in her hands, the other end of which was bound to this unhappy creature. It was not a pleasant feeling.

Burdock collapsed at their feet, panting.

'There I was, filching a few turnips for me supper, innocent as a babe in arms and I hears this buzzing in my ear. "Burdock!" it says. "Go away!" says I, but it keeps calling and the magic grabs me round the belly and drags me two miles across ditch and stye, and here I am. So what d'you want?'

'I'm sorry, but it's an emergency and I think you're the only one who can help us.'

'Is that so? What's the predict-ament?'

'My brother's gone missing,' said Rue.

'Little chap? Puffy cheeks, brown eyes, covered in toffee ice cream?'

'What have you done with him?!' Rue launched herself at the goblin, who scuttled away like a crab. Cassie had to restrain her.

'I done nothin'. I'm a filcher, not a nabber, never had the stomach for it. But you're not likely to see that little cherub again,' said Burdock.

'We cast a seeking spell and saw him with a goblin, somewhere in the Hedge,' said Cassie.

'Did you now? Well there's a lot of us in those woods, more 'n you witches guess at.'

'He was with a bunch of other children, there were lanterns, green lanterns.'

'Ah, so happens I might know where that is.' A grin spread across the goblin's face, revealing sharp yellow teeth. 'What's it worth to you?'

'Tell me where my brother is or I'll make you into goblin pie!' said Rue.

'No need to get your trousers in a twist. I'll help, never said I wouldn't. Just ain't gonna do it for free.'

'What do you want?' asked Rue.

Burdock grinned at Cassie. 'She knows.'

'No, you can't have the key.'

The goblin shrugged. 'No golden key, no golden boy.'

To Rue's credit, she didn't ask Cassie to give it up. It was enough that they'd used the lanthorn flower seeking Oliver. To hand over her mother's last gift would be too great an ask. Besides, they both knew whose hands it would fall into if the goblin had his way.

'You owe me a favour, remember? I let you go, I didn't call the Hedgewitch. I'm calling it in now.'

'Hmm, ask me for another then. Don't much like this one.'

Cassie sighed, nothing was ever straightforward with goblins. 'How about doing the entire coven's laundry, then? Soap, bubbles, you'll come out squeaky clean!'

Burdock stared at her wide-eyed. 'You wouldn't do that to a goblin.'

Cassie raised her eyebrows.

'All right, all right, I'll help you find the babe. But then my debt's cleared, right? No more talk of s-o-a-p.'

'Agreed.'

'You'll have to leave those flying sticks behind, they'll be a dead giveaway. You got any glamour?'

'That's faery magic. You know we don't.'

'Turn your cloaks inside out then, gotta hide those silly badges, and pull your hoods up. If anyone asks, you're my prisoners and I'm taking you to sell at the market.'

Chapter Twenty Three

The Goblin Market

'How do we know he's not leading us into an ambush?' whispered Rue, trudging through the dry leaf litter. They trailed after Burdock, pushing through thickets of blackthorn that scratched their faces, climbing over brambles that twisted around their ankles and caught in their socks. They had to trot to keep up – the goblin moved fast, and if they lost sight of him they'd have no chance of finding their way back.

'I don't trust him any more than you do,' Cassie whispered. 'But this is our best chance to find Oliver.'

By daylight the Hedge had seemed endless but at night it closed in around them, wrapping them in shadows. Creaking branches and rustling leaves took on frightening potential when they could not see the source of the disturbance. A nightjar called, spooking the girls with its eerie staccato whirr.

Burdock laughed. 'Don't tell me little witchlings is afraid of the dark?'

Cassie was just beginning to think the goblin might be leading them in circles when Rue called out.

'Look, Cass, lights!' Rue was pointing to a faint glow in the distance, between the trees. It was the same eldritch green they'd seen in the silver bowl. As they reached the first of the lanterns, Cassie saw it was a small cage made of twisted wire. Inside was the writhing, pulsing glow of a wisp.

'How awful, it's trapped in there!'

'Wisp-lamps, the copper turns them green,' Burdock explained.

Two rows of lamps formed a pathway, they followed it to a cluster of light and the sound of voices.

Cassie nudged Rue and they put their hoods up to hide their faces.

Burdock turned to them and grinned. 'Everything that crosses the border comes through here first, the rocks and leaves you need for your little charms and cantrips, the snuffwort your gardener smokes, the wood for your brooms – all traded by goblin spivies. An easy life they has, selling the human goods we filchers nick to the high and mighty on the other side. Just now there's a great fashion for your magic spinning orbs on string. Stolen several myself.'

'Do you mean yo-yos?' asked Rue.

'And of course, children. The lords and ladies love pretty human children.' Burdock grinned. 'Your precious Hedgewitch has been searching for the market for years, but it moves every night and only a goblin can find it.'

Before them was a clearing ringed with blackthorn. A dead elm stretched its skeleton branches above, strung with more wisp-lamps. The goblin spivies hawked their wares at stalls made of rotting logs and tree stumps sprouting fungus. More goblins, some of them carrying knives and nets, passed between the stalls. A slender, green-skinned goblin was playing an eerie melody on a double flute. But not all the market-goers were goblins, other hooded and masked strangers inspected the stalls as well.

''Tis busy tonight,' said Burdock. 'Folks waiting for all the new merchandise coming through from the other side.'

They came to the first of the goblin merchants. She had a braid of long, dirty hair with rings woven into it and her wares were displayed on a grubby blue cloth. Neatly arranged in rows were small pink and brown sausages, only there was something not quite right about them.

'Toeses! Toeses!' called the goblin woman. 'Finest toeses in the six kingdoms! All freshly plucked this week. Childers' toeses, big toeses, hairy toeses, with and without boils!'

They shrank back from the gruesome display. The next stall was more intriguing, it was loaded with baskets and barrels of ripe fruit. Large pink pears with yellow spikes, tiny lavender coloured berries, golden orbs with translucent skin that showed seeds like rubies inside.

Cassie touched the jewel-like fruit.

'That there's the valoquat,' explained a wizened old goblin. 'Makes you bold as a lion cub. Eat seven of its seeds and you will fear nothing. I sold one last year to a goblin maid who raided the nest of a moor wyrm. It ate her, of course, but even then she did not scream!'

Rue picked up a dark red ball with shiny skin.

'That's elli fruit. One bite and you'll grow a year older, if you finish it you'll end up like me!' The goblin

297

cackled. Rue dropped the fruit and wiped her hands on her cloak.

'I thought faery fruit made you immortal?' asked Cassie, who'd read this in a storybook.

'Ah, she speaks of the golden apples of the sun, the fruit of the aurifer tree, the rarest of all. They grow only in the orchard of the queen. If I had such a thing, the price would be too high for the likes of you.'

From inside his coat the merchant produced a handful of shiny jet-black berries, shaped like teardrops. 'I can offer you these though, black bittersweet. They says it's the most delicious thing you'll ever taste. Better than chocolate!' He sniggered. 'Of course, it's also the last thing you'll taste. Two of these will kill a horse, but you'll only need one for your rival!'

'She's not interested!' Rue dragged Cassie away.

'What happened to Burdock?'

They scanned the crowd but could not identify the small, stealthy goblin amongst the rest.

'Well, never mind, he brought us here. This must be the place we saw in the bowl. We'll just have to find Oliver on our own.'

They passed a tent made of animal skins and fur. Clouds of purple smoke issued from a flap in the side.

'Dreeeeeams!' called a goblin in a blue velvet cape that was far too long for him.

'Antique dreams! Three sprigg an hour! Dreams from before the wars, dreams of the golden age, milk-and-honey dreams!'

Cassie pulled Rue around the back.

'We ought to look inside, it's big enough to hide the children.'

Rue lifted the paw of a bear skin. They caught a glimpse of goblins reclining on rugs and cushions amidst the violet haze. A puff of smoke escaped, engulfing them in sweet scented air.

Cassie blinked, images formed before her eyes.

She was running through a field of blue flowers, stroking the grass with her fingertips. The flowers lifted off, took flight and turned into butterflies, dancing in the summer air.

Now she was riding a white horse, keeping pace beside her was a boy on a black steed, he rode bareback and was smiling at her with golden eyes.

She was seated at a table in a woodland clearing, beautiful, haunting music played on flute and harp.

Around her sat smiling goblins in fine clothes. They raised golden cups and toasted her health, drinking deeply. She tasted the liquid, it was cool, sweet—

'Cass!' said Rue, shaking her. 'Come on, before they catch us.'

They moved back into the cover of the trees.

'Did you see that? Was it real?' asked Cassie. 'The goblins, they were so different, and the world – everything felt so much more *alive*.'

Rue shrugged. 'I don't know, maybe. It's probably just the smoke though. We have to find Oliver.'

They made their way around the outside of the clearing, keeping to the shadows. There were goblins everywhere, haggling, arguing, attempting to steal from one another, but no children. They came at last to a stall at the edge of the market; it was stacked with cages, made of the same copper wire as the wisp lamps. The cages were full of animals: a roebuck, three hares, a badger, an adder, a tawny owl and dozens more.

Between the cages stood two goblins in the middle of an argument.

'But I don't wanna go back yet, we only just got 'ere.'

'It's your turn, Fleabane, you know what Kripper said, they got to be watched 'round the clock.'

'We ain't got no clock.'

'It's just an expression. Go on, old Charlock will be falling asleep by now and they say the Hedgewitch is about, with a wasp in 'er bonnet.'

'Ha, no Hedgewitch 'as ever found this place.'

'Still, better do what Kripper says, you know what happened to Spineweed.'

'Oh, all right, just let me have a tiddy mun for the road.' The two goblins set off towards a stall selling drinks.

Cassie and Rue hid behind the cages.

'I recognised the goblin with the pig-nose,' whispered Cassie. 'He was one of the nabbers who tried to catch me in London, I'm sure of it!'

'You think they were talking about the stolen children?' asked Rue.

'Yes, it is truue,' said a soft voice from above.

The girls looked up. There was no one there but the animals.

'Yoou are looking for your hooman chicks?' asked the tawny owl.

'You're not ordinary animals,' said Cassie. 'You're familiars!'

'Trooly. I am Nimblewing, pleased to meet yoou.'

'But why have they put you in cages, surely they're not going to sell you?'

'They have a uuse for us, as for your chicks.'

'Who? The goblins? The Erl King? What do they want with the children?'

'They are taking us throough to the other side. We shall be made to work for the masked one, to doo his bidding.'

So the goblins were not just selling the stolen children as pets to the gentry, the Erl King had some other purpose for them.

The owl beat her wings against the cage, rattling the copper bars. 'They will return sooon. The hooman young are in a cave, not far from here, follow the alder trees. Go quickly, if you would save them, the mooon is high and the old roads stand open!'

'But what about you?' asked Cassie, looking about her at the caged familiars. She knew all too well what it was like to live behind bars.

'The cages are locked, there is nothing you can dooo,' said Nimblewing.

'Perhaps there is,' said Cassie, reaching for her key.

The cacophony of hoots, barks, screeches and howls drew all the goblins in the market, who added to the clamour with shouts and curses as they tried to catch the fleeing creatures. In the tumult, Cassie and Rue slipped away, following the line of alder trees.

The Hedge was dark, little moonlight could penetrate the thick canopy. In the end they found the cave by almost falling into it. The path dropped away suddenly into a wide hollow, as if a great shovel had scooped it out, exposing tree roots and leaving a sandy bowl of earth and dead leaves. At its centre, a pile of coals glowed softly, emitting a ribbon of blue smoke. A single goblin sat warming his mitts before it.

The girls slid down into the hollow behind him, as quietly as they could. By good fortune, they'd come down the same side as the entrance to the cave and so did not have to pass the goblin. Communicating silently with witch signs, Rue agreed to wait outside while Cassie went in.

She crawled through the small dusty hole that formed the cave's entrance. Under ordinary circumstances, she might have mistaken it for a badger's sett. However, once Cassie was inside, the cave widened and opened so that she could almost stand up. She felt her way through the tunnel with her hands, but the earth was cold and crumbly and she tripped over a tree root.

'Ow! That's my leg, you beast!'

'Ivy?'

'Who's there? Oh, it's you, Cassandra. Don't tell me you were taken as well? I suppose that's no real surprise.'

'Actually, I'm here to rescue you.'

'Well, at the moment you're standing on my cloak. I don't imagine you've brought a light, or anything to eat? I'm not hungry, but this brat keeps complaining.'

'Oliver, is that you?'

The boy whimpered in reply.

'No food, no light and no way of getting us out of here, I shouldn't wonder. *A witch should always be prepared!*' Ivy quoted the Hedgewitch.

'Oh, and I suppose you were prepared when the goblins nabbed you,' Cassie retorted. 'How did you end up here, anyway?'

'I went for a walk, after the contest.'

'On Midsummer, in the Hedge?' asked Cassie.

'If you must know, I was looking for halewort, it can only be picked at midnight on Midsummer's Eve. It's a healing herb.'

Cassie did not have to ask why Ivy would risk her life to find such a plant.

'My sprite lamp began to glow and then I saw them, three goblins shoving this boy in a sack. The rest of you were busy toasting marshmallows, so I went after them.'

Cassie hated to admit it, but that had been brave of her.

'You should have called for help, you're not meant to go into the Hedge alone.'

'Unless you're the Hedgewitch's niece, I suppose?' said Ivy.

'I'm with Rue, she's outside keeping watch.'

'Rue?' said Oliver.

'That's right, we're going to take you home, don't worry.'

'That doesn't exactly fill me with confidence,' said Ivy. 'You two can barely light a cauldron fire without it blowing up in your faces. So, what is the plan? Have you got some way of contacting the Hedgewitch? Is she on her way now?'

'Aunt Miranda doesn't know we're here.'

'Oh, marvellous. You don't *have* a plan, do you?'

'Look, you're welcome to stay behind in this hole if you like, but we're going to get the other children out. There's still one goblin out there and the others are likely to return soon. So, if you want to stop grousing, we could use your help. How many children are there?'

'Twelve, most of them are sleeping at the back of the cave.'

'Wake them, but keep them quiet. Here, give me Oliver, I'll carry him.'

The other children were either afraid of the goblins or of Ivy, for they woke quietly and huddled together in the darkness. Cassie crawled back out through the tunnel, a difficult task with Oliver clinging to her.

When she re-emerged, the fire was still burning, but the goblin was gone.

'Rue!'

'You found Oliver!' Rue beamed, taking her brother from Cassie.

'What happened to the goblin?'

'Goblin bomb! I had a bit of the leftover witch salt wrapped in my handkerchief. Thought I'd try it out. It works, Cass! Got him right between the eyes! He squealed like a piglet and ran away.'

'We're only supposed to use witchcraft in self defence.'

'It was self-defence, I just did it first.'

Cassie made a witch sign in the mouth of the tunnel to let Ivy know it was safe to come out. Ivy led the rest of the children into the clearing, trying in vain to brush the dirt from her uniform. Some of her badges had been torn and would need sewing back on.

Cassie looked over the others in the pale moonlight. Some were dressed in their pyjamas, others in their Sunday best, all dirty and caked in mud. One girl wore the school uniform of Fowell House.

'Jane Wren?'

'How do you know my name?'

'I'll explain later. How did they bring you here?' Surely someone in the village would have seen the children if they'd come through Hedgely.

'There are tunnels,' said Ivy. 'There's one at the back of that cave, they brought the children through it. I don't know where it leads to, but it must come out somewhere beyond the Hedge.'

Cassie remembered how Burdock had used the rabbit holes to get past Hartwood's walls. The wards didn't extend below ground, he'd said. The same must be true of the Hedge.

'Come on, we need to get away from here before that goblin returns with the others. We'll find a stream and follow it back to the village.'

'Wait,' said Ivy. She held up her sprite lamp, it was glowing vivid purple. 'They're coming.'

Cassie started herding the children back into the cave, but it was too late. A swarm of goblins appeared around the edge of the hollow, nabbers and spivies from the market, closing in on them in a circle. There were dozens of them, they had nets and hooks, sacks and knives and their teeth were bared in angry snarls.

Chapter Twenty Four

The Netherwood

Oliver began to cry. Rue hushed him. 'This is your fault, Rue Whitby,' said Ivy. 'We could have handled one goblin, but you had to send him off to fetch a whole horde of them!'

'If only we had our brooms,' said Cassie.

Ivy put two fingers in her mouth and whistled. A broom rose from beside the fire and flew swiftly to her hand.

Cassie and Rue stared at her.

'What? You haven't trained your brooms to come when they're called? You really are hopeless.' Ivy sighed.

'They took my broom when they grabbed me, otherwise I'd have escaped hours ago.'

Cassie turned to Rue. 'Why don't you take Oliver and go find my aunt?'

'Look here, I'm not leaving you to face them alone.'

'As if I'd let either of you ride Vortex!' said Ivy. 'Give me the boy and I'll find the Hedgewitch. You can both stay here and be captured if you like.'

Neither Cassie or Rue were happy about it, but they had to admit Ivy was probably their best chance. However, she would need help to get away. Someone had to distract the goblins.

Cassie turned to the other children, huddled together before the entrance of the cave.

'Now listen, I need you to stick together and keep quiet.'

The eldest was about Cassie's age, but most were younger. They were tired and afraid. If Montague hadn't shown up and Cassie had been nabbed in that alley in Trite, she'd be amongst them, knowing nothing about Faerie or witchcraft, with no way to defend herself. Instead, she was wearing a witch's cloak and they expected her to save them. That's what witches were for – helping people, protecting them from things they didn't understand. She might be new to this, but she had to do what she could.

Cassie smiled at the children and turned to face the goblins. 'Who's in charge here?' she called out.

The goblins looked at each other. One tried to step forward but was pulled back by the others and had his ears boxed.

That was good, they had no leader. It was always easier to deal with people who weren't used to making decisions. She just had to keep these goblins confused for long enough to let Ivy get away.

'I want to negotiate the release of these children!'

The goblins laughed.

'You mean you want to make a deal?' called the toe-seller, her rings jingling.

'Them kids is worth more sprigg than you could carry, witchling,' said one of the nabbers.

Cassie took a deep breath. 'I have something that's worth even more, something the Erl King wants!'

The goblins hissed at the name.

'You're lyin'!' a goblin barked. 'What could *you* have that's worth anything to His High and Horribleness?'

'This!' said Cassie, pulling Oliver's baby spoon from her pocket. She held it up for them to see. The silver rabbit shone in the moonlight.

'What's that when it's at home, then?' asked the toe-seller.

'It's a powerful magic relic, passed on in secret from witch to witch in the ancient family of Whitby. Whoever has it will never go hungry, for any dish they eat will be instantly refilled. It is – the Spoon of Eternal Pudding!'

'I dunno,' said one of the nabbers, squinting at her.

'The Erl King has been seeking the spoon for years. He sent filchers to try and steal it, but they failed.'

'If that's true,' said the old fruit-seller. 'We'll take it off you and keep the children too. We can sell you along with them. Young witches is worth even more, I hear.'

'Do you imagine the Erl King hasn't thought of that?' said Cassie, thinking furiously of every faery tale she'd ever read. 'If you could simply take it, I'd be dead already. No, the spoon must be given willingly, if it is stolen all its power fades.'

'You're mad,' whispered Ivy.

'But brilliant,' said Rue. 'Half of them are starting to believe you!'

The goblins had begun a row. Cassie couldn't make out much of what they were saying.

'If you let us go unharmed, I'll give the spoon to the

bravest amongst you. I'm sure the Erl King will reward you well for it!'

'That's me! I wants it!' said one of the nabbers.

'You? You're as brave as a pickled cucumber, the spoon belongs to me!' said another.

'I saw it first, it's mine!'

A fight broke out amongst the goblins as each tried to prevent the other from going after the spoon. They reminded Cassie of a flock of seagulls battling over a potato chip.

Cassie nodded to Ivy who mounted her broom, Oliver clinging on behind her, and sprang into the air, shooting above the heads of the fighting goblins and off into the trees.

'Look out! They's getting away!'

'Lyin' little witchling! We'll scoop your guts out with your precious spoon and string them up for the crows!' cried a nabber.

'Their toes is mine! Little soft childer's toes!' screeched the toe-seller, wielding a rusty kitchen knife.

The goblins surged down the hollow towards them, shrieking and brandishing their hooks and nets. Cassie stood between them and the children, the spoon still clutched in her fist. Rue was at her side. The goblins were nearly upon them when they heard the sharp *kee-wik* of a tawny owl.

Cassie looked up. Nimblewing was beating the air above them, ghostly in the moonlight. With her were a dozen other birds – thrushes, magpies and woodpeckers, a kestrel, a hobby and a sparrowhawk. Then came the sound of hoofbeats and an antlered head appeared over the edge of the hollow. It was the roebuck and his herd, the badger, hares and all the other familiars they'd released from the goblin market. With them was a young witch riding side-saddle on her broom. She cried out and the familiars poured into the hollow, chasing, biting and clawing their former captors.

Cassie and Rue stood protectively around the children, but the faery creatures did not touch them, parting on either side in a wave of fur, feathers and scales.

An adder slithered past Cassie's foot, chasing the dream-seller, while Nimblewing raked the caps off two nabbers. Some of the goblins tried to fight back; the old fruit-seller waved his blackthorn stick at the roebuck, but the deer tossed it aside with his antlers. The toe-seller was throwing rocks at the birds until an angry badger charged and knocked her off her feet.

The sparrowhawk, silent and deadly, twisted and dived, ripping the nets from their hands and snapping at their ears.

Bruised, scratched and defeated, the goblins fled the hollow, pursued into the trees by the faery beasts.

The witch flew down to meet them.

'Tabitha!' said Cassie.

'I followed you. I'm sorry, only, I knew you were up to something when you crept away before the chanting, so I hid and watched. I saw you do the spell with the silver bowl and follow that goblin into the Hedge. So I trailed after you, until you went through some holly bushes and vanished.'

'There's a glamour protecting the market. You weren't with Burdock so the magic must have kept you out. However did you find us again?'

'The familiars. I met Nimblewing and asked if she'd seen you. She told me you'd set them free, but were heading into danger, so we gathered the others and came here.'

'Tabitha, I'm so sorry we didn't tell you everything from the start.'

Cassie elbowed Rue in the ribs.

'Yeah, sorry.'

'You're bleeding!' said Tabitha. It was true, Rue had a great gash on her left leg.

'One of them nicked me with his hook, it's nothing. I'll be fine.'

'Nonsense! I've brought some yarrow ointment, sit down while I clean this up.'

Tabitha tended Rue's wound quickly and expertly, tying it up with her clean handkerchief, while Nimblewing flew up to a branch above their heads.

'Thank you for returning to help us,' said Cassie.

'We owed yoou our freedom. The debt is now repaid. We must part ways. What will yoou doo?'

'We've got to bring the children to Hedgely somehow,' Cassie replied. 'Ivy said there were tunnels, that's how the goblins brought them here.'

'It is truue,' said the owl. 'The badgers and rabbits whisper of such places, deep beneath the tree roots. They are known only to the goblins and other shadowy creatures who love the dark and fear the sun. Our people do not venture there; they call it the Netherwood.'

Jane Wren spoke up, 'We couldn't see much, it was so dark, but I know where the tunnel starts at the back of the cave.'

'It doesn't sound very safe,' said Tabitha.

Cassie sighed. 'Probably safer than going back through the Hedge with the goblins after us and no idea which way is out. Ivy said the tunnel must end somewhere outside Hedgely and they're not likely to guess we'd return that way. It's our best chance.'

The children were not eager to re-enter the cave so Tabitha held the hands of the two youngest.

'If only we'd thought to bring torches,' said Cassie.

'How about these?' Rue held up the small pouch of carbuncles they'd won in the contest.

'Rue! You perfect genius. How do they work?'

'You blow on them gently, like this,' Rue took one of the scarlet stones from the pouch and breathed on it through pursed lips. Like an ember in the fire, it flared brightly from within and began to emit a cherry-red light.

They lit one each and gave the fourth to Jane Wren. It wasn't as good as a torch but provided just enough light to see their feet. The children drew close to the warm glow.

'We'd best get moving,' said Rue. 'Carbuncles store sunlight, but these only have a few hours in them.'

Cassie led the small party, with Jane to guide her. The tunnel entrance was low and they had to crawl through, one by one. The stone was damp in places and slimy to touch. Cassie bumped her head on the roof and dislodged clumps of dirt. She was afraid the tunnel would collapse on them, but didn't dare say so. The children were scared enough as it was.

'I don't like this at all,' said Tabitha. 'If they come after us, we're trapped.'

The narrow passage pitched down, deep beneath the wood. They were forced to crawl through a tight space of wet, slick mud. Some of the younger children began to complain but the witches urged them on.

Finally the tunnel opened out again. They were in a cavern, higher than the great hall at Hartwood and so wide the walls were swallowed up by darkness. They picked their way between broken stalagmites which, to their nervous imaginations, took on the lumpy forms of goblins squatting on rocks. Above them stalactites hung like serpent's teeth, dripping cold water into a curving stream.

'Don't drink it!' Cassie warned, guiding the children away from the tempting water. They were all thirsty, tired and hungry, but there was no question of stopping for a rest. They needed to reach the tunnel's end before the goblins had a chance to regroup and catch up with them.

They were following a narrow track of compacted earth. The ground sloped away from them in a scree of loose pebbles on either side, one false step would send them down into the darkness. Cassie held her carbuncle low to illuminate the path. Something glittered and caught her eye, pressed into the path; she stooped to pry it out. It was a gold pin, shaped like a shield. She handed it to Rue.

'It's a warden's badge,' Rue explained. 'We're not the first witches to find these tunnels.'

'What would a warden be doing down here?' asked Cassie.

'Probably tracking the goblins,' said Tabitha. 'My gran used to be a warden you know, before she retired.'

Cassie and Rue exchanged a furtive glance.

They kept on, in the eerie dimness of the cavern, with no sound but the drip-drop-drip of water. Cassie was sure that her carbuncle was not as bright as when they'd first entered the Netherwood.

Rue was giving one of the smaller boys a piggy-back ride, but the others were struggling to keep up and they had to set a slower pace than Cassie would have liked. It was hard to tell how long they'd been down there, without sun or moon to track the time. Every minute seemed to drag on as they listened out for the sound of goblin feet.

After a while, Tabitha joined Cassie at the front of their small group.

'I don't want to alarm you,' she whispered. 'Only, I think someone is following us. I've been hearing footsteps.'

'Goblins?'

'No, I don't think so, they'd have caught up with us by now. Whatever this is, it's in no hurry to catch us – it stops whenever we stop. I expect I'm just imagining it, it's too easy to start dreaming up all sorts of things down here. I'll be jumping at my own shadow next.'

But although she made light of it, Cassie could see the frown on Tabitha's face by the red glow of her carbuncle.

'Here, you lead for a while and I'll take up the rear.'

They switched places so that Cassie could listen out for anything behind them. At first there was no sound but the steady drip of water into the lake but then she heard it, a soft panting breath, the click-clack of claws on stone. Cassie stopped and the sound stopped too. Tabitha was right, something was following them.

Chapter Twenty Five

Wyrmroot

They reached the far side of the great cavern where the goblin path branched off in three directions. The first was wide and dry, the second narrow and lined with jagged stones and the third was little more than a foxhole.

'Do you remember which way you came?' Cassie asked.

Jane Wren shook her head.

'The wider tunnel looks well used,' said Rue. 'But it could be any of these.'

'I suppose we should take one each?' said Tabitha.

'If we do that, the children will be left on their own,'

said Cassie, mindful of their stealthy follower. 'Rue, I can see your leg is still hurting you. Stay with the children, Tabitha and I will each try one of the passages. If neither of them lead upwards, it must be the third.'

Tabitha chose the smallest tunnel, she had to crawl on hands and knees to enter it. Cassie decided to investigate the second passage, lined with sharp stones. She hoped it would lead her to a dead end and they could take the wide, dry path instead.

The light of her carbuncle was dim now, like the last moment of a sunset. It could not penetrate far into the darkness. Despite the rough sides of the tunnel, there was something unnatural about it, it was too even, almost rectangular. Cassie inspected the walls and saw they had been chipped away with a tool, leaving deep grooves in their surface. It wasn't a natural tunnel at all, but a corridor hewn into the rock.

The passage opened into a large chamber. The floor here was smooth, paved with coloured stones set in intricate patterns beneath a layer of dirt and dry leaves. Great columns rose above her, carved with flowering vines and strange symbols, bearing traces of faded paint. Between them were long stone tables, set in two rows, with a high table raised on a dais at the far end. A single dusty goblet stood on the last, as if waiting for its drinker to return. Moonlight filtered down from a crack in the stone ceiling, very high up, illuminating the hall. Every surface was encrusted with tiny, glittering crystals, like midwinter frost. Cassie reached out to touch a table and drew her hand away, covered in sparkling silvery dust.

Then she heard it once more, the clicking of claws on stone coming down the passage behind her.

'Dust,' said a low voice. 'All that is left of the glamour that once filled this place.'

Two yellow orbs appeared in the darkness as one large paw followed another into the light, revealing the heavy frame and unmistakable gait of a wolf.

'Dust and silence, where once there was music and dancing, beauty and magic. You stand in the great hall of Wyrmroot, where the lords and ladies of the Westernwood held their feasts. Few mortals were afforded such a privilege when they kept court here, only those who could play fine music or dance like aspen trees. Can you dance, Cass-sandra?'

The wolf's fur was as black as the shadows it emerged from.

'Glashtyn,' said Cassie, recognising the creature for

what it was. So that was who had been following them, slinking about in the shadows, waiting for a chance to catch Cassie on her own. 'There aren't any wolves left in England, you know.'

'No, not for five hundred years. Your people drove them off with fire and iron, as you do with all the wild things that frighten you.'

'Then you're not real, you're just taking that shape to scare me.'

'My teeth are real, my claws are real, what about me is not real?'

'What do you want? Why are you following me?'

'I want to help you, Cass-sandra. I have offered before, but you did not come.'

The wolf came towards her, forcing her further back into the hall. Cassie's boots crunched on the crystalline dust.

'A human boy found his way down here one summer,' said the wolf. 'He heard music coming from beneath the hill and crept in through a shaft. He hid and watched the dancers, but it was hot in the hall and he grew thirsty, so thirsty.'

Glashtyn was between her and the passage.

'He stole a goblet of wine and it put him to sleep.

325

When he woke on the cold hillside, it was winter. He ran back to his home, but a stranger answered the door. The boy asked after his mother—'

'Cassie!' Rue's voice echoed down the tunnel. 'Are you all right?'

Cassie wanted to run but the wolf was blocking her way. 'I have to go, my friends need me.'

'They cannot help you, Cass-sandra. They do not care about your mother, they have loving families of their own. Why should they risk all to aid you?'

Cassie knew the wolf was lying, but his words had teeth.

'If you would only put aside your fear, I could guide you to that which you seek. I am the only one who can help you.'

'Let me go.'

Glashtyn paced around her in a circle, holding her in his golden gaze. 'The little boy who stole the goblet, he spent the rest of his life searching for his mother, but he never saw her again. You see, a hundred years had passed while he slept, and she was long dead and buried.'

Cassie made a dash for the open tunnel. The rocks cut her arms and legs, but she pushed on, scrambling back towards the entrance.

She reached Rue and the children and turned, expecting to find the black wolf coming after her, all teeth and claws, but the passage was silent and empty.

'What's the matter, Cass?' asked Rue.

'Not that way, we mustn't go that way. It isn't safe.'

Tabitha was already back, her hands and face covered in mud. 'Mine was a dud too. I suppose that means we take the third passage.'

It was a relief to set out on the wide, dry path. It offered plenty of space for the small group to walk together. However, they'd not gone twenty paces when Jane Wren's carbuncle winked out. A moment later, Rue's followed.

One of the young boys began to cry.

'There, now,' said Tabitha, hushing him. 'We'll be above ground again soon, you'll see.' But her carbuncle promptly dimmed and went out like a candle. She blew on it again to no avail.

They were left in darkness, but for the tiny glow of Cassie's stone.

The path lead them uphill, over loose pebbles and scree which slid beneath their shoes as they scrabbled up the slope. Cassie was grateful for the grip on the boots

Brogan had given her for her birthday.

'Up here!' called Tabitha from up ahead. 'I can smell fresh air!'

They scrambled after her and soon the scree gave way to a series of large, flat stones. Pulling themselves up, using hands and feet, they found they were on a steep, uneven staircase cut into the rock.

'Look out, we've made it!' called Tabitha.

Indeed, they could now see a patch of light above them, pale-blue sky framed by stone. Tabitha climbed through, pulling her broom up after her.

Cassie, Rue and the children followed her out of the tunnel and into the fresh morning air. They were on top of a hill, surrounded by the ruins of an ancient building. Rubble and stones littered the grass and the crumbling remains of walls stood around them, roofless and open to the sky.

To the west they could see the wide swathe of dark woods they'd left behind, still lingering in the night. To the east was the first rosy glow of dawn, erasing the faint stars. Cassie's legs ached and her eyes stung with grit and dust. She sat down between Rue and Tabitha; their black cloaks were caked with mud and they had dirt and twigs in their hair.

'What is this place?' asked Cassie.

'Castle Hill,' said Rue. 'We're north of Hedgely. If you look that way you can see Hartwood and behind it is the Nix and the spire of St Aelfwig's.'

'So this is how the goblins have been sneaking the stolen children into the Hedge,' said Tabitha. 'I suppose no one comes up here, and it's outside the Hedgewitch's wards too.'

'Someone *has* been helping the goblins, though,' said Cassie.

Jane Wren sat down beside her. 'You're right, you know. I saw someone, a figure in a hooded cloak, talking to the goblins when they thought we were all sleeping.'

Rue glanced at Tabitha before turning to Jane. 'This person... were they old and cranky?'

'No, I couldn't hear what they were saying, but they were tall and slender, and walked very quickly.'

'We thought it might be your grandmother, Tabitha, but clearly we were wrong,' said Cassie.

Tabitha frowned. 'My gran? But why would you think that?'

Cassie told her of their encounter at Saltash & Son's.

'Well, that's simple enough to explain – selumbine isn't a poison, it's a powerful healing herb, they say it can cure any wound and extend your life for years. My gran must have hoped it would fix her back. Of course, it's a restricted substance now, because it only grows in Faerie.'

'But what about the gold she offered to pay with?' Cassie asked.

Tabitha sighed. 'My grandfather's watch, it's solid gold. She's always telling me she'll sell it and buy this or that, but she never does. I think she's actually quite sentimental about it.'

'I'm sorry, Tabitha, we should have just asked you.'

Rue gave her a sheepish grin. 'You know, you're not so bad, for a Blight. We'd never have made it out of there without you.'

Tabitha pointed. 'Oh! Look over there!'

Two black shapes were flying towards them, one larger than the other. As they drew closer, the shapes coalesced into the forms of Ivy and the Hedgewitch.

Miranda and Cassie herded the children back to Hartwood, where Mrs Briggs cooked a mountain of scrambled eggs with fried tomatoes and bacon, and soft white bread toasted over the fire, which the tired and hungry children ploughed through with glee.

The Hedgewitch sent a message to London with Elliot, reporting the recovery of the stolen children. Wayland Yard would contact their parents and make all the necessary arrangements. Meanwhile, Miranda arranged for them to stay with families in the village until they could be escorted back to their homes.

Jane Wren chose to stay at Hartwood. After breakfast, Mrs Briggs whisked her upstairs for a bath, leaving Cassie alone with her aunt. Miranda sat opposite Cassie at the kitchen table, a cup of steaming nettle tea before her; there were dark shadows under her eyes. Cassie was tired and in need of a bath herself. There was mud in her hair and she felt as though she could sleep for a week.

'The morning you arrived here,' Miranda began, 'I gave you three simple rules to follow. I don't suppose you remember what they were?'

Cassie's heart sank. 'You told me I was not allowed to enter your study, to stay out after dark or to go into the Hedge alone.'

'And now, tell me, which of these rules have you broken?'

Cassie considered this. 'Well, all of them I suppose.

331

Only, you see—'

'What on earth possessed you to behave in such an irresponsible manner? You're as reckless as Rose, putting yourself and your friends into danger. Did you even once stop to think what might have happened had the goblins captured you as well? And on Midsummer's Eve, no less.'

'But we had to do something. Rue's brother Oliver—'

'There you go again! Do you imagine yourself some sort of heroine, immune to the dangers of the Hedge? Or perhaps you consider yourself a prodigy, beyond the witchcraft we teach in coven and ready to handle spells from my grimoire?'

'That isn't it at all. I only wanted to find my mother but you wouldn't help me and then Oliver went missing and Rue needed the spell – I couldn't let her down.'

'Oh, so now there are two Hedgewitches in this house, I see. It is clear to me that you cannot be trusted to abide by the simplest instructions. If you are so determined to throw yourself at every possible threat then perhaps I should send you back to that school, at least you were safe there!'

That wasn't fair. Cassie had broken her aunt's rules, but only because Miranda wouldn't help her find Rose.

Ivy and the girls in Thorn Patrol might think she got

special treatment for being the Hedgewitch's niece, but she had nothing of the sort. Instead, she was expected to struggle along on her own and never put a foot wrong. Well, she'd had enough. It didn't seem to matter what she did, whether she followed the rules or broke them, Miranda was never satisfied. All her aunt cared about was the family reputation, all she talked about was duty and responsibility. Well, if that was what being a Morgan meant, then maybe Cassie didn't want to be one any more.

'I wouldn't have to break your stupid rules if you'd helped me in the first place. I just want to find my mother, but you don't care about her. You don't care about either of us!'

Cassie regretted it the moment she said it.

Miranda raised her eyebrows, her grey eyes wide. She looked away and she no longer seemed angry, just tired.

'Or maybe I care too much and could not bear to lose you as well.'

Miranda stood up and left the room, her tea still steaming on the table.

Although she'd been up all night, Cassie found she could not get to sleep. Mrs Briggs had drawn her a hot bath and scrubbed her hair with honeysuckle soap, brushing it until is shone like new pennies. Cassie had changed into fresh pyjamas and was lying in bed with Montague curled up beside her. The afternoon light poured through a gap in the curtains.

Montague yawned. 'If you're not going to sleep then read a book. Some of us have been fretting over your fate all night and could do with a rest without you wriggling about like an eel.'

'Montague, did Aunt Miranda notice I was missing tonight? I mean, before Ivy fetched her.'

'Of course she did. After that little boy vanished, she came back to the house to check on you. When she found you gone, she was afraid you'd been taken too. So she took your nightgown and set off into the Hedge. I would have gone with her, but someone had to be here in case you returned home.'

'She took my nightgown?'

'I'd wager your aunt knows more than one seeking spell.' The cat kneaded the bedclothes. 'She always comes to check on you at midnight and renews the wards on your door. Of course, you're usually snoring like a cave wyrm by then.'

Cassie threw a pillow at him.

Chapter Twenty Six

The Fledgling Test

'Y ou've got to see this!' called Rue, running into the coven hall. 'We're in the *Herald*!'

She waved a copy of the local newspaper. On the front page was a photo of Cassie, Rue, Ivy and Tabitha in their uniforms, accompanied by a piece on the rescue of the stolen children. It was passed reverently around Ash Patrol.

In Thorn Patrol corner, Ivy was giving her own version of the rescue. She skipped rather quickly over her capture by the nabbers and described her daring flight to find the Hedgewitch in great detail, as if her role had been the most dangerous and important of all.

Rue was telling Ash Patrol, for the third time, how she'd chased the goblin guard off with witch salt when Miranda came into the hall. The coven hurried to form a circle and sing the opening chant together. Cassie knew all the words by now and was struggling not to laugh as Rue grinned at her over the cauldron.

'I hope our new girls are prepared for their Fledgling Test today,' Miranda announced once the song had ended.

Cassie felt a cold wave of horror wash over her – she'd forgotten all about the test. Between the seeking spell, the Midsummer contest and the stolen children she'd barely spared a moment's thought for the upcoming trial. She should have been practising and now she'd run out of time. If she failed, Rue and Tabitha would go to coven camp without her and her aunt would have yet another reason to be disappointed.

'We have two candidates for today's test,' the Hedgewitch continued. 'Anika Kalra and Cassandra Morgan. Both have yet to swear their Witch's Oath and demonstrate the skills necessary to earn their hats. We shall begin with warding, then test your brewing and finally, your skill on the broom.'

Cassie caught Anika looking at her and wondered if the other girl was just as nervous, or keen to show her up.

'You may not refer to your handbooks during the test and I remind the coven that the candidates must complete these trials entirely on their own, with no assistance or advice from their patrol.'

The girls in the circle nodded solemnly. Tabitha squeezed Cassie's left hand and Rue gave her an encouraging wink.

'Very well, if the candidates would step forward.'

Cassie and Anika left their friends to stand before the Hedgewitch. She gave them each a piece of chalk. In her other hand she held an hourglass filled with black sand.

'The first and most vital skill we teach young witches is to protect themselves. You cannot hope to defend others if you place yourself at risk. To that end, we learn the skills of warding, those signs and materials the folk fear, so that you may guard against any faery threat. Today you will create a ward for safe travel. You have until the sand runs out.'

Miranda flipped the hourglass. The test had begun.

Cassie looked blankly at the chalk in her hand. It was ordinary white chalk, the sort Miss Featherstone used on the board at school. There was nothing magical about it. All the protective amulets they'd learned to make had involved herbs and wood, magical stones, iron and thread. She tried to remember the chapter on wards in the handbook. You could use witch salt to make a ward, if you sprinkled it around you in a circle. Maybe you could use chalk in the same way? Should she draw a circle on the floorboards of the hall? But no, that wouldn't work, it was meant to be a ward for travel. You wouldn't get far if you couldn't leave the circle. Cassie thought of the other wards she had seen – her aunt walking around Mr Bellwether's chicken coop, the weirstones in the Hedge. The runes! That was it! There were faery runes for protection: Bord, the shield rune and Hert, the stag. There were runes for travel too, depending on whether you went by land, sea or air. She could only remember the one for land: Hof, the horse rune. If she used all three runes, that might be enough to form a ward, but what would she draw them on?

'Your time is up,' announced the Hedgewitch, holding up the hourglass. 'Present your wards.'

Anika came forward first, holding out her broom. She'd written runes along the handle – some of the protection runes Cassie had remembered and Fugol, the bird rune, for flight.

'Very good, Anika, although your Bord is a bit rough, practise that one. This would indeed grant you some protection in flight for as long as the runes remained clear and un-smudged.'

Thorn Patrol cheered and clapped Anika on the back.

'Cassandra, what have you done to your boots?' asked Miranda.

Cassie's black boots were covered in chalk runes. She thought they looked rather nice actually, but she could hear Ivy snigger behind her.

The Hedgewitch had to crouch down to examine her work. 'Well, that is certainly one of the more original interpretations I've seen, but it is acceptable. You would receive some protection while wearing these boots, although you'd want to avoid walking through wet grass.'

'Hurrah!' cried Rue.

Cassie had passed the first part of her Fledgling Test.

The next test was brewing potions. There were a dozen basic recipes in the handbook and Miranda might pick any one of them. Cassie and Anika would have to work together over the great cauldron at the central hearth.

Cassie smiled at the small, serious girl from Thorn Patrol, but Anika had her eyes fixed on the Hedgewitch. Cassie couldn't help wishing she was working with Tabitha instead.

'Brewing is an ancient art, one that requires care and concentration. Over the generations witches have learned the powers of herbs and stones, fire and water, and brought them to life in the cauldron. We brew potions to heal and restore, medicines against fear, pain and sickness. Mending is the path of cooperation and so you will work together to make a Sweet Dreams Syrup, to drive away nightmares and bring healing sleep,' Miranda announced.

They'd made the syrup only a month ago and Cassie was sure she could remember most of the ingredients.

She followed Anika to the herb cupboard at the back of the hall. It was filled with jars and boxes, baskets and bags of all the magical ingredients they'd collected throughout the summer. There were dried toadstools and cat's whiskers, bloodstones and willowbark, mockthistle and red madder root. Cassie took down lavender and chamomile, spring water –gathered on a new moon, lime blossom and honey.

'Is that everything? asked Anika, her voice unsure.

Cassie scanned the rows of jars and bottles, looking for anything they'd missed. 'I think so.'

Anika lit the fire beneath the cauldron with her spark stone, using a handful of tindergrass to get it nice and hot. Carefully, Cassie filled the cauldron with spring water. It glistened in the dark bowl and reflected their faces back at them. Anika measured out the right amounts of the sweet scented herbs while Cassie stirred them in with a long wooden spoon. They simmered the liquid down until it was a beautiful golden colour, like liquid sunshine. Cassie strained out the herbs and added the honey, a whole pot full, thickening the brew to an amber-coloured syrup.

A rich scent filled the hall; it was like lying in a meadow on a summer's afternoon, listening to the hum of bumblebees, with the grasses and flowers nodding over your head and the sun on your back – at the same time, it smelled like the warmth of an open fire on a snowy night, as you sat wrapped in blankets with a hot drink in your hands.

'There's something missing,' said Anika.

She was right. The potion smelled delightful, comforting and sweet, but it wasn't making them drowsy. Cassie ran back to the cupboard. Rifling through the shelves, she hunted for the missing ingredient but there were so many bags and bottles and boxes and she didn't know what she was searching for.

Looking up, she saw Rue pulling a strange and tortured face. Beside her, Tabitha was making a gesture with her hands. They knew what she'd forgotten, but they couldn't tell her, the Hedgewitch had forbidden it. Nonetheless, her friends were trying to communicate some hint, some clue. Rue wasn't terribly good at potions, so if she remembered the ingredient, they must have used it recently. Perhaps in the witch salt? Tabitha picked up her familiar, Wyn, whose soft white fur reminded Cassie of the flowers of—

'Angelica,' said Cassie to the Hedgewitch. 'There isn't any in the cupboard and we can't complete the potion without it.'

Miranda smiled and produced a small cotton bag from her pocket.

'Here you are. You will not always find what you need at hand and must learn to ask for help.'

Cassie knew her aunt was referring to more than just brewing potions. Rushing back to the cauldron, she sprinkled a pinch of the scented root into the liquid. Anika stirred and the syrup took on a shimmering, opalescent quality.

Cassie recited the incantation over it:

'Flowers of field and new moonbeams,
Honey sweet and linden tree,
Grant respite from the terrors of night,
Banish fear and bring sweet dreams.'

She sat down, exhausted by the effort. She couldn't do any more tests today, she needed to lie down, to close her eyes for a moment.

'Cassie, you've done it. You've passed the brewing test.' Tabitha was shaking her shoulder. 'Oh, do wake up, there's still one more to go!'

Someone opened the windows and a cool breeze blew away the heady scent of the syrup. A few of the other girls were being shaken awake by their coven mates. Miranda was ladling the last of the syrup into two bottles; she stoppered each with a cork.

'A potent Sweet Dreams Syrup,' she said, handing them the bottles. 'Congratulations, you both pass. Only one test remains.'

Cassie had been dreading the final part of the Fledgling Test. There would be no tricks or surprises here, it was purely a measure of flying skill. The coven filed out of the door and gathered in the grassy field that lay between the coven hall and the Hedge.

'Do you want to borrow my broom, Cassie?' offered Tabitha. 'It's always been a steady flier.'

'Thank you, but no. I need to do this on my own.'

Ivy brought over their brooms. 'Here you are,' she handed Tantivy to Cassie. 'It's a lovely broom, seems a pity to waste it on a second-rate witch.'

'Ignore her,' said Rue. 'You'll be spectacular.'

Cassie grasped the broom. She was glad she'd spent some time repairing it – the brush was neatly combed and the handle polished, and you could barely see the scratches from where she'd gone through the rosebushes. Tantivy trembled in her hand, excited and ready to fly.

'The final test is simple – a witch is not a witch without her broom. For centuries we have tamed these branches of whifflewood with their inherent power of levitation. They have given us flight and speed, allowing us to go quickly to the aid of those in need or to escape great danger. Flying brings us closer to the stars and gives us freedom from the rules that confine earthbound creatures. To demonstrate your skill and control over the broom you will make three circuits around the hall in a clockwise direction and land, gracefully, where you took off. Anika, you may go first.'

Anika Kalra mounted her broom, speaking soft and encouraging words to it. She rose above the coven and sailed towards the hall. Keeping the pointed roof of the building to her right, the young witch made one slow and careful circuit.

Rue yawned dramatically.

'She's playing it safe,' said Tabitha. 'Going slowly to avoid any mistakes. Anika's a gifted flyer, but she's not showing off. The Hedgewitch doesn't want to see tricks, just good flying. That's smart.'

'But dull. We'll be here until Christmas at this rate,' said Rue.

Anika made another circuit. Thorn Patrol clapped. Cassie watched her closely, noting the way she leaned into the right, just slightly, to keep her balance.

Anika completed her final circuit and landed, with a little bow and a flourish, before the Hedgewitch.

'Well done. You were a touch crooked on that landing, remember to bend your knees, but a satisfactory effort over all.'

Anika nodded solemnly to the Coven Mistress and went to join her patrol. Eliza, Ivy and the rest welcomed her with open arms, praising her and talking excitedly amongst themselves.

'Cassandra,' Miranda called. 'It is your turn.'

Cassie felt her stomach turn to lead.

'You'll do splendidly,' said Rue. 'Just remember what I told you, heels to the earth, head to the stars!'

Tabitha gave her a smile and nodded vigorously.

Cassie walked a few paces away from the coven. She wanted a quiet word with her broom.

'Look here, I know we've not always got along and you'd probably rather have a really good flyer like Ivy riding you, only, this is important. All I'm asking is that you don't try anything silly while I'm up there. If you behave I'll give you a nice rub down with linseed oil tonight, all right?'

The broom stood motionless in her hands. She was pretty sure it had understood her, whether it would obey was another matter.

'Cassandra, we are waiting,' called the Hedgewitch.

With a sigh, Cassie mounted the broom. 'All right, here goes.'

It was higher than she'd flown since that first time in Trite, on an old broken broom with Montague clinging to the brush. Surely, if she could survive that she should be able to manage a few laps of the hall?

Cassie corrected her balance, holding tight with her legs as Rue had taught her. A really skilled witch could fly hands-free, only, there was no way Cassie was going to risk that today. The sun was warm on her back and the wind played with her hair. She was over the roof now, the grey slates looked like the scales of a wyrm, spotted with green moss and lichen. The peak of the roof sported a weathervane shaped like a flying witch. It swung as the wind changed. Cassie banked to the left, readjusting her course. Thankfully, it wasn't a strong wind and she flew on, keeping the roof to her right. Tantivy was flying smoothly, turning at the lightest touch, it had so far shown no inclination for its usual antics. Before she knew it, Cassie had completed her first circuit of the roof. She could hear distant clapping and Rue's loud hoot of triumph but she didn't dare take her eyes off the broom. She still had two laps to go.

The wind had picked up, it was blowing from the west, bringing the deep green scent of the wood, of pine and oak and something else wild and strange. The breeze filled out her cloak and blew her hair in her face as she turned. Cassie did her best to compensate for it, she was halfway through her second circuit, nearly there now.

There was an odd shadow in the corner of her vision, but she ignored it.

Tantivy was speeding up, as if it wanted to race the wind. She couldn't keep to the careful pace Anika had demonstrated and was forced to lean in even further to keep her balance. Cassie's broom, her mother's broom, made by one of the finest broomsquires in England with a handle of lively whifflewood, was not designed for plodding along steadily towards its destination. She could feel its restless energy, it wanted to go faster, fly higher, spin and loop and do something impressive. It was taking all Cassie's willpower just to keep it on course, her knuckles white as she held it steady.

Now there were two shadows below her on the roof, her own and a smaller winged shape. She tried not to look down, that never worked out well for her. She needed to keep her eye on the spire and the weathervane. The second shadow rose above her, coming between her and the sun, Cassie risked a glance up. It was a rook, a big black bird with golden eyes, and it was flying right at her. If she didn't change course they would collide.

Cassie tried to veer out of its path, but her grip on the handle slipped. The broom dipped and she grabbed it again just in time to pull it back on course.

She was on the final circuit, if only that bird would leave her alone and let her finish. Cassie cast the rook a furious glance. The wind had picked up again, the rook swooped beneath her and then came up, crying at her in its hoarse voice. The broom bucked, spooked by the bird, and veered right at the weathervane. It was too much, Cassie lost her balance and felt the broom slide out from under her. She was falling.

Miranda caught her. Astride her own broom, the Hedgewitch had leapt into the air the second Cassie lost her grip. Together they returned safely to the field below. The rook was gone and Cassie's broom was still in the air, doing gentle loops of the hall roof without her.

'I'm fine,' said Cassie, while Tabitha fussed over her, but her heart was still thumping as the horrible realisation came over her. She'd failed the final test.

Chapter Twenty Seven

Operation
Grass Snake

Cassie sat in the Hartwood kitchen, staring at her breakfast. Mrs Briggs had served up eggs and ham, slabs of soft white bread and a steaming pot of bramble tea. There was even a bowl of plums, the first of the season, brought in from the orchard by Brogan, but Cassie couldn't eat. She'd barely slept either, the events of the previous day – the Fledgling Test and her failure – played over and over again in her mind.

Rue and Tabitha had tried to comfort Cassie, they'd

even complained to the Hedgewitch that it wasn't fair and Cassie should be allowed to try again.

But those were the rules: a Fledgling candidate was allowed one attempt at each part of the test and if she failed she had to wait three whole months to try again. It didn't matter that the wind had changed, or that the rook had interrupted her flight path; a better witch would have kept her balance, would have finished the test even if a dozen birds flew at her, a fact Ivy explained loudly on the way home. Everyone in Hedgely would know of Cassie's failure by now, would be talking about the Hedgewitch's niece who couldn't even fly a broom without falling off.

Across the table, Jane Wren was having no such qualms about her breakfast. She was going back to Fowell House and seemed intent on hoovering up every crumb of Mrs Briggs' cooking before she had to return to mutton and mushy peas. Around her neck she wore an amulet from the Hedgewitch to protect her in London. Cassie almost envied Jane; at Fowell House no one had expected anything of her. If she failed a test there would be dish-washing duty or a few hundred lines to write, but no one would look at her the way her aunt had, with bitter disappointment.

Cassie pushed back her untouched plate, thanked Mrs Briggs and went out into the garden, taking a reluctant Montague with her.

July had arrived, bringing the rain with it. A damp cloud hung about the hill and the leaves of the horse chestnut dripped. It was bad weather for flying, Rue would say, not that Cassie could even look at a broom right now. She stomped through the kitchen garden where happy snails left silver trails and hydrangeas bobbed like pink and blue lollies. After stopping to check on Peg, warm and dry in her stable, she wandered down the drive. The gravel made a satisfying crunch under her boots.

'If you're going to sulk all day, you could at least do it indoors by the fire,' said Montague.

'I'm not sulking, I'm thinking.'

'Another activity you could pursue equally well in a dry room.'

The sound of flapping fabric and the whistle of wind through birch twigs made Cassie look up. A witch was flying down to meet her. She wore a mackintosh over her uniform and her pale hair was dripping wet. Cassie felt a pang of envy as the witch executed a perfect landing, her robin familiar perched on her shoulder.

'Well, hullo there!' said Renata Rawlins. 'Abominable weather for flying, this. Good thing I waterproofed my broom last week. I've come to fetch Jane Wren.'

'She's inside, eating breakfast,' said Cassie.

'It seems you've had a few adventures since we last met, care to fill me in?'

Cassie told her all about the lanthorn flower and the seeking spell, about the goblin market and the familiars. She described the Netherwood and explained how they'd got the stolen children out through the tunnels.

'My goodness, you have been busy! I suppose I have you to thank for the safety of my young charge, then.' Renata gave her the witch's salute, touching the brim of her hat with three fingers. 'Well done, from one witch to another!'

Cassie sighed. 'Only, I'm *not* a witch. I failed my Fledgling Test.'

'Surely you're not going to let that stop you? You performed a spell from the Hedgewitch's own grimoire. You outwitted a whole horde of goblins and brought those children home. If that doesn't make you a witch, then I don't know what does.'

'I don't think my aunt sees it that way.'

'Then show her – take the test again. We all fall off our brooms sometimes, I failed my Fledgling Test the first time too, you know.'

Cassie stared at her in disbelief.

'It's true, always been useless at brewing. Had to make a Lionheart tonic, I put in too much cinnamon and the whole thing exploded! I was cleaning orange goop off the hall ceiling for a week; you can probably still see the scorch marks.'

Cassie laughed.

'But the second time around I passed with flying colours. That's one element of witchcraft you won't find listed in the handbook, good old-fashioned stubbornness!'

'But what if I fail again, with everyone watching?' Cassie wasn't sure she could bear that.

Renata put a hand on her shoulder. 'You're Rose Morgan's daughter, your mother never gave a fig what anyone thought of her. When she wanted something, she'd pursue it to the ends of the earth. Over the summer you've demonstrated you have every bit as much heart as Rose. That's why she chose you to protect the key, she believed in you.'

As Cassie watched Renata enter Hartwood she felt a little flicker of hope kindle inside her. She might not be able to go to coven camp, but if she practised flying every day, maybe she could take the Fledgling Test again in the autumn. After all, she'd have passed the first time, if it hadn't been for that bird.

'How did that witch know about the key?' Montague asked.

'Oh, she saw it the first time we met, at Fowell House...' Cassie trailed off. It was true that Renata had glimpsed the key, and Cassie had told her it belonged to her mother, but not who her mother was, or why the key was important. And Renata had spoken as if she knew Rose.

Montague narrowed his eyes. 'You mean to say, that warden knew you had the key before I brought you to Hedgely?'

Cassie nodded. Seeing Renata again, telling her about the Netherwood had reminded her of something else. Cassie bolted through the great oak door and up the stairs, Montague close behind. Bursting into her bedroom, she pulled her *Witch's Handbook* from the shelf. In the back was tucked the cutting she'd found in Miranda's study, the story from the *Hedgely Herald* about Elm Patrol, the young witches who'd saved a boy lost in the Hedge. There was her mother, with her mop of curly hair and a big grin. Standing just behind her was a slender girl, her fair hair in two long braids. Cassie hadn't seen the resemblance at first, but if she looked beyond the grown-up Renata's fashionable hair and lipstick, it was unmistakeable.

Renata had been in 1st Hedgely Coven with her mother, in the same patrol.

Cassie retrieved the warden pin she'd found in the Netherwood.

'We thought this was Mrs Blight's, but what if it belonged to Renata?'

Montague placed a paw on the newspaper cutting. 'If Renata grew up in Hedgely she might have discovered the tunnels for herself.'

'And if she was friends with my mother, she could have known about the key.'

'It has always troubled me, how those goblin nabbers found you in London and why they were so eager to catch you,' said the cat. 'I never believed it was a random attack, far more likely someone told them about the key and sent them to bring you in.'

Cassie frowned. 'Renata was in Hedgely on Midsummer's Eve too, when Oliver was taken.'

Renata had been tasked with recovering the stolen

children, but what if she'd been helping the goblins all along? And they were about to hand her Jane Wren.

Cassie reached the kitchen to find Mrs Briggs kneading dough and Miranda reading a book at the table.

'Where are they? Renata... Jane?' Cassie gasped.

The Hedgewitch looked up. 'They left a few minutes ago.'

'Renata is the warlock, the one who broke the weirstones. She's helping the goblins – she's going to give them Jane!'

Cassie feared that Miranda would doubt her, would waste precious time telling her that Renata was a respected witch and warden and that she must be mistaken. But the Hedgewitch rose from her seat immediately. 'Get your cloak and meet me on the drive.'

Riding pillion on a broomstick is not a comfortable experience. Cassie was perched awkwardly behind Miranda, clinging to her waist. She'd never been this close to her aunt before. The Hedgewitch's dark cloak smelled of lemons, rosemary and woodsmoke. Malkin sat before his mistress, like a ship's figurehead, peering into the clouds. Miranda's broom, Zephyr, was a fast and steady flier, yet Renata had a good lead on them and was nowhere to be seen in the sky over Hedgely.

Cassie assumed that Renata would take Jane straight into the Hedge, but Miranda was flying due north. Soon, the familiar shape of Castle Hill appeared, the ruins stood out like a row of broken teeth. As they descended, Cassie's hair and eyelashes were strung with tiny droplets of water. They touched down and Cassie half-leapt half-fell off the broom.

'Renata!' called the Hedgewitch.

'Help me!' cried a small voice.

Miranda ran into the ruins with Cassie close behind.

Renata stood by the entrance where, not long before, Cassie, Rue and Tabitha had emerged with the stolen children. The day after their return, Miranda had overseen four strong farm labourers as they blocked the tunnel with a great stone, inscribed with warding runes. The stone was still there, sealing the entrance to the Netherwood.

Renata had changed. Gone was the friendly smile and nonchalant air; she scowled at them, her body tense and angular. Pinning Jane's arms behind her with one hand, she held a silver knife in the other. 'Stop right there,' she said, bringing the blade to Jane's small throat.

The Hedgewitch raised her empty hands. 'Renata, let the child go.'

Renata laughed. 'I don't take orders from you, Hedgewitch. I report only to the true king.'

The Erl King, thought Cassie, *she's working for the Lord of Rags and Tatters.*

'What has he promised you, that you would hand him innocent children?' the Hedgewitch asked.

'Innocent? She's *human,* none of us are innocent. But this girl has a chance, a chance we never had. I'm doing her a favour.' Renata smiled and pulled Jane closer. 'She's lucky, she'll see wonders you and I could only dream of, she'll help to right the wrongs of the past.'

'What does he want with the children, Renata?'

Renata ignored Miranda and turned her attention to Cassie. For a moment her expression softened and Cassie caught a glimpse of the friendly young warden she'd met at Fowell House.

'You should join us, Cassie, you'd like to see Faerie, wouldn't you? You'd like to see your mother again.'

Cassie's heart skipped a beat.

'Don't let her fool you.' Miranda laid a hand on Cassie's shoulder. 'Renata, you are a warden, sworn to protect and shield, have you forgotten your oaths?'

'It is you who have forgotten, Hedgewitch,' said Renata. 'You've forgotten what we were in the past, the great witches and what they could do. You waste your time on petty cantrips and wart cures. But on the other side of that wood there is still real magic, the magic of Faerie.'

The Hedgewitch took a step towards the pair. 'Nonsense. Faery magic is illusion, nothing but smoke and shadows. The Erl King is full of lies. Let the child go and we will return to Hartwood together. I will ensure the Assembly gives you a fair trial.'

Renata sniffed. 'Witches and their rules, as if you can bind magic. You do not know what is waiting on the other side of that wood, what is coming for you, for all of you too blind to see. This is only the beginning.'

The warden removed the knife from Jane's throat, and, for a moment, Cassie thought she might give in, but instead she struck the stone with the blade. A clear, cold note rang out, followed by a crack, like the breaking of bones. The stone that had blocked the tunnel split in two.

Cassie looked at her aunt, expecting her to cry out, to do *something,* but the Hedgewitch just watched, her face betraying no emotion.

'Your mother knew everything, Cassie,' said the

warden. 'She knew the truth behind the lies they teach us, she knew the taste of real magic and what had to be done. Someday, I hope you'll finish what she started, but until then, farewell!'

Renata gripped Jane tighter, pulling her towards the crack in the stone, but there was a small, dark shadow behind her. Renata screamed. Malkin, creeping up from around the stone, had sunk his teeth and claws into her leg. She dropped the knife and Jane pulled free, running towards Cassie and Miranda. Renata's robin familiar dived and pecked at the big black cat, who snarled and hissed, swiping at the bird.

With blood running down her leg, Renata clambered through the opening and disappeared below ground.

Cassie started after her.

'No,' said Miranda. 'We must get Jane away from here. Our first duty is to keep her safe. Quickly, pick up the knife – but don't touch it, use your handkerchief.'

Cassie retrieved the blade and brought it to the Hedgewitch. It was made of some white metal that held a bright sheen, the handle was of antler.

'Weregilt silver, I should have known – that is how she destroyed the weirstones. We must hope the Erl King has no more such blades.' Miranda took the knife, wrapped tightly in the handkerchief, and tucked it into her belt.

'We have to go after her!' said Cassie.

'Renata is free, but she has lost. She used her position with the wardens to aid the goblins and abet their kidnapping. Now she will be of little use to the Erl King and every witch in Britain will be after her.'

Cassie looked back at the split in the stone. 'But she knows where my mother is.'

Miranda shook her head. 'Don't be a fool, Cassandra. Renata would say anything to win you to her side. If you go after her she'll hand you over in place of Jane.'

Cassie stared at the dark gap, her heart thumping and Renata's words still echoing in her mind.

Elliot came on the afternoon express train, summoned by an imp from the Hedgewitch. They met him at the station.

'I still can't believe it.' He shook his head. 'Such a promising young witch, so full of enthusiasm and talent. Well, I suppose you never can tell.'

'There will be others,' Miranda warned. 'You should examine your new recruits closely, Elliot.'

'Oh, I'm sure there's nothing to worry about. One over-imaginative and slightly unhinged witch who believed some nonsense about a goblin king and took it a step too far. We'll make a full investigation, of course, see if we can't bring her in, but no need to cause a general panic.'

Miranda pursed her lips in that disapproving way Cassie knew only too well.

Her uncle ignored her, herding Jane towards a first class carriage on the return train to London. 'Anyhow, well done, Cassie, for figuring it all out and saving young Jane here – for the second time in a row! I will make sure the higher-ups hear of this, we'll have to think up a suitable reward for you and your friends.'

But Cassie was less interested in a reward than what Renata had said about Rose. Miranda might not have believed the warden, but to Cassie it confirmed her darkest fear – the Erl King had her mother.

Chapter Twenty Eight

The Lonely
Tower

The clouds cleared in the evening, granting them a vivid orange and purple sunset. After dinner, Cassie made her way through the Hartwood gardens. The long grasses were golden now and the vegetable patch full of nodding sunflowers and fat, juicy strawberries. The orchard trees bore clusters of ruby cherries and small green apples. In the rose garden, the white and pink blossoms that had dominated in spring were replaced now by rich red and gold blooms that smelled of ripe peaches.

Cassie sat on the carved bench, rubbing the key between her fingers. There had to be another way to find her mother. Some spell or charm that could lead Cassie to her.

She could summon Burdock once more, ask him to take her to the Erl King and demand he release her mother. But the goblin had already fulfilled his favour to her and she did not think he would help her of his own free will.

No, there was only one option left to her. She had to make a deal with the creature who had haunted her since her arrival in Hedgely, the faery beast who'd appeared as a pine marten, lynx and wolf. Even now, the thought of those golden eyes frightened her, but he was the only one who'd offered to help her, the only one who could. There was no other way to get her mother back. She would wait until the camp, she decided, when everyone was busy and would not notice she had gone. Miranda would be away from Hartwood and neither she, nor Tabitha nor Rue, could stop Cassie from going. She would enter the Hedge alone and seek out Glashtyn.

On the day of the camp, Rue and Tabitha came to see Cassie at Hartwood. They were trying to cheer her up, but there was nothing they could say to change the fact that they would be sleeping under the stars in Mr Bellwether's field, cooking their dinner on an open fire and singing silly chants without her.

'I 'spect it will rain,' said Rue. 'My mum said her knees were aching this morning and that always means a downpour. Last year, the tents leaked and we all looked like river hags in the morning.'

They glanced out the window at the pastel-blue sky, dotted with the smallest puffs of cloud.

'It really won't be the same without you,' said Tabitha.

Cassie changed the subject. 'We had an imp from my uncle this morning. Jane is safe, but they still haven't found Renata.'

'I can't believe she was the one who stole Oliver. She seemed so nice at the fair,' said Tabitha.

Rue frowned. 'If she's hiding in the Hedge, we'll find her. I'll show her what happens when you mess with my brother.'

Montague came into the room. 'The Hedgewitch is looking for you two, she wants help with the tents.'

Cassie watched them go, Rue bouncing down the stairs and Tabitha carrying Wyn in her arms. She listened to their voices fading and the sound of the great oak door downstairs closing behind them. Then she began to pack her satchel.

'Of all your poorly considered, rash and foolish plans, Cassandra, this is the worst by far,' said Montague.

The road was empty between Hartwood and the village. The moon hung in the branches of a lime tree like a silver peach with a bite taken out of it and the air smelled of freshly cut hay. Cassie adjusted her cloak and hoisted her broom over her shoulder.

'I have to do this, Montague. It's the only way to reach my mother. The Erl King has her, I'm sure of it.'

'Then speak to the Hedgewitch; get her help.'

They crossed the Nix and followed the river uphill towards the woods.

'Aunt Miranda will only try and stop me. Besides, I don't need her, there's someone else who can help me.'

'Not that thieving goblin again?'

'No, someone much cleverer.'

They had reached the tree line. The Hedge was already deep in shadow; the last glow of the setting sun cast a purple gloaming over the forest. This time, Cassie did not pause, crossing into the darkening wood, she walked on.

'Glashtyn!' Cassie cried into the shadows. 'Glashtyn! I'm here, I need your help!'

'Wonderful, now every nasty thing in the Hedge will be after us,' said Montague.

The wood was silent. Cassie could feel the trees waiting, listening. Then, slowly, the leaves above her began to rustle. A gentle susurrus passed from one tree to the next; there was no wind to stir the air, the leaves were moving on their own.

A small blue flame appeared on the path before them, just a few yards away. A wisp, twisting in the air and burning with a cool light. The wisp did not try to fool her with voices, scents or visions of her heart's desire, it just waited.

'You're not going to follow *that*? It'll lead us off a cliff.'

'It's all right, Montague. I think he sent it to guide me. Remember what you told me when we first met? Not all faeries are wicked.'

'I was speaking philosophically.'

As soon as Cassie took a step forward, the wisp danced up the path ahead of them, painting the tree trunks with blue light. They followed.

'This is madness, you're going to walk right into the Erl King's trap.'

'He has my mother. This is the only way.'

'Haven't you learned anything about the faery folk? They don't play by human rules. He'll trick you.'

'Then I'll just have to be careful. I know it's dangerous, Montague, and you don't have to come with me, but I don't have any choice. I have to do this, it might be my only chance.'

Montague sniffed. 'Just don't complain to me when the Erl King turns us both into beetles.'

The Hedge was unnaturally silent. They heard no birds, no scurrying of small creatures, only Cassie's footsteps on the path. The snap of a twig beneath her boot startled them both.

Montague clung to her side. His small, warm presence against her legs was a comfort.

The wisp led them away from the path, into the deep woods. The branches of the larger trees reached out towards each other but did not touch. Cassie picked her way over the net of roots and pushed through tangles of bindweed and nettles, struggling to keep up. The wisp was impatient, if she did not hurry, she would lose it.

Cassie sighed and grasped her broom. 'Get on,' she said to Montague, 'quickly.'

'If I lose one of my lives on this fool's errand, I shall hold you entirely responsible.'

When they were both perched on the broomstick, Cassie leaned in and whispered, 'Fly, Tantivy, fly.'

The broom crashed through the trees, branches whipped her face and arms, forcing her to keep her head down and shelter the cat with her body. They flew through a dark tunnel of leaves, the blue light of the wisp speeding ahead. Cassie's stomach lurched as they skimmed over a fallen log, the broomstick twisted and she nearly lost her grip. Tantivy was clearly enjoying the challenge, diving under branches and rising over the undergrowth, the wisp leading them on, deeper into the woods. They were flying too fast for Cassie to get more than a glimpse of her surroundings. Every muscle in her arms and legs ached with the effort of clinging to the broom and she scarcely had time to breathe.

The wisp flickered and vanished. Cassie tugged on the broomstick, pulling it out of its headlong flight with a struggle. She tumbled off into the soft leaf litter, Montague leaping after her. When she sat up, she found they'd reached a clearing. The ground sloped up to a grassy mound dotted with daisies, all silvered by the moonlight. Above them, at the crest of the mound was a tower. It was silhouetted black against the sky and cast a long shadow that pointed, like a finger, to where they stood.

The tower was built of grey stone, greened over with moss and ivy. Aside from the weirstones, Cassie had never seen any mark of human presence inside the Hedge, nor any buildings. The tower was partly ruined now, the windows held no glass and the archway over the door had crumbled, its stones lying in the shadows. She wondered who'd built it and why. Perhaps it had been the home of a hermit witch or maybe it was a watchtower, keeping an eye out for faery armies, or even a prison designed to hold some frightening foe.

'You're not going *inside*?' Montague hissed.

'I think I have to.'

'I don't like this place, Cassandra, it makes my fur stand on end.'

Cassie stepped through the doorway and felt cobwebs brush her face. She was at the foot of a winding stair. Montague remained outside. 'I can't enter. The wards are too strong.'

Indeed, there were runes carved into the remaining stones of the doorway. Cassie clasped the key, dangling from its chain, it was warm. The key had let her past the wards that protected the threshold.

'Be careful, Cassandra,' said the cat. 'Listen to your head as well as your heart.'

Cassie nodded and began to climb. The stairway was narrow, the stones worn smooth by centuries of footsteps. As she climbed higher, Cassie could hear a humming sound, like gentle music, or someone singing a lullaby, coming from above her. The song had a soft, rocking melody, strangely familiar. She was sure she'd heard it before, it filled her with warmth and she hurried up the stairs, eager to find the source of the music.

Cassie came out into a circular chamber, walled and floored with bare stone. There were no windows. The only light came from a green wisp-lamp, hanging from a chain above. Beneath the lamp in a high-backed wooden chair, singing softly to herself, was Cassie's mother.

Chapter Twenty Nine

The Phooka

C assie's mother rose from the chair. She was dressed in a black gown with long sleeves that fell in soft folds behind her. Her bright hair was unbound and formed a halo of rose gold about her head. She had tears in her eyes. 'Cassie?'

'Mum?'

The woman swept forward and embraced her, enveloping Cassie in soft fabric, curly hair and the smell of lilac. That scent brought memories flooding back, it was as much a part of her mother as the smile on her lips. Cassie let herself be held, feeling like a little girl again, warm and safe from the outside world.

'I knew you'd find me, you clever thing,' said Rose.

'But I don't understand, why are you here?'

'I tried to cross the border to Faerie, but the Erl King was waiting for me. Someone betrayed me to his spies. I fell into his trap and was imprisoned here.'

'For all these years, you've been here in this tower?'

'Yes, darling. It has been torture, trapped halfway between Faerie and our world. Having no way to reach you, or even send word that I was alive. But I knew that someday you would find me.'

Rose released Cassie from her embrace and looked her in the eye, her face serious.

'I'm sorry, Cassie. I'm sorry for leaving you behind, for all you've suffered alone. I've missed you so much.'

Cassie's eyes were blurry, she brushed them with her sleeve.

'It's going to be all right now,' said her mother. 'We can go home together, we can start over. I'll find us a house by the sea, like that cottage you loved so much, with the orange tree. I'll never leave you again, my darling.'

'Let's go now,' said Cassie, tugging on her mother's hand.

'I cannot. See the runes on the floor? I am bound here by a spell.'

'Then how can I help?'

'The key! You must give me the key,' said Rose, eagerly.

Cassie's hand went automatically to her chest. The key had let her into the tower, it could set her mother free. Surely it would be right to give it back? After all, it belonged to Rose.

'Please, Cassie, we haven't got much time. The Erl King will be back soon, I couldn't bear for him to hurt you. Give me the key and we'll leave this place together.'

Cassie lifted the string over her head. It would be good to give it back, to be released from the burden of keeping so precious and powerful an object.

A high pitched caterwaul came from outside the tower. It was Montague, warning her.

'The Erl King!' said Rose. 'He's coming. Quickly, Cass-sandra, give it to me!'

But the yowl woke Cassie, as if from a dream. She looked at her mother again. In her joy she'd missed something, one little detail that wasn't quite right. Rose's eyes should be grey, like her own, like Miranda and Elliot's, but the eyes of the woman before her were a dull gold, like ancient coins.

'No,' said Cassie. 'You're not her. It's a good try, you even smell like her, but as much as I want it to be true, it isn't.'

Anger flashed behind those golden eyes for a second, then dissolved once more into pleading softness.

'What are you saying, Cassie? Of course it's me. I know it's been a long time, we're both older now. I may not look exactly as you remember me, it has been seven years after all, seven long years under this enchantment – but I'm still your mother. I love you, Cassie!'

'Stop it!' Cassie stepped back, clutching the key in her fist, her eyes stinging. 'Stop pretending to be her! You have no right.'

Rose Morgan froze, the expression on her face blank. She turned to the high-backed chair, sitting down, she faced Cassie once more. But Rose was gone; in her place sat the Garm.

'You stupid child,' said the headmistress of Fowell House. 'How many times do you have to be told? Your mother is dead.'

'My mother is alive, but she isn't here in this tower.'

'If you do not give me the key, she will die!' The Garm curled her claw-like hands around the arms of the chair, her knuckles were white. 'And it will be your fault.'

'I don't believe you. I don't believe you even know where she is! If you had my mother, if the Erl King had her, you wouldn't need to pretend to be her.'

The only thing about the woman before her that had not changed were her eyes. They watched Cassie with the same inhuman gaze as a fox or a goat. She needed to know who – or what – she was truly facing. Cassie stepped towards the seated figure and began to recite the chant of revealing she'd seen in Miranda's grimoire, walking clockwise around the chair.

'Glamour glowing, glamour fading
Through the veil of shifting mist.
Shine the light of witching power,
All enchantments are dismissed.'

The Garm laughed, a loud, unpleasant sound that echoed in the small chamber, cutting her off.

'What do you think you are doing, little witchling?'

Unperturbed, Cassie raised her voice to recite the second verse:

'By the candle of my art,
With witching sight I see anew.
Shades and phantoms must depart,
Banish the false, reveal the true.'

'That cantrip can only reveal the true form of one who has such a thing. I have none. I am the wind at night, I am the shadow of the screech owl, I am a current in the ink-dark sea. You could not see me if you had the sight of an eagle.'

Cassie shook her head. 'You are a lie and so is everything you say.'

'Give me the key, Miss Morgan, and I may let your mother live,' the Garm commanded, rising to her feet again.

'No.'

The headmistress took a step towards her and as she moved she shrank in height, growing thicker and wider. Her face contorted into the sneering grimace of Lizzie Bleacher. Strong hands grabbed Cassie by the shoulders and shook her.

'Give me the key, Morgan, or I'll make you into mincemeat.'

The creature before her wasn't Lizzie, any more than it had been Cassie's mother, or the Garm. It must be Glashtyn himself, his power to change shape greater than she had ever imagined.

Cassie knew the Bleacher wasn't real and yet the same old fear washed over her, paralysing her. The Bleacher's fingernails dug into her flesh and her hot, rancid breath made Cassie turn her face away.

'Think you're clever, don't you? Think you've got it all figured out? But you're still small and weak. No one's going to come through that door and save you this time, Morgan.'

Lizzie shoved her against the hard stone wall and held her there.

'You're going to give me the key or I'm going to dash your head against these stones and leave you here to die. No one will find you in a hundred years. Not that anyone would even notice you're missing.'

If Cassie handed over the key, Glashtyn might let her go, but without it she wouldn't be able to leave the tower. She would be trapped there, she might never see Rue or Tabitha or Miranda again. She would never find her mother.

But if the Erl King gained the key he would be able to walk through any door in Britain, break through any witch's ward. No child in the country would be safe, and it would be her doing.

She met Lizzie's gaze. The Bleacher's yellow eyes betrayed the illusion, but the pain in Cassie's arms was real enough.

Cassie kicked Lizzie in the shin. The girl shrieked with rage and loosened her hold for just a moment. Cassie squirmed away from her and ran for the stairs, the key clutched tight in her hand. The Bleacher was behind her, horrible heavy footfalls followed her down the tower stairs, hands grabbed for her flying hair. She was out, through the open arch, into the silver moonlight.

Montague rushed to Cassie's side as she turned to face the tower. Through the doorway stepped a tall, straight-backed figure in a black cloak.

'I'm very disappointed in you,' said the Hedgewitch.

Montague hissed.

The shadows made it impossible to see the woman's face clearly. She was outlined in darkness, like the tower behind her, but her voice rang clear and true.

'I had such high hopes for you, the next Morgan witch. If I was hard on you it was only because I wanted to make you stronger, to push you, to find out what you are capable of, but you have failed me.'

Cassie held her ground but her eyes were blurred with tears. It couldn't be Miranda, she would never help the Erl King, yet doubts crept into Cassie's mind. Like Renata, the Hedgewitch had failed to find the missing children – what if she too had been helping the goblins all along?

'Don't listen to it Cassandra,' Montague urged her. 'It's using your thoughts, your memories, to gain power over you.'

'I had hoped to make you the next Hedgewitch, someday,' said Miranda. 'I had hoped you would follow in my footsteps and those of your great-grandmother. But you can't even pass the Fledgling Test. You are an embarrassment to our family, to your name, to me!'

It was true. Deep down, Cassie knew she'd failed her aunt. She'd wanted to fit in at Hedgely, to do well at coven, to make her aunt proud, but she'd failed her at every turn. She was useless as a witch.

'You might as well give up, Cass-sandra, give me the key and run away, like your foolish mother,' said the tall black figure. 'You are worthless to me.'

'No, she is not,' said the same voice, only this time it came from behind Cassie.

She looked back to see her aunt standing at the edge of the clearing, her broom in one hand and the goblin Burdock at her side.

'Cassandra is reckless, headstrong and an indifferent flyer, but she is also a brilliant young witch. She has entered the Hedge and returned safely no fewer than three times. She has performed spells that would challenge witches twice her age. With help from her friends, who admire her greatly, she saved a dozen children from the goblins, and I am very proud of her.'

This Miranda seemed less real to Cassie than the angry one, but she had the clear, grey Morgan gaze. Behind the Hedgewitch stood Rue and Tabitha, frowning and silent, but holding their ground.

'You know that isn't me, Cassandra. It's only a shadow that forms itself from fears and memories. It cannot really hurt you, unless you allow it. Use the key.'

Cassie turned back to the false Hedgewitch, but she was gone. In her place was a figure, six feet tall and robed in tattered black. Where its face ought to be it wore a mask, the skull of a stag, hollow-eyed with vast branching antlers.

Cassie had seen it before, in the pages of Widdershin's book.

Behind her, Burdock screamed. 'It's him! His High and Horribleness!'

Montague brushed against Cassie's leg. 'The goblin is wrong. That is only a shadow of the Erl King. The creature goes too far in attempting to mirror its master – see, it is fading.'

The cat was right, the tattered edges of the figure

were transparent, the moonlight shone through them. The very effort of producing the illusion was hurting it.

'Now, Cassandra, use the key!' called Miranda.

The revealing incantation had failed her. Cassie would need another, but she'd learned so few spells. She would have to make it up as she went along.

The Erl King stood still and silent before her. Cassie held up the key, silently begging it to help her. She needed the right words. A melody still lingered at the back of her mind, the tune that Glashtyn had been humming in the tower, a tune he'd stolen from her own infant memory, granted by the stream called Gnost. Her mother's song, her childhood lullaby:

'Your own true self, your face so fair,
I'd give a purse of gold to see,
And from the shadows sing you forth,
Oh, when will you return to me?'

As Cassie sang the key began to glow, shining brighter by the second. It was pure gold, the only colour in the moonlit landscape, and nearly burned her hands with its heat. The clearing, tower and trees were lit as if at midday. She repeated the verse and the Erl King cowered, holding up arms made of shadow to hide its face from the light. The figure shrank, folding into a small dark bundle. As Cassie finished chanting, the key's light faded.

At first, she thought the creature who'd been her mother, the Garm, Lizzie Bleacher, the Hedgewitch and finally the Erl King had vanished, leaving behind only a hairy black skin. Then she saw it move; a small, furry head appeared from the folds. It was black as soot, with long ears and little stubby horns. The creature looked up at Cassandra with round, yellow eyes; its whiskers twitched.

'A phooka,' said Miranda, coming to stand beside her. 'The cleverest of the faery shapeshifters, they can assume the form of any bird or beast, though it is a rare individual that can imitate humans so well.'

Cassie thought of the pine marten, the lynx, the wolf, even the rook who had made her fail the Fledgling Test. They were clearly just skins worn by the phooka, the way she might put on different coats.

The small furry form before her was shivering. It was a pathetic creature, beneath all those disguises. No wonder it changed its shape to appear bigger and stronger.

'No doubt we have also discovered the mysterious thief of Brogan's radishes – phooka have a notorious fondness for them,' said Miranda. 'Go back to your master, shifter, and tell him the key is lost to him. The wards of the Hedgewitch stand and we are not afraid.'

The creature scurried away, its tufted tail vanishing into the undergrowth at the edge of the clearing.

Rue and Tabitha rushed forward to hug Cassie.

'We went back to Hartwood, to bring you some toffee from camp, but Mrs Briggs said you'd gone to bed early,' said Tabitha.

'We didn't believe that for a minute!' said Rue.

'We sort of broke into your room,' admitted Tabitha. 'We were so worried when we couldn't find you! Then Rue noticed your broom was missing.'

'And so was Montague. We guessed you'd gone into the Hedge.'

Tabitha interrupted. 'We had to tell the Hedgewitch everything. She summoned Burdock to lead us to you. He wasn't very happy about it.'

'But she threatened to roast him over the campfire!'

'We're so glad you're safe.'

'You better not go into the Hedge again without us,' said Rue.

Cassie promised. The phooka had been wrong about one thing – she had been missed.

'Come now, I believe we have a camp to be getting back to,' said the Hedgewitch.

Chapter Thirty

Coven Camp

1st Hedgely Coven had transformed Mr Bellwether's field into a bustling hub of activity. In the centre of a circle of tents was the campfire, over which a large cauldron hung on a tripod. The smell of tomato soup bubbling inside drifted up the valley. Girls in black hats and cloaks scurried about, fetching firewood, carrying water and chopping herbs and vegetables. The tents were black too, except for the yellow and purple flags that marked out those belonging to Ash and Thorn Patrols. Mr Bellwether's Hedgely Blue ewes had been shepherded into the neighbouring pasture where they watched the cavorting witches with placid eyes, chewing mouthfuls of grass.

'They're roasting sausages!' said Rue. 'I can't believe they started without us.' Rue and Tabitha raced downhill to join the rest of the coven.

'Cassandra, a moment,' said the Hedgewitch, before Cassie could follow.

They stood together on the crest of the hill, Miranda gave Cassie a tired smile. 'I wanted to speak with you alone. I know you have had a long night, but there is still one thing we must resolve. The key, Rose gave it to you?'

'Yes, before she left.'

'May I see it?'

Cassie slipped the cord over her head and handed the key to her aunt.

The Hedgewitch cupped the small golden object in her hand. 'Did Rose tell you what this is, or where it came from?'

Cassie shook her head. 'Only that I was supposed to look after it until she came back.'

'This is one of the great and ancient treasures of Faerie, they call it the *Auriclys*. Cassandra, do you know what a skeleton key is?'

'I read about that in a book once. It's a key that opens any door in a building.'

'Indeed, the Auriclys is something like that, but aside from mundane locks it can break any spell of binding, any ward or magical protection. Some old stories suggest that it can not only open doors, but create new ones, doors between worlds. That may be why the Erl King seeks it.'

Cassie frowned. At present, the goblins had to wait until the Crossing Nights to smuggle goods and people into Faerie, they had to evade the wardens and the Hedgewitch. But if the goblins could cross the border at any time, or anywhere, then no child in Britain would be safe.

'What does he want the children for?' Cassie asked, thinking of those who had already been taken to Faerie, those children they had not been able to save.

'I do not yet know what the Erl King plans for the children, but it will not be good. He hates humans and witches and cares only for his own kind. I fear he is plotting some great trouble for us.' Miranda handed the key back to Cassie. 'As long as you wear the Auriclys, he will pursue you. You were only safe all those years in London because he did not know you possessed it.'

'Why did my mother have the key?' asked Cassie. 'Where did she get it?'

Miranda turned to face the Hedge, looking away from Cassie as she answered. 'The key has long been the secret possession of the Hedgewitch, kept locked and safe within Hartwood. Your great-grandmother, Sylvia Morgan, was its last keeper. One night, I caught Rose sneaking out of the house with it. We fought, argued, and Rose ran away, taking the key with her. That was over thirteen years ago, the last time I saw her.'

Cassie rubbed the key with her thumb. It had helped her escape Fowell House, had woken Ambrose and freed the familiars at the market. The phooka had feared its power and been forced to reveal his true nature and the Erl King desired it for himself. The key was also the last thing her mother had given her and she'd kept it close for seven years. It was a symbol of her mother's promise and Cassie's hope that one day they would be reunited. There was nothing in the world she treasured more. Yet she knew it wasn't really hers, it belonged with the Hedgewitch. Cassie held it out to Miranda again.

'Will you look after it for me?' she asked.

'I will keep it safe and hidden, and in doing so I hope to keep you safe.'

Miranda slid the golden key into the inner pocket of her cloak. Cassie watched it glimmer as it vanished into the dark folds.

'I was not going to give you this.' The Hedgewitch pulled a crinkled envelope from her pocket and handed it to Cassie. 'I hoped that if I deterred you from going after Rose, you would be safe from the forces that pursued her. But my caution has not stopped you seeking her. Now I see that I may have been wrong, that you deserve to know. I received this from your mother's solicitor, a few days before you came to Hedgely.'

The seal was broken. Inside was a letter, a single sheet of lilac paper covered in her mother's looping handwriting. Cassie held her breath as she read.

Miranda,

If you are reading this, then I have failed. I am either dead or beyond your reach.

I know we have not been on speaking terms these past years and I am sure you have not yet forgiven me for what I've done. But know that despite all that was said that night, I am still your sister. I have stayed away, not from hatred or anger — those have long passed — but from fear. Fear that being so close to the Hedge would tempt me to leave behind all that I love and go looking for what I have lost, fear that in revenge He would take all I have left — you and Elliot and Cassandra.

Cassandra is my daughter, my bright star, and for her sake I have given up witchcraft, have stayed far from the border and kept silent and safe. He does not know of her existence and, for this reason, I have told no one, not even you. Forgive my secrecy, it was always to protect her. I planned to stay away, to keep her from ever knowing Faerie and its dangers, but now I have been called back. I received a message last week from a friend who has offered to help and now that Cassie is a little older, I find I must take this chance. I have left her in the safest place I could find, the address is on the back of this letter. If anything should happen to me, please take her in and watch over her. You are the only one I trust.

Yours always,
Rose

The letter was dated April 30th, in the year Cassie had entered Fowell House. On the back was the school's address. So this was how Miranda had known where to find Cassie, why she had sent Montague to fetch her.

'So the Erl King *was* after my mother, but why? What had she lost that was so important? Why did she leave?'

The letter had given her more questions than answers. She stared at her aunt, begging for an explanation.

Miranda shook her head, her eyes downcast. 'Rose and I drifted apart over the years, she no longer shared all her secrets with me.'

'Do you think she's still alive?' Cassie asked.

Miranda sighed. 'I have tried every seeking spell I know. If she is alive, then she is beyond my ability to find, which means there is only one place she could have gone.'

'Faerie,' said Cassie. 'Then I'll go after her, I'll cross the border, I'll find her on the other side.'

Miranda took Cassie by the shoulders, looking her in the eye. 'The phooka showed you only illusions and you barely escaped him. You are not yet ready to face the Erl King and his servants, or any of the myriad dangers of Faerie. If you want to help your mother, work hard at your witchcraft training, earn your licence and then we will talk of this again.'

'But that will take me years! I can't wait that long.'

'If you tried to save her now, you would fall into the Erl King's hands and I cannot allow that. Rose would never forgive me. No, if you must pursue her, be sure that you have a way to defeat him. I am not ready to lose you too.'

Miranda released Cassie and turned her gaze on the camp below. 'Let us join the others, we do not need to talk any more of this tonight.'

The Ash Patrol girls waved and cheered as Cassie met them by the fire. Harriet handed her a sausage on a stick. A slab of bread and bowl of herby tomato soup were pressed upon her. Rue and Tabitha joined her on a log bench, exhaustion and the crisp night air adding relish to their meal.

'What is *she* doing here?' asked Ivy. 'She failed her Fledgling Test.'

The Hedgewitch ignored Ivy. 'Come now, it's time to form the circle.'

They spread out in a ring around the fire, not separated into patrols but all mixed together. Cassie, Rue and Tabitha held hands and joined in with the coven song, their voices carrying in the open air:

'For we are witches, one and all,
And we are not afraid
Of goblins, grigs and gwyllions,
Our wards and charms are laid.

For we are witches, one and all,
A coven of the best.
Good friends who stand together
Through any threat or test.

For we are witches one and all,
We know, protect and heal,
With noble hearts, loyal and kind,
And courage true as steel!'

As they sang, Cassie's heart soared with the words and the rising sparks of the fire.

'Tonight we celebrate the achievements of 1st Hedgely Coven, the skills you have learned and badges you have earned,' said the Hedgewitch. 'We meet, as witches have done for generations, around the open fire to share food and stories, chants and spells. We have grown as a coven over the past year and welcomed new members. Anika Kalra, please come forward.'

The youngest member of Thorn Patrol stepped into the circle.

'Who presents this fledgling to the coven?' asked Miranda.

'I do,' said Eliza Pepper, taking her place at Anika's side. 'This is Anika. She has trained hard this year to join Thorn Patrol and pass her Fledgling Test. She is an exceptional flyer and has proven herself capable and skilled.'

'Anika, will you swear the Witch's Oath?'

Anika recited the oath in her soft, clear voice.

The Hedgewitch smiled and Cassie felt a pang of jealousy. She'd learned the oath too – if only she'd passed her test, she would be up there now with Anika.

'Every witch must have a familiar, a partner in her work, a creature born of faery stock who will guide, aid and protect her.'

The Hedgewitch raised her arm and a bird flew out of the darkness into the circle. It landed on Miranda's wrist and turned an inquisitive eye on Anika. It was a jackdaw.

'This is Cheo. May you work wisely together.'

Anika raised her arm and the jackdaw flew to perch on her shoulder, making her laugh as its feathers brushed her face. The small black bird whispered something in her ear.

Cassie looked at her feet so no one would see the expression on her face. She would have to work extra hard to pass the Fledgling Test next time and be awarded a familiar of her own.

Miranda was bending over Anika, attaching something to the collar of her cloak. 'This pin marks you as a member of the coven, and this pin shows you are a fledgling witch. Wear them with pride,' the Hedgewitch continued. 'And finally, the hat.'

Ivy passed Miranda a brand new black felt hat. It had the purple band of Thorn Patrol.

'When you wear the pointed hat, you are one of us, a part of the sisterhood of witches. We expect you to behave with honour and dignity, to help those in need, to know, to protect and to heal. Wear it well.'

Anika, who'd been solemn throughout the entire ceremony, broke into a gap-toothed grin the moment the hat was placed on her head. The whole coven cheered.

'Both Ash and Thorn Patrols have done their leaders proud this year, but they have grown too large. It is time to create a third patrol, so we may welcome new witches to our number.'

The circle broke into excited chatter over this news.

Cassie turned to Rue, but her friend did not look surprised, she waited patiently for the Hedgewitch to continue.

'The new patrol shall take the oak tree for its badge and wear green in their hats. Oak Patrol will be led by Rue Whitby, a witch who has proven that, despite her pranks, she has a good head on her shoulders and is a patient and capable teacher. Joining her will be Tabitha Blight and Cassandra Morgan. These three have already demonstrated their friendship and ability to work together – the seeds of a good patrol – and I expect to see them flourish in the coming months.'

Rue winked at Cassie and Tabitha. The Hedgewitch must have told her already.

'Of course, no witch can officially join a patrol until she has passed her Fledgling Test and Cassandra failed her first attempt.'

Cassie's heart sank.

'However, the test exists not only as a measure of training and practice, but of the qualities that make a good witch: a brave hand, a kind heart and a bright mind. This very night, Cassandra has demonstrated each of these qualities in facing one of the most dangerous and treacherous creatures of Faerie, a far more difficult test than any I could set her. Her trial was to see the truth, even when the lie was more appealing. Therefore, I ask Cassandra to step into the circle.'

Cassie wasn't sure she understood. Tabitha grinned and Rue led her by the hand towards her aunt, who appeared to be smiling at her. It was the oddest thing that had happened in that strange night and for a moment Cassie wondered if she were dreaming.

'Who presents this fledgling to the coven?'

'I do,' said Rue. 'This is Cassie, she's a pretty rubbish flyer, but she's good at everything else and I'd trust her with my life.'

'Cassandra, will you swear the Witch's Oath?'

Cassie nodded.

'I swear, by the seven stars,
To stir my cauldron in healing,
To weave my wards in defence,
To fly by the light of wisdom,
Standing with my sisters
In service of this land.'

'Your familiar, as it turns out, has been by your side since you first came to Hedgely.' Miranda stooped to pick up Montague, who was lurking behind her. The cat squirmed in her arms. 'He will continue to watch over and protect you. In future, perhaps, you may better heed his advice.'

The Hedgewitch handed her the large grey cat who dug his claws into Cassie's arm until she put him down. Montague, like all self-respecting cats, hated to be picked up.

Miranda pinned two badges to the collar of Cassie's cloak. One was shaped like a feather, the fledgling pin, and the other was a brass triskele, the design on *The Witch's Handbook*. Miranda turned to Ivy who passed her the hat reluctantly.

'You've earned the right to wear this, Cassandra – wear it with pride and honour your oath.'

The Hedgewitch gave Cassie the witch's salute, which she returned in kind.

'And finally,' said Miranda, 'the Witches' Assembly have seen fit to award these three members of Oak Patrol with the Argent Star.'

There was a collective gasp amongst the coven and whispered exclamations.

'The Argent Star, as many of you are aware, is awarded in recognition of bravery, skill and service to the community. It is given only to those who have performed above and beyond their training. In this instance, it recognises the courage shown by these young witches in rescuing a dozen children from their goblin kidnappers, at great risk to their own lives. I would ask you all to applaud them for their efforts, but not to emulate them, for they placed themselves in great danger. Rue Whitby, Tabitha Blight and Cassandra Morgan, please step forward.'

Cassie and Tabitha did their best to look serious and solemn but Rue was grinning from ear to ear as the Hedgewitch pinned a shiny silver star-shaped badge to each of their cloaks.

The ceremony over, they broke the circle and handed around mugs of hot cocoa with chocolate digestives and marshmallows to toast over the fire. Nancy Kemp pulled out her tin whistle and began to play a faery reel, her frog familiar croaking along. The girls danced around the fire until they were dizzy and tired. As the fire died down to crackling embers, the patrol leaders told stories about ancient witches and wicked faeries haunting old houses and lonely moors.

It was well past midnight when they finally dragged themselves away from the fireside to their tents. Cassie spread her bedroll between Tabitha and Rue's in the newly designated Oak Patrol tent, but although she was exhausted by the night's events, she could not sleep.

Cassie tugged on her boots and pulled a blanket around her shoulders, moving carefully so as not to disturb Rue, who was snoring, her face buried in the pillow. She slipped silently out into the night.

All that was left of the fire was a circle of white ash and glowing charcoal, but the sky was heavy with brightly burning stars. A river of light stretched from east to west. Could they see the same stars in Faerie? Cassie wondered. As if in answer, a single falling star made its mad dash away into the night.

'Can't sleep?' asked Tabitha, coming up beside her.

'No.'

'Me neither. Want to go flying?'

Cassie smiled. 'I'll get my broom.'

Acknowledgements

I am deeply grateful to the friends who have supported and believed in my work, especially Bethany Bryce, Alice Nelson, the Daphnistas, and Neil, my constant support and belief.

Acknowledgements

Although one witch can write a story, it takes a whole coven to transform it into a book. My heartfelt thanks (and a witch's salute) to the 2nd Hedgely Coven: my agent, Philippa Milnes-Smith, who has the power to make dreams come true; my editor, Felicity Alexander, whose dedication and kindness mend all things; illustrators: Saara Katariina Söderlund and Tomislav Tomic, enchanters both; designer Thy Bui; Jane Harris and the rest of the team at Welbeck Children's, including Margaret Hope who waved her artistic wand over everything.

I am likewise grateful to the individuals who have supported and believed in my work for many years: Bethwyn Grey, Alice Nelson, Rosemary Atwell, the Unpublishables and Neil, my patient partner and encourager-in-chief.

Skye McKenna

Skye McKenna grew up in the iron ore mining town of Newman in the Australian outback. Surrounded by the red dust of the Pilbara, she developed a healthy respect for wild things and wild places at a young age. Longing for adventures of her own, she travelled to England and fell in love with the British countryside.

Skye now works in heritage and recently curated the Magic & Mystery exhibition for Barley Hall, York, introducing visitors to real and legendary wizards and alchemists and developing activities for school children and families visiting the exhibition.

HEDGEWITCH is her debut novel.

WOODWITCH

'The writing is as magical as the story.' Piers Torday

SKYE McKENNA

WOODWITCH

Witches aren't born, they're made . . .

The magical story of Cassie and
her friends continues in *Woodwitch*.
Read on for a sneak peek.

Chapter One

Fledgling Witch

Cassandra Morgan was brewing potions in the potting shed. Bent over a softly simmering cauldron, she measured out an ounce of powdered peppermint, a drachm of dried rosemary and thirteen drops of tincture of ginger. She'd been there for hours, so long, in fact, that Montague had given up chasing woodlice and was taking a nap amidst the cabbage seedlings. Now and then, the cat opened one golden eye to check on her progress and make helpful comments like: 'You've miscounted, that's fourteen peppercorns,' or 'I'd grate the lemon peel finer, if I were you.'

Cassie was working in the potting shed because she had been forbidden by Mrs Briggs, the housekeeper, from using her camping cauldron indoors after accidentally setting fire to the moss-green rug in her bedroom. It was only slightly singed, but as Mrs Briggs explained, there was a lot of wood in Hartwood Hall and a lot of antique furniture. Cassie had complained that she couldn't possibly work out-of-doors because she was trying to brew an Enlivening Elixir which required very steady temperature control – and it had been blowing a gale all week.

Brogan, the groundskeeper, had taken pity on her and let her use his shed. So there she was, amidst towers of terracotta pots and salmon coloured geraniums, carefully feeding tinder grass to the fire beneath her small copper cauldron.

'It's supposed to be turning a shade of warm apricot,' said Cassie, checking her Witch's Handbook once more.

'It would, if only you would give it sufficient time and *keep stirring*,' said the grey cat. Montague was Cassie's familiar; he could do a little magic of his own, but mostly he was there to provide annoyingly practical advice at every opportunity.

'I haven't *got* time,' said Cassie, glancing at the clock on the potting shed wall. 'I need to get to coven after this.' Cassie was determined to arrive with a bottle of perfectly brewed elixir and complete the tasks required to earn her white Potioner badge.

'You have ample time. You're only thirteen and the

witch's craft takes years of hard work to master. Humans aren't like cats,' said Montague, grooming his whiskers. 'We are born with agility and grace whereas you must develop your skills through constant and persistent practice. There will be plenty more badges to earn and tests to pass after this one.'

But that was just the problem. As a matter of fact, Cassie had three problems.

The first was that she had started behind compared to the rest of the young witches in her coven. They had all grown up in the village of Hedgely, or in witching families elsewhere in the country, and had known about the world of Faerie and its dangers since they could walk. Cassie, on the other hand, had spent half her life in a boarding school in London. Her teachers had told her there was *no such thing as faeries* – but her teachers had been wrong, and when it came to the dangerous and deceptive faery folk she had a lot of catching up to do.

Cassie's second problem was that her mother, Rose Morgan, was still missing. It had been seven-and-a-half years since Cassie had last seen her, but now she at least knew *where* her mother had gone. Cassie had seen a letter in which Rose explained that she planned to travel to Faerie, to find something precious she had lost, and that a friend had offered to help her do so. Cassie didn't know what her mother had been searching for, or who had

413

helped her cross the border, but she was sure Rose had intended to return home.

Which brings us to Cassie's final, and most insurmountable problem: her aunt. Miranda Morgan was Cassie's guardian, the coven mistress and the Hedgewitch; the warden who guarded the Hedge; the great tract of forest that formed the border between England and Faerie. She was the only person who could help Cassie follow her mother to Faerie, but Miranda had forbidden her from going, that is, until Cassie had earned her licence and was a fully qualified witch.

And so, Cassie needed to earn this badge, and all the others that stood between her and that final test. She had to prove that she had all the skills necessary to travel across the border, to survive Faerie and return safely home again.

'*Cassandra...*' said Montague, softly.

She had to learn and learn fast if she wanted to prove herself to her aunt. There was no time for mucking about on broomsticks with the other girls or playing silly games like Blinkers. She had read the Witch's Handbook cover to cover, and she was determined that she would master every rune, every spell, every potion in it.

'CASSANDRA!' Montague hissed.

'What is it?' asked Cassie, drawn from her thoughts back to the potting shed and the geraniums and the orange flames that were licking up the sides of her cauldron.

'Oh no... no, no, NO!' she cried, blowing on the fire, but this only made the flames rise higher. The purplish-brown liquid inside was bubbling to a rolling boil, rising over the rim of the cauldron and pouring out, hissing as it reached the flames and letting off clouds of rosemary-scented steam.

'The watering can. Quickly!' said the cat.

Cassie emptied its contents over the potting shed table, dousing the flames and flooding the workbench. The geraniums had been splashed with the diluted elixir and, one by one, lifted their pink petals and began to sing. A wordless tune filled the potting shed as the plants formed a chorus, nodding their blooms to the strange melody.

Cassie sank down on her stool and sighed. In one careless moment she'd lost hours of meticulous work and the potion wasn't the only thing she'd ruined; her witch's handbook was soaked through, its pages dyed with clouds of aubergine.

'You'd better tidy this up before Brogan sees it,' said Montague, batting a paw at one of the singing geraniums which was rather off-key, 'Or you'll be brewing potions outdoors all through the winter.'

By the time Cassie had mopped up the potting shed, raced upstairs to change into her pointed hat and witch's cloak and back down to the kitchen to hang her sopping handbook by the fire to dry, she was already running late.

'Here now, hold your kelpies!' called Mrs Briggs, turning from the bread she was kneading to pull a tray from the oven. 'I've baked hazelnut rolls; you can take them along to the coven hall for afternoon tea. Oh my, whatever happened to this?' She peeled away the cover of Cassie's handbook to inspect its sodden contents.

'I had a little accident in the potting shed.'

'Another?' said Mrs Briggs. 'Well, it will dry, but you can't go along without a handbook. Wait here a moment.'

'But I'm going to be late!' called Cassie, as the housekeeper disappeared through the scullery and up the back stairs.

Mrs Briggs returned a moment later with a small black book and passed it to Cassie. It was a Witch's Handbook, just like her own, with the swirling silver triskele on the front cover, only it was older, its pages dog-eared and yellowing.

'It was your mother's copy, found it last time I was in the attic and put it aside, just in case. Alright, straighten that hat and don't forget the rolls!'

Cassie's broomstick, which was named Tantivy, thoroughly enjoyed the break-neck flight down the hill from Hartwood, over the river Nix, through the village of Hedgely and up to the Coven Hall. Cassie could still barely control its enthusiasm, but just now she was grateful for its speed as she and Montague skidded to a halt outside the hall. Normally, she would come to coven straight from school on a Friday afternoon, but today was the last day of the summer holidays and their first coven meeting since July.

The coven hall was a low, round building of yellow stone, situated on the outskirts of the village between the last row of houses and the looming shadow of the Hedge. It had a pointed slate roof, like a witch's hat, and was surrounded by a garden of flowering herbs. Just now there were poppies, pennyroyal and purple loosestrife, but Cassie did not have time to stop and admire them. She could already hear singing coming from inside the hall.

'The sky is clear as we fly on,
Beneath the dazzling stars.
We know their names and stories,
Their wisdom, it is ours.'

A dozen voices were raised together in the coven song, the meeting had already begun. Leaving her broom outside in the September sunshine, Cassie crept up the stone steps and slowly pushed the door ajar.

Look out for

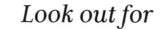

SEAWITCH

Available from 2024

HAVE YOU READ
THE BUTTERFLY CLUB SERIES?

WOULD YOU RISK THE FUTURE
TO CHANGE THE PAST?

Members of **THE BUTTERFLY CLUB** are time-travelling thieves, stealing artefacts from the future to bring progress forward. But small changes in history can have a big impact and only time will tell the consequences. That's the Butterfly Effect.